THE WAY

LUCAS GORTON
MCINTIRE

THE WAY

Lucas Gorton McIntire

CONTENTS

1 — Molding a Mind
1

2 — The Depravity of Man
7

3 — Another Day and Another Day in Hell
21

4 — A New Hope
30

5 — Rage of the Desperate
38

6 — Collision
43

7 — A Coupon from God
54

8 — Building Hope
65

9 — Devine Purpose in Debauchery
75

10 — Faith in Dead Branches
81

CONTENTS

11 — Irrational Love
96

12 — Horror Stories & Delusions
105

13 — Renovating a Heart
114

14 — Changing Seasons
122

15 — Date Night With Jennifer
128

16 — A Victory for the Devil
136

17 — Wounds of Memories
141

18 — Reasoning of the Flesh
152

19 — Skin Deep
167

20 — Puzzle Pieces
177

21 — Serpents in Shining Armor
184

22 — The Descent
191

23 — A Crumbling House of Lies
203

CONTENTS

24 — Joshua versus Jesus
214

25 — The Good News
220

26 — Tiffany Rejects Katrina
223

27 — The Broad and Narrow
230

28 — The Men's conference
238

29 — As the Sun Sets
250

Epilogue
257
About the Author
263

MOLDING A MIND

Sitting on his bedroom floor, five-year-old Joshua Nickel played with his Legos. Elevated voices from down the hall penetrated his bed room door as he assembled his multicolored high-rise. It's not an unfamiliar sound to his little ears but, nonetheless, it grabbed his attention and curiosity compelled him to leave his room. He meandered down the short apartment hallway to his parents' bedroom door. He placed his ear to the door to listen, though he really didn't need to. He slowly turned the knob and cracked the door open and peeked into the bedroom just in time to witness his father defending his alcoholic drinking habits—among other cyclical proclivities—then slamming his fist into the mirror on the dresser across from the bed. Joshua quickly shut the door then ran hastily back into his room, and in the manner in which he witnessed his father hit the mirror, Joshua put his fist through his assemblage of Legos, dismantling the mini-skyscraper.

Shortly thereafter, the shouting noticeably left his parents' bed room and approached his door. Then his mother burst into the room followed by his father. The volume and level of hostility immediately dropped in Joshua's presence. His mother, Trisha, quickly began rummaging through Joshua's dresser, throwing all the clothes she could into a duffle bag.

"Are we going to go visit Grandma and Grandpa again?" Joshua asked his mother.

She turned and, with a little mascara running down her face, smiled—as best she could—and replied, "Yeah, we're going to go visit Grandma and Grandpa again." At that, Joshua ran to his closet and quickly grabbed his shoes, as this, too, was not un-common.

"You're not taking my son away from me," Mark, Joshua's father, said in as much of a calm voice as he could.

"He's my son too, and if you really gave a damn about him—or me for that matter—you would sober up and get help with your temper," Trisha responded in the same tone. She threw the duffle bag over a shoulder, grabbed Joshua's hand, and led him out of the room with haste. As she stopped by the dining room table to grab her purse, Mark blocked the door to the apartment. "You're not leaving with my son," he again said, as they approached the door.

"Move or I'll call the police—again," she responded. He then timidly moved from the door. Trisha opened the door and picked up Joshua with one arm.

"Can I at least give him a kiss?" Mark asked, to which Trisha hesitated at first but then came forward allowing Josh and Mark to quickly exchange kisses, then pulled him back and left.

"I love you, Daddy. See you later," Joshua said. Mark, at first, simply stood in the doorway but then, emotionally, ran out after them. He followed them down the exterior stairs of the inner-city apartment complex, which was in desperate need of repair, pleading for them to stay—and by them meaning Trisha, for Joshua was more of an accidental burden to Mark. Trisha ignored him as much as she could on her way to her small Toyota and buckled Joshua into the back seat of the car. Meanwhile, Mark's emotional outcry was inviting onlookers from other apartment homes as he began crying and getting on his knees, which was nothing more than his normal manipulative routine.

"Look, Mommy, Daddy's crying. Can't he come to Grandma and Grandpa's house with us this time?"

"Not today," Trisha simply responded, as is the usual answer. She did her best to maintain her composure as well as to fight off the feeling of embarrassment, among other feelings, that Mark was creating. She closed the back seat door then looked around, seeing others staring through their windows at the dysfunctional family. However, this also isn't something new. She then faced Mark and said, "Get up. You're embarrassing me and your son. Get it together—"

"I'll get help!"

"YOU NEVER DO! We just go in circles. I can already tell you what's going to happen. I'm going to leave, then you're going to go up there and get drunk—until you're passed out! You'll go to AA for one week, then call me the next weekend to say that you're better, you've changed, yada, yada, yada. Then, like the loser I am, I come right back. And a few days later you're putting your fist through walls and getting drunk again."

"Not this time. I promise," Mark emotionally reassured her.

"I can't believe you anymore."

"I'll do anything I swear."

"Okay. All the alcohol in the house...in the dumpster...right now!" she said, crossing her arms with a vile expression across her face.

"All of it?"

"That's what I said."

"Why all of it?"

"Do you hear yourself? I just now gave you a way to keep me from leaving. And you can't do it!"

"You used to drink too..."

"Oh, here we go. The: *you-used-to* defense. Yes, I used to do a lot of stupid things. Oh, but what happened? That's right, you knocked me up. And I stopped all of that. Oh, and what did you want me to do when I told you I was pregnant? Or do I need to remind you of that too?"

"You thought about it too, remember?" Mark, likewise, reminded Trisha of her part in once thinking about terminating the pregnancy, to which she looked off to the side. She then opened the driver's side door to get in, but again Mark pleaded with her, to which she stopped and repeated her earlier offer, "I told you what you need to do."

"What if I get rid of most of it?"

"Most of it! You could get rid of ninety percent of the alcohol in the apartment and there'd still be more alcohol than food! The milk is nearly a week past its expiration date! We've been living off of oatmeal and water. It's a treat when I can make Joshua a grilled cheese sandwich!"

"Well, you're not working to help," Mark attempted to excuse himself.

"YOU WANTED ME TO BE A STAY-AT-HOME MOM! My goodness, Mark. Do I have to remind you of everything? Oh, and I'm just talking about the alcohol. I didn't even say anything about your porno magazines! Of which three times now, I found Joshua looking at because you leave those on the back of the toilet bowl."

"You used to like those too."

Trisha put a hand over her forehead over Mark's remarkable ability to bring up the irrelevant past. "Yeah. I used to like a lot of things. I used to think I loved you. But I was only infatuated with you."

"Mommy?" Joshua shouted from the back seat.

"Yes, hunny, we're leaving." She then threw her purse to the passenger seat and got in and closed the door. Mark bent down to the window continuing to plead for her not to go. "What's your secretary's name at the auto shop again? Sheila or something? Maybe she can come to keep you company."

"What are you talking about?" Mark responded in a manner which revealed he actually did know what she's talking about. Trisha then reached out of the car window and grabbed the collar of his white shirt in which there's a faded stain and pulled it for Mark to see.

"I. Don't. Wear. Purple. Lipstick!" she said through her teeth. Then she let go of his shirt and drove out of the parking lot, her Toyota sputtering along the way. She watched Mark through the rear view mirror fall to the ground ridiculously and screaming profanities.

Shortly thereafter, Mark returned to the apartment and swiftly went to the fridge, which was nearly completely full of alcohol, as was the freezer and many cupboards. He scooted the expired milk out of the way of a jug of vodka and proceeded to chug it right where he was. Then, enraged, he threw the jug across the room and then slammed his fist into a wall, which was already inundated with holes associated with his fists.

****

Later

Bill, Trisha's father, was sitting in an old wooden rocker on the porch as his daughter and grandson began driving down the lengthy winding dirt driveway toward the country house. He sat simply watching them pull up with his hands through the straps of his coveralls. He appeared as if he spent the day doing yard work. As Trisha and Joshua exited the vehicle, Bill stood up to greet them.

"Grandpa!" Joshua shouted excitedly then ran up the few steps to meet his grandfather who scooped him up. Bill took his straw hat off and placed it on Joshua's head, which covered even his chin. Josh lifted the hat off and said, "It's still too big for my head."

Bill smiled and responded in his deep yet gentle tone, "Not as big as last time."

Trisha finally made it to the porch after getting a few things out of the car. Bill turned to her but didn't say anything. She looked off embarrassed to be there under the circumstances—again. He then smiled and, with his free arm, embraced her as well.

Just then, Trisha's mother, Tina, came out the front door, saying, "Are they here? I heard a car"—but then seeing them, said—"Trisha, you can't keep doing this." At that statement, Bill looked up at Tina who realized that she wasn't being very loving, then joined the group hug. "Well, dinner is ready, so why don't we eat, then we can talk later," she said in a more welcoming tone.

The rest of the evening was fairly pleasant for Trisha and Joshua; some tears from Trisha fell as she told her mother everything while Bill alternated playing catch-and-tag with Joshua on their five-acre property while talking to him about being a man, to which, being five years old, Joshua's primary response was, "ice cream?"

THE DEPRAVITY OF MAN

Twenty Years Later...

The arena was packed with thousands of belligerently scream-ing fans. Jumbo-Tron screens lined the interior of the arena and in the center, below the video cube, was the encaged octagon fighting ring. The music was fast, heavy, and loud—very loud. The atmosphere could have been mistaken for being that of a death metal concert. Tonight's fight was also to be a unique one.

The competitors were on opposing sides of the ring outside the fencing. Their agents, trainers, and close supporters stood with them. Cameras were flashing, and videos were recording. Two-time title champion, Brett Karmal, who goes by the fight name Jawbreaker, was restless, eager to get in the ring. Hanging on him was a woman stroking his vein-populated arms and chest provocatively. But this wasn't just any woman, it was supermodel Tiffany Love. Tonight was her debut live appearance after being voted the sexiest woman in America. Up until now, her face had only been viewable in magazines and photos.

"Ladies and gentlemen, we thank Glamour Entertainment for sponsoring tonight's title event!" an announcer broadcasted throughout the arena's PA system. "And your pre-title candy—for all you men in the house—Glamour Entertainment's pride and joy, who was also voted this year's sexiest woman in America! Tiffany Love!" Electronic music blasted through the speakers accompanied by a diversity of lights—pulsating, strobes, and lasers—and in a multitude of colors as a handful of provocatively dressed girls enter the octagon in a choreographed dance sequence.

Tiffany Love left Brett's arm to walk around the ring, allowing fans to glimpse the red-headed beauty. As she approached the entrance to the cage, she provocatively kissed her hand and waved it to the crowd. Then turning and stepping up into the ring, she became the center of attention as she twirled and moved in harmony to the techno-rock melody, which the crowd lustfully hollered at her over.

Meanwhile, live commentators of the event compared the stats of the competitors as well as gave background information for those watching the event live.

"Tonight's card, we have Karmal versus Nickel for the title. A unique quality about tonight's match is that both competitors are local residents. Both competitors are known for their speed although this will be the first time we'll see Joshua in action since retired, former boxing champion, Cad Arris discovered him after putting a guy in a coma in the old Brick Town Community Center."

"That's right. Joshua Nickel, in fact, just wrapped up a two-year parole sentence six months ago for that, which has made it difficult for Cad to secure a professional sponsorship for him."

"Not to mention that Cad had to pull a lot of strings to convince the UFC to let Joshua fight in a title event for his debut performance—"

"Which, interestingly, it's rumored that Joshua doesn't do any martial arts, so either this kid is ridiculously overconfident or he's got a secret weapon in his fists. When asked why he doesn't do boxing instead, his answer was, he felt claustrophobic in boxing gloves."

"Well, we'll see how he does tonight. It looks like Ms. Love is about to wrap up her little set."

"Speaking of Tiffany Love, who's also a local resident, her whole family died in a plane crash four years ago."

"Poor girl, that's gotta be tough."

"I don't know about poor. Her father, Daniel Love, was CEO of the international aerospace company Skyward Industries. Tiffany actually inherited the company after her father passed."

"Well, I guess the title of Chief Executive Officer wasn't her calling."

"Apparently not."

Tiffany wrapped up her entertainment by walking over to the fencing in which Joshua was on the other side. She bent over with her hands on the links then, with a finger, signaled for Joshua to come up to her. He glanced at his trainer, Cad, then nonchalantly walked over and put his ear near her to hear what she had to say.

"Brett is going to mop the ring with your pretty little face."

Joshua then looked at her and watched her provocatively lick the plastic-coated fencing links before winking at her, to which she then noticed his eyes—silver. She already had a glaze over her eyes, but Joshua's eyes appeared to have an effect on her. It lasted just a moment, then she stood back up and headed toward the ring exit while waving at the crowd again but looking back one last time at Joshua before stepping out of the octagon.

"What was that about?" Cad asked.

"I have no idea. But she's hot. Screwed up in the head and most likely on drugs, but hot," Joshua responded, having deducted something was off with the woman. "I think I'll take her home tonight."

"Normally, I'd believe you, Josh, but this chick? I'm doubtful."

"I'll bet you ten bucks. You know why they call me the mechanic," Joshua responded confidently.

"Maybe because you own an auto service center and fix cars?"

"I'm talking about the other reason," Joshua said with a smile.

"Would you shut up, you pervert," Cad said sarcastically. "Now listen, this isn't the community center. This is the real deal. There was a lot of pulling strings to get you in here tonight. Brett's a professional martial artist. Stick to your defense strategy for now and we'll see how that fairs. But you have to at least get one shot in every round. If it doesn't appear to be effective by the fourth round, you'll have to go in offensively," Cad explained. Joshua nodded then headed inside the ring.

"Standing six foot, five inches and weighing two hundred and fifty-five pounds, give it up for two-time season title champion, Brett...the Jawbreaker...Karmaaaaal!" the announcer shouted over the PA, to the screaming of thousands of fans—though there were boos mixed in. Brett walked around his side of the ring yelling, "yeah! yeah!" as he flexed his muscles and beat his bare chest. His face was almost deformed—a result of more hits to the head than could be accounted for—and it appeared as if he had no neck due to the enormous shoulder muscles. "And standing five feet, eleven inches and weighing in at two hundred and fifteen pounds, give it up for Joshua...the Mechanic...Nickel!" again the announcer shouted through the PA to more blistering scream-ing. Both yays and boos, about evenly, came from the crowd. Joshua, unlike Brett, just stood there focused—this was his first professional fight after all. He always had a lite grin on his face, sometimes it was hard to determine if he was happy or if he was smirking at something—or in this case, someone.

The two competitors met with the referee in the center of the octagon. The rules of the fight were explained, then the two fist bump and immediately Brett threw his first punch at Joshua's face, but Joshua was prepared and blocked it. Joshua had vigorously studied Brett's fighting technique. And just as Joshua suspected, Brett followed through with a hook, which he also blocked. A roundhouse came up, and again Joshua blocked that as well. Joshua didn't throw a single hit until the last few seconds of the five-minute round when he got in a body shot, though a weak one, just to get it on the board. Joshua had successfully deflected every headshot that came at him but had taken a few body shots from Brett, though nothing he wasn't expecting.

The second round began with much of the same thing. Joshua, again, maintained his defensive technique. This was indeed an unusual fight. Watching someone just block punches and not throw any? What kind of MMA fight was this? The third round, the same thing. By the fourth round, Joshua could tell that Brett was getting angry at the fact that Joshua wasn't throwing any punches or kicks or any kind of offensive move, except for a body shot near the end of each round. He could also tell that Brett was getting worn out, as he continually insulted Joshua. "Come on! fight me! fight me!" Brett would shout. But Joshua maintained a cool head. He was focused. He didn't say anything the entire match; he only nodded when Cad spoke to him between rounds. The fifth round came and gone—the same thing. Likewise, the sixth round, and by the seventh, Brett was so angry he was beginning to flail his punches and kicks—he was indeed burning out.

Finally, the eighth and final round. They fist-bumped, and again Brett came at Joshua's face with a right hook, which Joshua blocked, but this time, immediately Joshua came right back with his first right hook to Brett's face—contact. Blood flew out of his mouth. Joshua pounded on Brett's face until Brett began protecting his head. Then Joshua began body shots—and this time, they weren't weak. Brett had let his guard down during this round. Finally Brett got a roundhouse up, but Joshua caught it and twisted his leg, sending Brett to the floor. The crowd was astonished and suddenly began rooting primarily for Joshua. Brett stumbled back onto his feet, and immediately Joshua's fists came at him, having had no time to even get an arm up. Brett landed back on the matt, his face bloodied and his body red and bruised. Finally, after laying face-first on the ground for several seconds, a tentative knockout had been declared and Joshua was deemed the winner. The crowd roared. Joshua's little grin was the same, however—no emotion was expressed. Cad and a few other supporters climbed into the ring, praising Joshua.

Then, lastly, Tiffany Love reentered the octagon and, without hesitation, went right up to Joshua, pulled his head to hers, threw a leg around his waist, and began kissing him. The crowd roared even more as the exotic scene was displayed on all the screens. Brett, coming around, looked up and saw his—supposed—woman kissing Joshua. Enraged, he sprung to his feet to tackle Joshua out of hostility. Joshua's quick reflexes, however, compelled him to move Tiffany to safety, then turned to slam his fist into Brett's face, sending him again to the floor with a bloody and broken nose. Medics attended to Brett, while Tiffany, highly aroused by the action, resumed her passionate gratitude toward Joshua for protecting her—or so she thought. While Joshua was allowing Tiffany to climb all over him, he held his hand toward Cad indicating that he owed Joshua ten dollars. Cad laughed and pulled out ten and put it in his hand, which then Joshua promptly put the cash in his pocket then placed his arm around Tiffany. The cameras were flashing, and the intimate scene would be on the front page of many sports magazines around town the next day.

"Josh! Just remember, the after-party's at the clubhouse," Cad reminded him. "Try not to be too late." Joshua gave him a thumbs-up as his mouth was preoccupied. "Oh, and put a dress shirt and cologne on...it's going to be classy."

****

The party had been active for a few hours when Joshua finally arrived at Cad's clubhouse. It was filled with supporters, close friends, and a few members of the local press. It was a mildly formal event as most of the invitees were dressed in either a classy dress or business-type apparel, except Josh. He wore jeans with the dress shirt Cad told him to wear though untucked with the cuffs rolled up a bit. Cad smiled and shook his head over Joshua's casual look as he walked in. Cad then handed him a champagne glass as he approached. Joshua was used to more informal parties, which generally included a far less classy dress code with much stronger alcoholic beverages.

"Seriously? A glass? Where's the bottle?" Joshua asked rhetorically.

"Calm down, this is just for the toast. You know everyone's been waiting for you for a couple of hours."

"Sorry about that. It took longer than I anticipated."

"I bet." Then Cad said to the invitees, "Can I have your attention! A toast to Joshua Nickel, who, on his first MMA fight, took out a two-time season title champion."

"Twice!" one of the invitees added, to the laughter of all who were there, then they drank up.

"Josh, a couple of things. One, don't be a jerk when a journalist asks you questions," Cad advised.

"When do I ever act like a jerk?"

"Like, all the time."

"Oh, well, I was born that way?"

"Yeah, I don't think so, kid. Second, keep the alcoholism to a minimum. I really don't want to have to drag your drunken butt out of here in front of camera phones after a good performance. Plus, two potential sponsors are here. You best figure out how to balance your I-don't-care about-the-world vibe with at least a *minimum* amount of compassion."

"I'll do my best."

"And thirdly, you owe me five bucks."

"Five bucks? For what?" Joshua asked, opening a beer.

"You said ten bucks if you took *her* to *your* house. *She* took *you* to *her* house...you owe me five bucks."

"Dude, that's low," Joshua responded with a laugh while rummaging around his wallet for a five-dollar bill. "Don't spend it all in one place."

"Speaking of which, how was she?" Cad probed for juicy details.

"Once we got to her bed, it was pretty wild. You think she was programmed for sex. It was awesome until she started going on about her daddy, her daddy's house, then wanting me to stay with her, and blah-blah-blah."

"Did you?"

"Does it look like it?"

"No, man, I mean you gonna go back afterward?"

"Yeah, right! I stayed with her until she fell asleep. That's as good as I get."

"She was probably just drunk," Cad considered.

"I have to tell you, I've never seen so many empty bottles of wine in a house that big in my life. But I'm convinced that she was more than just drunk. She was like a shell. Her eyes were, like, blank. Like no one was there. Admittedly it was kinda freaky...and not in the hot sexy way either."

"Doped up?"

"On something. You deal still, right?"

"Some but not downers. Besides, I don't even know that chick. That's the first time I've ever seen her in my life...outside of a bill board or an almost-porn magazine," Cad informed.

"I hear ya. I didn't even know she lived in town. I thought all the models lived in Cali or New York. She must keep a low profile."

"I would too if I were her," Cad responded.

"Liar," Joshua said.

Cad chuckled then admitted, "Mostly a low profile," laughing. Then, as Cad earlier predicted, a young journalist walked up to Joshua. "Oh, here you go. If you don't know what to say that sounds intelligent, just tell her how good you are at fixing engines—and I'm talking about actual automobiles. Or just don't say anything at all."

"Hi, Joshua, my name's Suzi. I'm a local sports journalist. Could I get a couple of statements from you? About tonight's fight?" she asked.

"You sure can," he responded. "That, by the way, was a statement," he joked. Suzi laughed.

"That's a good one. Short but clever. So you are quite the entrepreneur, you're an auto mechanic, own your own business, now your first MMA fight...and you're just twenty-five years old. Pretty impressive."

"Thank you," he politely responded.

"In regards to tonight's fight, which is one for the books, we're you at all nervous before the fight?"

"Not at all," Joshua simply responded. Suzi waited for a second before asking another question believing there would be a few more details.

"Okay, simple enough. So for a little background on you, I have a statement from the court that you had to spend five days in jail and two years on parole for random acts of violence, particularly for put ting a man in a comma. Can you tell me a little about that?"

"I learned my lesson. Everything else is in the court record," Joshua simply explained.

"Okay. How about a good sob story to tug at the heartstrings of some of the readers and would-be fans?"

"I don't cry."

"Okay. So no tragedies in life that you had to *fight through* to get you to where you're at?" she inquired with emphasis.

"My dad passed away when I was seventeen."

"Did you cry then?"

"Not that I recall," he assured her.

"All right. Well, that was short and to-the-point. On one hand, you're going to make my story easy to do, and yet you're still a mystery. Thank you, Joshua." Suzi closed her notebook, then left.

Cad returned, saying, "Hey, man, she was pretty cute. You should have asked her to stick around."

"For me or for you?" Joshua sarcastically commented.

"Ha ha. Well, brown hair, brown eyes—"

"Yeah, I avoid them like the plague."

"Seriously? I thought they were your favorite?"

"I get attached. The weirdest thing. I can't figure it out."

"Heaven forbid anyone cracks your stone heart," Cad added. "Oh, and speaking of the whole random violence thing, the news reported two more guys in the hospital—with their faces banged up. You wouldn't have anything to do with that, would you?" Cad asked in s serious tone.

"Not at all," Joshua again simply responded.

"Uh-uh. Better not. That's where I draw the line, kid," Cad warned.

"I find it ironic where your line is drawn, especially when selling dope isn't crossing it."

"Well, that's the difference between being beat to death and feeling good to death in my opinion."

"I suppose, just don't overdose anytime soon."

"I don't plan on it."

"Good, 'cause I need you for the next fight. I am fighting again, right?" Joshua asked, still learning the nuances of the UFC.

"Actually I need to talk to you about that. I'm looking for a martial arts trainer for you."

"Why?"

"Josh, buddy, listen. First of all, I'm a boxer, so I train you to box. But you're doing mixed martial arts...and you can't even do martial arts. That's what's really ironic. Your speed and defensive tactics won the day and, beyond that, are pretty impressive. Period. But, dude, you really need to learn other fighting techniques to get in the points. Plus, your left hook still needs work."

"So I'm not fighting again?"

"Ha ha, yes, you are, tentatively in six months. But I need to get you another sponsor. I'm going to go broke doing this on my own."

"I thought you said if I did good tonight, they'd come out of the woodwork."

"Josh, let's face it, you have done a lot of stupid stuff. And that makes some people with deep pockets a little nervous. Public image is a big deal, man. Besides, you took some pretty good body shots. You need a little time to heal up, and hopefully, we'll get someone to train you on some other stuff."

"You're the boss," he responded, continuing to drink.

Just then two of Joshua's random flames entered the club-house with a third unfamiliar face. Cad commented on the three attractive ladies. "Oh, dang."

"What?"

"Well, if you're avoiding brown hair, don't look at what two of your fb's just brought to the party," Cad warned, but Joshua glanced over anyway, though remained across the room where the majority of the alcohol resided, which he's already consumed several bottles of. Cad went over to greet the ladies.

"Good evening, ladies, or should I say good morning. I guess it's after midnight now, isn't it?" Cad said to Sandra and Kara. Sandra and Kara knew Joshua from when he was in college getting his ASE certification so he could open his own auto mechanic shop.

"Hey, Cad," they said.

"Who's this?" Cad asked about their friend they brought. She had long brown hair with a few highlights, brown eyes in which her glasses lightly magnified, and wore a classy, business suit-type dress. She looked very professional than that of sexy.

"Oh, this is our new roommate. She just transferred from a university in Florida; her name is Jennifer," they replied.

"Jennifer, it's nice to meet you. Come in, have a drink. I'd offer you some food, but I think it's all gone."

"Thanks, I don't like to eat late anyway. Kara and Sandra mentioned a social gathering. They're friends with Joshua. And I thought...it's Friday night, I need a break from homework."

"I hear ya. Do you follow the sport?" "Oh, no. Honestly, I think these things are pretty barbaric—no offense."

"Ha ha ha. None taken. You're not the only one who thinks that. There were some here this evening who believe the same thing, but they're mostly investors, so it's just a moneymaker for them."

"That makes sense."

"So what are you going to school for?"

"I'm a math major."

"Yikes!" Cad responded sarcastically.

"I know, that's what a lot of people say. I'm here on a scholar ship though."

"Well, Jennifer, great to meet you, and feel free to converse, have a drink, or whatever you want."

"Thanks," she replied, and then Cad left to converse with some others.

Jennifer glanced around the clubhouse. When she spotted a tall, attractive, and casually dressed man, she took notice. He was talking to another gentleman and drinking beer.

"Who's that?" she said, immediately drawn to the individual.

"That would be Joshua," Sandra answered.

"What a dream," Jennifer added.

"Um, sweetie," Kara and Sandra interjected, "in your case, try...a nightmare."

"Huh? Why?"

"Listen, we know you're a confident chick, with how easily you convince guys to do things for you, but no one dates Josh," Kara said, to which Sandra added, "You just sleep with him."

"Girls, it's not my first rodeo...I got this," Jennifer said confidently.

"I'm telling you, Jennifer, he'll be gone before you wake up."

"How would you know that?" Jennifer asked.

"You know our motto: boys are toys," they responded with smiles. Then Jennifer headed over to introduce herself to Joshua.

"Maybe we shouldn't have brought her," Kara said. "I think it's kind of cute—like watching someone drink out of a carton labeled strict nine," Sandra added.

"You're screwed up," Kara said, to which Sandra responded, "And you're a slut."

"Touché."

Joshua was still conversing with the same individual when Jennifer approached.

"Hi, sorry to interrupt, my name's Jennifer. You're Joshua, right?"

"That would be correct," the gentleman Joshua was talking with answered, noticing the attractive lady may have an interest in Joshua, "I think I better get going," he said, winking at Joshua.

"Wait!" Joshua responded, not wanting to be left alone with a woman with brown hair.

"You mind if I have a drink with you?" Jennifer asked.

"No," Joshua simply responded, pointing to the fridge. She got herself a beer, hit the top of the bottle on the edge of the counter, knocked the cap off, and chugged it in front of him. She then grabbed another beer and again popped the top off on the counter but this time just took a sip. That indeed impressed Joshua.

"So what would you like to talk about?" she asked.

Joshua avoided direct eye contact with her, and she could tell. "Whatever you want," he said, taking another swig of his twentieth-something beer.

"Are you okay? You seem intimidated by me."

"I'm great. No intimidation here," he responded.

"That's good. The last thing I'd want is to intimidate you. I have to say, you don't necessarily seem like one to fashion these types of parties."

"Yeah, my parties are normally a lot less formal," he replied.

"I hear ya. I'm not much for dressing up myself. I'm more of a jeans-and-t-shirt-type a gal."

"Well, I have to say, you look really nice...although—"

"Although what?"

"You kind of look like a teacher."

"I could be," she smiled, leaning on the counter in front of him.

"Could be?"

"I could teach you a few things," she added with a wink. Joshua then noticed her eyes that her glasses slightly magnified—brown, darn it.

"I'm sure you could," he responded. They both then continued drinking and talking about random subjects the rest of the night.

ANOTHER DAY AND ANOTHER DAY IN HELL

"Hey! Wake up!" Cad said, slapping Joshua with a pillow.

"What the—" Joshua responded.

"It's almost noon and I got a business appointment in two hours."

"What does that have to do with me?" Joshua inquired half asleep still.

"Two things. One, the business meeting is with a potential sponsor. He drew up a preliminary contract. I'm gonna check it out. And two, because you're in my bed."

"What! How'd I get here?"

"Jennifer and I dragged your drunken butt from my club-house to my bedroom. You're lucky Jennifer stuck around, or I would have just left you out in the grass. What you two did after that, I don't even wanna know. Just make sure my bedding is dry cleaned by the time I get home this evening," Cad explained.

Joshua sat up in the bed, pulled off the comforter and sheets, then noticed something odd for having supposedly slept with a woman—his clothes were still on.

"Cad, I honestly don't think we did anything," he responded.

"Either way, I don't want to smell your cologne when I go to bed tonight either," Cad added as he left the room.

"Fair enough." Joshua then got out of the bed and began pulling the bedding off when he saw a piece of paper laying on the sheet. It had Jennifer's name on it and a phone number along with the phrase, *for free tutoring*, and a hand-drawn winking smiley face.

"I don't think so," he said to himself, fully aware of the kryptonite effect that women with brown hair and brown eyes have on him. He then crumbled up the torn piece of paper and tossed it on the floor. He then took the bedding to his truck and drove off. Cad, a little while later, walked back into the room looking for clothes in his closet when he noticed the paper on the floor. He picked it up and read it. He then heard a truck pulling up into his driveway. The front door opened, and Joshua came walking back into the bedroom, grabbed the paper out of Cad's hand, put it in his pocket, and left again. Cad nodded and laughed to himself over the action.

****

Meanwhile, in another wealthy suburban area of town, Tiffany Love was also waking up—without the assistance of a pillow of course. Upon opening her eyes, Snuggles was visible across the room in the corner on a chair. Snuggles was a gift from her only two friends. They gave him to her about a year earlier. "Good morning, Snuggles," she said with a smile. The smile, however, would soon vanish as she felt behind her presuming that Joshua indeed stayed with her, but no one was there. She rolled over to see the remainder of her king bed empty. Her hand flew to her stomach clasping the flesh as the anxiety returned in full force. She fought back the tears as she had learned to do over the last four years.

"It's okay, Tiffany, you're okay. Just breathe," she told herself. She then grabbed the bottle of maximum strength anxiety medication that was prescribed to her and threw a pill in her mouth. On the floor next to her bed were bottles of wine, most were empty, but she grabbed a full one and chugged it. She then laid there, clasping the bottle as if it were her friend while continuing to tell herself that everything will be okay. After some time had passed, the numbness set in replacing the overwhelming sadness and anxiety. She then placed the bottle back down on the floor and got out of bed.

This was not an uncommon morning for Tiffany, as every morning normally starts out with tears. In fact, most mornings don't even start with a smile, just the ones in which she expected to wake up next to someone that she had, again, given herself to, the previous night—a result of her seemingly desperate desire to fill an ever-widening void absent of love.

Tiffany rarely left the house most days unless her employer, Glamour Entertainment, required her to fulfill a contractual assignment, which generally involved photoshoots. However, her new contract now included making provocative appearances at events—primarily large venues—as she did the night before, which was her first. Other rare instances of her leaving the house were to buy new apparel or visit her favorite restaurant in which she routinely got kicked out of for getting drunk and making wild scenes. Occasionally she would attempt to work in one of the many flower beds surrounding the mansion that her mother, when alive, kept in perfect condition.

Tiffany would spend hours getting herself ready for the day. Sometimes the majority of those hours was simply her taking a shower in which she would scrub herself profusely, followed by makeup, prepping her hair, and dressing in gorgeous outfits—just to walk around the house while occasionally talking to herself—and today was no different. By the time she had completed getting dressed for the day, it was late in the afternoon, just about time for her two friends to show up for a visit...

"Knock-knock!" On the front door, then two girls enter on their own. "Tiffany!" they said, announcing their presence. "It's us— Kara and Sandra."

"Just a minute," Tiffany said from elsewhere in the house.

Unbeknownst to Joshua and many others, Kara and Sandra knew Tiffany as she was their old college dorm roommate before she dropped out due to a multifaceted nervous breakdown. Tiffany at one point was good at math and routinely helped them with their math assignments. Tiffany wasn't always *glamorous* either. She had bad eyesight, which required her to wear glasses that magnified her eyes more than average since she was in middle school. However, contacts have since replaced the glasses as spectacles dampened her *sexy* appearance—at least according to Glamour Entertainment.

Sandra and Kara relaxed on the couches in the formal living room, which were lined with more wine bottles, until Tiffany came down the stairs.

"Wow, Tiffany! Is that a new dress?" they said.

"Yeah, do you like it?"

"It looks beautiful!"

Tiffany smiled at the comment.

"But you always look beautiful, Tiffany," they reassured her. "We brought salmon...we know that's one of your favorites."

"Aww! Can you cook it the way you did last time? It was so yummy!"

"Of course, Tiffany," Kara responded.

"Anything for you," Sandra added.

"How much do I owe you for the salmon?" Tiffany was about to go fetch her purse, but they responded, "Tiffany, we're you're friends. You don't have to pay us for it. We just want you to be happy." Tiffany smiled and hugged them. They can always tell when she's medicated by her glazed-over eyes as they currently were but never say anything.

Kara and Sandra cooked dinner for the three of them while Tiffany sat at the island orating random subjects mostly indicative of her delusionary need for self-gratification.

"So is Brett going to be over tonight?" Kara asked.

"No, we're done. He's a loser now," Tiffany straightforwardly said.

"Oh really? What happened?" they responded, though happy to hear it. They didn't like Brett much. His short temper combined with his inability to form complex statements—most likely a symptom of being hit in the head over the years via being a professional fighter—was annoying to listen to.

"Glamour e-mailed me and said to dump him. He's not good for my public image anymore," she simply explained.

"That must have been hard to do," they assumed as Tiffany is always looking for a man to stay with her as she equated that to love.

"Not really, I was going to dump him soon anyway. Six months was about all I could handle of his ugly face. And he stunk. I wanted to vomit every time I slept with him," Tiffany explained with zero remorse.

"Wow, Tiffany. That's pretty brutal," they responded.

"What? I just know what I like and what I want," Tiffany added.

"Fair enough. So what do you want?"

Tiffany rested her head in her hands, and her face lit up indicating she had a lustful desire for someone in particular. "Hmmm, Joshua."

Sandra and Kara glanced at each other at hearing that. "Are you referring to Joshua Nickel?"

"Uh-huh," Tiffany confirmed.

"Tiffany, listen. You don't want to get involved with him. Please listen to us this one time. He's going to hurt you, probably worse than anyone else," they attempted to persuade her from getting attached to Joshua; unfortunately, it was too late.

"He already did."

"He did what? Did you two—"

"Yeah."

"Wow! And I thought I was fast at getting a guy in bed with me," Sandra said, to which Kara responded, "That's because you're a slut."

"Excuse me? You're calling me a slut? I lost track of how many guys you brought to the dorm last month," Sandra rebutted.

The two of them then began arguing over who the more promiscuous one of the two were before Tiffany interjected aggressively, "Stop arguing in my daddy's house!"

"Sorry, Tiffany," they responded, concluding their argument.

"Besides, you're both whores," Tiffany vindictively added.

"Dang, Tiffany, that's pretty harsh," they responded.

"Well, isn't that how you two pay your tuition still?"

They looked at each other secretively then responded, "Not... anymore."

"Oh well, as long as I'm not part of your income schemes," Tiffany concluded, to which they glance at each other secretively again.

"But, Tiffany, you get attached. We don't. And either does Joshua."

"How would you know that about Josh?"

"Well, we know him personally."

"You do? How personally?" Tiffany further inquired.

"Very...personally," they reluctantly divulge. Tiffany scowled at hearing that. "Besides, Tiffany, you might have some competition. Our new roommate has taken to him too."

"But I'm the sexiest woman in America—"

"According to fifty or sixty thousand Glamour entertainment social media followers, Tiffany. That's a far cry from a national consensus. You can't let that go to your head."

"I need him though."

"But why?"

"He protected me from Brett."

"Are you sure he protected you? It could have been reflex," they responded. Dinner was about ready. Kara grabbed some plates and Sandra filled them up with food. They all sat at the island and began eating, that is except Tiffany. Kara and Sandra's attempt to talk a minimal amount of reality into Tiffany—though their reality isn't much less shallow—appeared to offend her resulting in her appetite for the salmon to waiver. Tiffany instead just sat there and poked at the fish with the fork while staring at it with her glazed-over eyes. Kara and Sandra could tell they upset her, so they reversed course to lift her up.

"Tiffany, we're sorry, we didn't mean to upset you. Maybe you're right. Maybe he will fall in love with you and all that. If you want we can talk to him for you the next time we see him."

Tiffany didn't respond, she just looked up and focused on them with a blank stare. Looking into her eyes was like glancing into the eyes of a soulless creature that was wearing a mask of a human female at times. It had become a familiar sight for Kara and Sandra, but occasionally it was still eerie.

"I'm gonna go watch a movie," Tiffany softly orated. "You can have whatever you want," she added, then left the island as well as the uneaten salmon. Kara and Sandra then began arguing over who upset her, to which Tiffany angrily shrieked as she descended the basement stairs, "*STOP ARGUING IN MY DADDY'S HOOOUU-USSSE!*" The sudden outburst sent chills down their spines.

"Maybe we should leave," said Kara. "I'm not leaving. She said we could have whatever we want. I'm eating her salmon, and she's got awesome wine," Sandra responded.

"You're such a moocher, Sandra."

"Keep talking gold digger."

Tiffany, on the other hand, remained downstairs the rest of the evening watching homemade movies of her family, which had become almost ritualistic over the last four years, cuddled up in the crux of her couch. Boxes filled with random things were placed in unorganized locations throughout the basement. Family photos that once decorated the walls were randomly stacked on the floor upside down. It was an obvious yet failed attempt to vanquish the source of her innermost emotional pain—and it obviously didn't get too far. A desk sat in the back of the basement. Two stapled packs of paper laid in one of the desk cubbies—they were glamour entertainment contracts. The tops of them were dusty, as was the desk, the computer, and most of the surfaces in the basement.

Next to the couch near where Tiffany sat, zoning into the TV laid several bottles of wine—most were empty. In her hand rested a glass of wine which laying on her thigh was the open wine bottle which the wine in the glass came from. She had every word in the video memorized and repeated them with the video. Watching the videos allowed her to go back in time to be with her family—unfortunately the videos acted more as a suppressant, reinforcing a false reality that she would be reminded of the next morning in which she'll grab her medication and the cycle would continue.

While Tiffany was engrossed in the family films, this particular evening, her phone rings and she answered it; it was Brett.

"Why, why, Tiffany" was all that he said.

"Because you're a loser now. I tolerated your stinky ugly face when you were a champion, but you lost to a rookie fighter half your size...you're an embarrassment. Now leave me alone," she said, with zero remorse, still zoned into the TV.

"I lost everything."

"You didn't have anything to begin with."

"I had you."

"Not anymore."

"I can't live without you."

"Then shoot yourself." His continual pleading with her aggravated her to the point she viciously informed him, "Oh, by the way, I brought Joshua Nickel home last night, and it...was...awesome." At that, he began shouting profanities through the phone to which she slowly lowered the phone and disconnected the call. Then as if nothing had interrupted her activity, she continued talking in unison with the TV, saying, "you protected me from the bee, Daddy," little Tiffany in the movie said.

"Of course, sweetheart, I'll always be here for you and I'll always protect you," her father in the video responded.

"You have pretty eyes, Daddy—"

She continued watching the videos and drinking glasses of wine until she was so incoherent that she had to crawl to her bed on the second floor.

CHAPTER

4

A NEW HOPE

Hope Community Church was near the heart of the inner city. Most of the congregants were from the surrounding area, which the locals called Brick Town. The area nickname spawned from the number of old brick buildings and apartments spanning roughly ten city blocks. Most of the buildings were in bad repair, and the poorest of individuals lived here. Conversely, the wealthiest areas of town bordered around the edges of the city limits.

The rising problems plaguing the city in general but Brick Town, in particular, ranged from homeless children to increased violence among teens and young adults—much of which can be attributed to the further deterioration of the family unit year after year, decade after decade. Not uncommon were weekend news reports detailing incidents of murder, rape, and theft, among other criminal activities.

Hope Community Church's paper-thin budget made a reliable outreach program somewhat difficult. Other churches in the area were just as broke and of course, the lack of interest in God, or anything remotely related to the subject, kept many away, especially the younger individuals who found sex, drugs, alcohol, theft, and so on, more enticing than sitting in a pew Sunday mornings listening to a preacher explain why they *shouldn't be doing* those things. Nevertheless, Hope Community Church maintained its commitment to reaching the community, though attracting would-be candidates to fill the role has been difficult. The last couple left after only six months in the position—unable to adequately face the community challenges. Now the position has been vacant for several months. But God's timing is not always ours.

An old Toyota Camry pulled up in the church parking lot. The occupants of the vehicle entered the church and waited outside the church office on a bench. Being Monday afternoon, there wasn't a whole lot of activity in the church. A secretary came walking down the hall toward the office and noticed the couple waiting on the bench next to the office door. Assuming they were looking for handouts based on their appearances, she said to them, "I'm sorry, our feed-the-homeless program are Wednesday evenings in the cafeteria."

The couple looked at each other, smiled, and then responded, "That's good to know. We'll make sure to be there Wednesday evening." The secretary then walked through the office doors.

Shortly thereafter, the pastor came out of the office after the secretary informed him of the couple in the waiting area. "Can I help you two?" he said.

"Yeah, I'm Chris Belvu. This is my wife, Katrina Belvu."

"We're here to meet with Pastor Richard Myer," Katrina added. As soon as Pastor Myers heard their names he knew who they were. He greeted them and led them into the office. "I apologize for the misunderstanding. I wasn't expecting you for a couple more days."

"None needed. We decided to drive straight through...fewer expenses that way."

"That's a good sign," Myers responded to their statement, indicating frugality. "This is Connie, my secretary," Myers introduced.

Connie sprung up out of her seat. "I am so, so sorry," Connie apologetically exclaimed for mischaracterizing the couple, especially Chris as he had a shaved head and a multitude of tattoos on his arms and on his neck that appeared to rise from his back along with a few ear piercings. His jeans were worn and his shirt looked as if it had been used to check the oil. But at least he smelt good. Katrina's hair was frizzy. Her makeup was worn off. She had a faded Jesus Freak T-shirt, most likely obtained from a *DC Talk* concert decades ago. They were both in their forties.

"No worries, Connie. We've been on the road for about eighteen hours, so I'm sure we look the part," Chris graciously responded.

"Hunny, you always look the part whether we've been on the road eighteen hours or not," Katrina said to Chris, to which he thought for a second before responding, "That's not true. I wore a flannel shirt once."

"That you bought from a thrift store on our way to the court house to be married...or did you forget that," Katrina reminded him with a smile.

"I did not forget that. I bought you a rose on the way out of the store...remember that?" The two of them smiled at each other as they briefly divulged one small part of their past. Katrina then turned to Connie, smiling, and added, "It was a fake rose."

"Fake?" Connie inquired.

"Because fake roses never die. That was twenty years ago, and I still have it," Katrina further explained with a bright smile, then kissed her husband on the cheek.

"Wow, you two seem like you've had a perfect run," Connie, again, mischaracterized the two of them.

"Not quite. We've had some close calls, but our first commitment was always to the Lord and his will for our lives...that's gotten us through a few problems over the years," Chris added.

"And saved his life a few times," Katrina added with humor.

"Well, I'd love to hear more of you two's testimony sometime," Connie responded.

"That's always fun," replied Katrina.

"Let's head back to the study and go over a few things, and then I'll walk you over to the parish," Myers said, then he led the couple to his study where he sat down behind his desk and Katrina sat in one of the two chairs in front. Chris, having sat for several hours straight, walked around the room looking at pictures, seminary certificates, and doctorate degrees belonging to Pastor Myers and glanced over the binders of the vast amount of apologetic and theological books on the bookshelves.

"So, Katrina, you have a pretty polished resume. A master's degree in theology from seminary. High GPA. I only have one thing to say about this resume." Myers then ran the paper through a shred der next to his desk. Katrina was perplexed by the action, but Chris, however, laughed at the illustration. Then, picking up two more pages that accompanied her resume, Myers continued, "But this is how I knew you were the right fit for the job. You two have spent ten years working with troubled youth and young adults. And your testimonies are powerful. Katrina, I've known few who've been through similar circumstances and even fewer who've come out of it as you have. And you, Chris, we're in a gang at one point?" Chris nodded. "Well, we have some of those problems here as well. I'd definitely like to hear more of your testimony sometime, but I'm sure the two of you are exhausted from all the driving. How about I show you the parish. It's not far...just on the south end of the church property passed the basketball court. Then you guys can get settled in."

"Sounds good to me," Chris responded.

****

The parish was small. A thousand square feet at best. The dwelling sat right next to a small slab of concrete that had a pole with a basketball backboard attached to the top, but the rim hung on it vertically without a net. It had two small bedrooms. The living room and dining room were connected. The kitchen was narrow and a wall separated it from the living room. Hardwood flooring was throughout the house—though in need of repair.

Rink! the hinges on the screen door sounded like they needed oil when Pastor Myers pulled it open. The house was a little dusty as well as humid; the window air conditioning unit hadn't been in operation in a while. After entering the parish, Chris attempted to turn on the AC unit, but it wouldn't start.

"Sorry about that, I can see if our maintenance man can fix or replace that for you," Myers said. Chris, however, without thinking twice, unplugged the unit from the outlet, pulled the front paneling off, played around in the wiring of the machine, plugged it back in, pressed the power button, and air—though it blew some dust out of the vent initially. Chris then placed the panel back over the front of the unit.

"Not a problem," Chris said. Pastor Myers was already impressed with the couple as he could deduct that they were apparently quite resourceful on their own—something the church needed considering their paper-thin budget.

"He likes fixing things," Katrina explained to Myers. "It gives him something to do with his hands...that's quite opposite than his former trade," she added.

"I can see that. So there is some furniture here...though fairly old. But the bedding is new. One of our congregants wanted to donate these to you. Beatrice. Nice lady. Speaking of gangs, her oldest son was shot to death nearly a year ago. He was seventeen. So she's a big supporter of community outreach."

"Oh goodness," Katrina exclaimed.

"I'm guessing that the father was absent?" Chris assumed.

"Yes, but he died in a work-related accident about fifteen years ago." Katrina and Chris expressed their condolences via facial expressions. The pastor then turned the subject to the topic of expenses.

"Now the church council agreed to a stipend of six hundred dollars a month. Being that the parish is on the church property, it and all its utilities are part of the church buildings' expenses, so you won't have to worry about those. Food and other amenities, however, well, that will have to come out of your monthly stipend."

The couple looked at each other, then Chris responded, "Looks like we're getting a raise, babe."

"It's about time," Katrina responded jokingly. She then went and sat down on the couch, which was nothing more than an old wooden frame with a few vintage cushions on it.

"So, Pastor, I'm curious as to what you have against seminary graduates? Aren't you one of them?" Chris asked rhetorically.

"On principal? Nothing. I think education is a wonderful thing...if you're going to be a teacher. We've had young people, fresh out of some sort of theological training in this position before. I believe with all my heart that their initial intent was good, but many of them came from pretty well-off places with little...if any...real-world experience in dealing with the kind of problems we have here...or in many cities for that matter," Myers continued. "They believe that miraculously everyone that comes in contact with them will be in awe of their biblical/theological knowledge and immediately repent and turn to God. But that's simply not true. Not to mention they never seem to be able to relate to those they're here to minister to. And honestly, during the last council meeting last month, they initially decided to end the outreach—to save some money. However, when it came in front of the congregation, the idea was not received well at all. Beatrice was one that didn't want to see the program shut down. Fortunately, we do have a couple of committed givers that are very well-off. One of which agreed to increase their giving in order to keep this going."

"That's awesome. We'll have to let him know of our appreciation," Chris responded.

"No need. He prefers to be anonymous. Anyway, with all that, we decided to give this one more go, but only if we could find someone, or in this case, a couple that had some real experience in this area. I was happily surprised to get a letter of reference from your former church pastor, Pastor Wesley, if I remember correctly. Which begs the question, why did you want to come out here when it appears you've had real success within the community you came from?"

Katrina looked away after hearing the question; obviously, there was a secret the two of them we're not going to divulge at the moment, but Chris wittily replied, "It sounded like a good place to retire." Pastor Myers took the phrase as having a sarcastic bent but didn't inquire any further, perceiving their ultimate reasoning to something of a private nature; thus, he simply nodded his head and smiled.

"Well, if you need anything—within reason of course—don't hesitate to see me in the office, or call. And for maintenance needs on the parish though, it appears you have that covered, but just in case, you can call the church and Connie can connect you. We don't have anything going on tonight, but Tuesday evenings there's a men's Bible study, Wednesday evening, of course, is the Food for the Homeless program, Thursday evenings we have a women's Bible study, and Friday is youth night—though rarely do any show up on Friday nights. Service starts at ten forty-five. I'll introduce you to the congregation this Sunday."

"Sounds great, Pastor. This really is a nice little place," Chris said as he too went to sit on the couch next to his wife.

"Have a strategy to get you started?" Myers further asked.

"Fixing the basketball goal is going to be my first priority, but besides that, we'll get our assignments soon," Chris replied.

"Assignments?"

"It's a mission, right? Missions always come with assignments," Chris explained.

"All right, sounds like you two kids know what you're doing."

"Did you hear that, hunny? He called us kids?" Katrina said, smiling.

"I'm sixty-five, anyone fifty and younger is a kid to me," Myers added.

"I won't argue with that," responded Chris.

"Ha ha, have a good evening, you two." Myers then exited the small parish home.

"Well, I say after dinner we go for a walk around town, what do you think?" Chris asked his wife.

"Sounds good to me," she replied.

"You know this couch is pretty comfy," Chris said before all four legs gave out sending them to the floor on the cushions startling the couple before laughing.

RAGE OF THE DESPERATE

"Former boxing champion and trainer for Joshua Nickel, Cad Arris, was found dead earlier this week. Police uncovered several kilos of black ice at his villa. Blood samples indicate that he overdosed on the drug. This just one week after his student, Joshua Nickel, made a historic UFC debut defeating two-time title champion Brett Karmel. The death of Nickle's trainer leaves in limbo Joshua's future with the UFC as his newly obtained and only sponsor pulled his financial backing for the new fighter. The revelation of a possible drug trafficking scandal in which Cad may have been a part of sent the sponsor backing out and other potential sponsors withholding their support. Mr. Nickel voluntarily submitted himself for drug tests of which all came up negative repairing some of the negative publicity he sustained earlier this week. However, his connection with Cad Arris, combined with his former police record of violence, is sure to leave a black mark on his reputation for a while," a news anchor reported from the street in front of Cad's villa.

Joshua turned his TV off and then tossed the remote at the wall, dismantling the device upon contact. He then lifted the bottle of alcohol to his lips and finished it off. Boiling with anger he bolted from the couch and began pacing around his living room; then finally, accompanied by a verbal outburst, he threw the empty bottle of alcohol at the same wall as the remote, shattering the bottle as well as putting a hole in the drywall. Fighting in the UFC was his only outlet for his anger that would not accompany legal problems. Thus, with that at least temporarily out of the question, keeping a lid on his temper seemed to be problematic. Shortly thereafter, however, the phone rang—with some seemingly good news.

"Brody?" Joshua said through the phone. Brody was his best friend and lead mechanic at his auto service center. "Did you find one?"

"Oh yeah. You'll like this one. Six-seven, three hundred pounds —not in the best shape. He has a temper too."

"Did he sign?"

"Yeah. And he's awfully confident. He's dropping 5k in cash."

"Is he ready to go?"

"He's headed to the junkyard right now."

"I'll be there in twenty minutes." After hanging up Joshua immediately left his house and headed to the junkyard.

The junkyard was equivalent to that of a playground for Joshua. Growing up, he made many trips to the junkyard, mostly to find exceedingly cheap parts to replace worn-out/nonfunctioning hardware for his mother's vehicle. It was also one of his first jobs as a kid. Mr. Grizzly, the old half-hill-billy/half-hippy took a liking to young Joshua. Joshua still did a lot of business with Mr. Grizzly as he still routinely buys replacement parts from the old man for customers who are looking to have repairs done as cheap as possible. Joshua had twenty-four/seven access to the junkyard as a result of a trusting relationship with Mr. Grizzly. However, the owner wasn't aware of the occasional extracurricular use his junkyard provided Joshua.

A nice Lexus rounded pile after pile of junk cars and other scraps until it reached the back of the junkyard, where Joshua was sitting on the hood of an old rusted truck. A burly-looking dude popped out of the driver door and slammed it shut. He had a smirk on his face. He had slacks and a dress shirt on. He looked as if he had just left an office job—I guess it's lunchtime. He pulled off his dress shirt and threw it on the hood of his car. Shortly thereafter, Brody rolled up to meet them in his truck after locking the junkyard gate behind the Lexus. Brody was also the regulator of these unethical events as Joshua could easily lose control.

"You must be the *Joshua*," the burly man said, to which Joshua simply nodded. Brody showed Joshua the contract and the five thou sand dollars in cash. Joshua looked the burly man over. He indeed was a big fella—strong-looking but not very toned or conditioned. Joshua then pulled two rolls of bills totaling ten thousand dollars to raise the stakes.

"What's that for?" the burly man asked, more anxious to get to the pummeling rather than talking.

"I thought you'd like the idea of making 10K instead of just five," Joshua responded.

"I only got the five."

"That's a nice ride you got there," Joshua commented.

"That car's worth more than ten thousand."

Joshua then pointed to his truck several yards away, which was obviously worth more than the burly man's Lexus. Brody then whispered, "Are you sure you want to do that? There's always a chance..."

"How many times have I lost?" Joshua interjected his friend who chuckled briefly and nodded.

"Never...that I can remember."

"Are we going to do this or what!" the burly man shouted. "I don't have all day!"

"Just between you and me," Joshua responded, "you should have taken the whole day off."

"Ha ha ha! You cocky kids. All right, my Lexus is up. When I leave you laying in the dirt, I'll take your 10K and your truck." He then pulled out the deed to his Lexus and set it with the rest of the money and the contract. The contract was to ensure that no one would take legal action against Joshua for sustaining injuries.

A roughly twenty-foot-diameter circle was made with white spray paint on the dirt ground. Joshua and the burly man stepped inside. Brody then explained the rules; they were pretty simple. "You have to stay in the circle. You have three minutes to get Joshua out of the circle or put him on the ground. Good luck."

At that, the burly man swung with a growl. His hooks were powerful but wide and slow—easily predictable by Joshua. The man came at Joshua continuously with high intensity. Joshua ducked, swerved, and blocked his offenses. He was putting off his own offenses toward the burly man until the last minute. Brody counted down notifying them of each minute. "Sixty seconds left!" Brody informed just as one more hook came at Joshua, which he caught then twisted the man's wrist followed by a plethora of fists to the man's face. It wasn't long before the man was on the ground bleeding out of his mouth and nose with both a detached jaw and septum.

Joshua's anger encouraged him to continue beating the man's face while yelling at him, "I HOPE YOU REMEMBER THIS THE NEXT TIME YOU DECIDE TO HIT YOUR LADY!" The man was next to limp on the ground only being held up by Joshua's grip on his undershirt so he could continue socking the man. Finally, Brody, observing that the burly man was motionless and Joshua was losing control of his anger, tackled his friend.

"Man, you need to learn when to stop!" Brody lectured Joshua.

"You know what kind of man this is?" Joshua responded.

"Do I have to remind you how you ended up on parole for two years? You lucked out that you didn't get a major sentence for putting that guy in a coma."

"That's why they sign a contract now," Joshua again responded.

"Josh, I still highly doubt these contracts would stand up in court. I'm just saying, the last thing I want on my conscience is to know my best friend beat some guy to death, you know?" Joshua simply nodded. His temper was finally starting to cool down, and the two of them stared at the burly man on the ground in the middle of the scuffed circle with his face, shoulders, and under-shirt covered in blood. He was moving but like that of someone without an equilibrium.

"You should probably take him to the hospital," Joshua said to Brody.

"Me?"

"Yeah, you." Joshua then unbound the wad of five thousand dollars the man bet and gave fifteen hundred to Brody and put the rest with his other ten thousand and the deed to the Lexus.

"All right. Nice doing business with you," Brody responded then went to clean up the mess, which was the burly man, while Joshua got in the Lexus and drove it to the shop where he would begin detailing it to sell.

CHAPTER

6

COLLISION

Swoosh! Another goal. Chris finished fixing the basketball rim and cleaned up the concrete half court as much as possible, which was primarily removing the overgrowth of grass and weeds from around the concrete slab and from hundreds of cracks throughout.

Swoosh! Another goal.

"Looks like you still got it, babe!" Katrina shouted, walking from the parish with a glass of tea.

Chris stopped his hoop shooting to take a drink of the iced tea Katrina just made. "Yeah, it works a lot better with the rim straight. Ha ha," he said. Chris then grabbed the basketball and began shooting again.

"Hey, man, you're really good!" a kid about thirteen or so years old shouted from the street. Chris and Katrina turned to the kid.

"Thanks," Chris shouted back, then held out the ball toward the kid and said, "Would you like to play?"

"Nah," the kid responded. "I'm going to the community center to play. A whole bunch of us play there every day. You should come and play with us. We usually have uneven teams anymore since Josh doesn't come by that often...since Cad died."

Chris and Katrina glanced at each other at the kid's story. "Assignment time maybe?" Chris said.

"Maybe," Katrina responded.

"Yeah, I'd love to come play," Chris told the kid. Then he ran to meet up with the kid and headed to the community center.

"Have fun!" Katrina shouted. "Lord, protect Chris and all these kids. Amen."

The young boy and Chris conversed as they made their way to the community center. The kid told Chris everything he knew regarding Cad Arris and how since his death the community center had fallen into disarray as Cad kept it going, sort of. As they approached the community center, Chris observed the grass hadn't been cut in a while, cracks in the sidewalks, graffiti on the building and even the basketball court.

There were several kids on the court; they ranged in age from ten to seventeen and consisted of different ethnicities. Most were boys; a couple of girls were there as well—though they were there mostly to lust over the shirtless boys playing ball. The doors to the community center were locked with a chain around the double doors. The windows were boarded up from the inside as much of the glass was broken out. A sign detailing the bank that repossessed the property laid on the ground next to the court.

"Hey, guys!" the kid shouted to the others on the court. "I found another player!" The others rejoiced, in their own way, to the news. As Chris approached the court, however, the others noticed that he was quite a bit older, even though he still looked athletic.

"Man, you're old," they said. Chris just smiled. He's been called a lot worse by kids before.

"That just means I'm a *real wise guy*," he rhetorically responded.

"Guys, he's really good. I saw him playing at that church a few blocks away," the thirteen-year-old defended him.

"Let's see your moves," one of the older kids said to him, tossing him the ball.

"You don't believe this young man?" Chris asked.

"We just want to see if you're good."

"I'll tell you what, let's play and then you can judge whether or not I'm good."

"Aight." Then the two oldest kids became captains and started picking the teams. Chris was the last one picked. Then the game was on. Chris didn't let them down; he was pretty good as the thirteen year-old had said.

After a while, a big expensive-looking truck pulled up in front of the community center. The truck definitely looked as if it didn't belong in the area. One of the kids at seeing the truck yelled excitedly, "josh is back!" The driver, who was Joshua, got out of the truck. The entire group of kids ran to meet Joshua. Chris was impressed at the apparent magnetic quality this man had on these kids. He greeted them pretty warmly, a few profanities, though in a brotherly love way, accompanied his un-classy greetings to the group. Other kids and teens came from down the street to see Joshua as they heard he was there. Unfortunately, Joshua also attracted one particular individual, who appeared to be about the same age as him.

"JOSHUA NICKEL!" the man shouted in an aggressive tone. He had his shirt off; he was a big guy—bigger than Joshua even— and built. He had a scowl on his face. His chest was puffed out. He stepped onto the community center property heading right for Joshua and shouted his name again. All the kids backed off behind Joshua. Chris, however, just watched, preparing himself if he needed to get into the middle of a conflict. Joshua saw the man coming and stood unafraid. The man then picked up speed across the court to attack Joshua. At that point, Chris got in the middle of the two. Both the man and Joshua looked at Chris, who neither of them knew, as if he just broke up a party.

"What's going on here?" Chris asked the man who towered over both Chris and Joshua.

"This fool touched my woman!" the man shouted at Chris.

"Ah. Well, in that case, by all means." Chris then got out of the way anticipating the big guy to pummel Joshua, though prepared to stop it if it got too out of hand.

"Trevor!" Joshua said back to the man. "I did *not* touch your woman!" Joshua corrected him.

"Then why did my neighbors see her all over you in your truck?" Trevor shouted.

"Because she was touching me—big difference, homie! And she couldn't get enough of this either!" he added, kissing the air. Joshua's response not only antagonized Trevor, as well as caused Chris to reconsider stepping in at all if Trevor pummeled Joshua. Immediately Trevor swung at Joshua. Joshua caught his arm, turned, and pulled, dislocating Trevor's shoulder, then turning back again, socked Trevor in the stomach which caused him to buckle over to which Joshua grabbed the back of Trevor's head and slammed his face into his knee. Trevor collapsed to the ground.

Chris had not anticipated the brutality that would have come from this Joshua fellow, and when he saw Joshua grab Trevor's hair and raise his opposite fist to begin an onslaught of power punches to the already incapacitated Trevor, Chris rushed at Joshua, knocking him over onto the ground. Chris stood in between Joshua and Trevor as a protector of the guy he never met. Chris getting in the middle of Joshua's anger streak further enraged him. He jumped to his feet and ran up to Chris to intimidate him. But Chris stood unafraid, not blinking once. Joshua was a little shocked at the lack of intimidation but didn't express it. They stared at each other. Then one of the kids shouted, "Oh man, this cat's about to get *bombasted*!"

Another said, "Josh is going to kick your butt! He's a UFC fighter!"

Chris took note of the comment and said to Joshua, "UFC huh? I'd like to see your roundhouse."

"Listen, punk!" Joshua said to Chris's face, accompanied by some spit. "We don't like outsiders." Outsider was a term used to describe people from outside the Brick Town neighborhood.

"Outsiders like you? I haven't seen too many seventy thousand dollar trucks around here, kid."

"This is not your playground," Joshua continued. Then he pointed to the street. "You gotten seconds to get out of here...or I'll remove you." The statement drew antagonistic "*ohs*" from the other kids. Chris was half-tempted to count to ten just to call Joshua's bluff but felt prompted to not escalate the situation any further, so he turned and headed away from the court. He passed the sign with the information for the bank who owns the property and made a mental note of it, then continued home.

"Hey, hunny. How was the game?" Katrina asked Chris as he entered the house from the kitchen. She was doing dishes.

"It was fun. It got really exciting actually. Oh, and I picked up the mail," he responded.

"Anything important?"

"We're preapproved for a car apparently," he said rhetorically. "And a fifty-percent-off coupon from a *Sassy Fashion* Store."

"Sassy fashion, huh," she chuckled.

"Yeah, sounds like your type of store," Chris added, laughing. She took her hands out of the water and threw some of the soapy liquid at him, then continued with the dishes. "The game got exciting, huh. Usually, *your* idea of exciting and *mine* are two different things."

"This guy, Joshua, shows up in a truck. And all the kids just flocked to him. It was pretty incredible."

"And then?" Katrina urged, suspecting trouble.

"And then, this other guy, Trevor—he was a big dude—comes barreling down the road screaming at Joshua."

"Was there a fight?" "Oh, yeah. Apparently, Josh had gotten friendly with Trevor's lady. I thought the big guy was going to clobber Joshua, but Josh put this guy down in seconds—it was pretty impressive."

"The things that impress you, sweetheart."

"Yeah, well, I thought he was going to kill him, so I got in the middle of them."

"You're not allowed to get into a fight, Chris!" she reminded her husband.

"I didn't get into a fight. But I wasn't going to let that guy kill him either."

"Good, 'cause if you had, *I* would've killed you!"

Chris chuckled at her rhetorical then responded, "Ha ha, I know. But then, after I'm gone, you can finally start your incarcerated woman's ministry." Chris meant the comment as a joke, but Katrina didn't find it funny.

"Would you stop saying that?" she said, pounding a fist on the bottom of the sink.

"Sorry, I just know the prison ministry thing is your passion."

"That's not what I'm talking about!" "Oh, right. I was just joking about that," he said in reference to the statement '*after I'm gone.*'

"I told you to stop joking about that!"

"All right, babe. I'm sorry. Sometimes I just think you should prepare for—"

"I'm preparing for it in my own way. I'm not going to spend all my time living in the future just to miss what I have here...now."

Chris then went over to his wife and put his arms around her. She had paused doing the dishes. "I'm sorry, babe. I don't think sometimes." He then kissed her neck. Then she smiled.

"Hey, tomorrow's Saturday, how 'bout we go on a date tomorrow evening? We've been so busy fixing things, and with church stuff, we haven't had much *us* time," Chris suggested. That expanded her smile, and she turned to face him and put her wet and soapy hands around his neck.

"That sounds great," she simply responded. Then she gave him a kiss on the lips. She then turned back to the dishes.

"Oh, I have to go talk to Pastor Myers real quick. I'll be back soon though," Chris informed.

"Okay, I'll see you in a bit." She then turned the water back on to rinse the dishes off, but then the seal broke at the base of the faucet and water shot out at Katrina, drenching her clothes. "Ah!" She turned off the water and grabbed a towel to dry herself off. Then she looked down at the mail; the fifty-percent-off coupon was lying there.

"Sassy fashion, huh. Sounds like my kind of store."

****

Meanwhile

"What can I do for you, Chris?" Pastor Myers asked.

"I have an odd request for you."

"Is that so? I was under the impression that you didn't need help with anything," Myers sarcastically replied.

"Yeah, well, this involves a purchase."

"What kind of purchase?"

"The community center over on Ivy St.," Chris asked, somewhat hesitantly.

"Chris, you do remember I said, within reason?"

"I know it's an unusual request—"

"Unusual? How about an impossible request."

The comment struck Chris fairly oddly as he doesn't believe in impossible things. "You know what else is impossible? Being stabbed fifty times and surviving," Chris said, to which Myers lightly nodded. "Look, Pastor, that place is dilapidated. It's in an area that no real investors are going to set up shop in or whatnot. The bank is obviously making property tax payments on it, I'm sure. If we bring it under the church, we can use it for the youth program. Besides, I just have to be real with you about youth night here...it sucks. I'm just saying. And I'll even fix up the center. It can be like a faith center or something."

"Chris, that sounds great. But we would still have to purchase it and the odds of the bank selling it for what we can afford—well, agreed that it's not impossible, but I would think it's unlikely."

"I'll make you a deal." He then pulled out some cash and set it on Pastor Myer's desk. "That's a hundred and twenty dollars. Double our tithe. If they won't give it to you for sixty dollars, pretend we never had this conversation," Chris responded in confidence.

Myers nodded, then said, "All right. I'll go to the bank." Chris then got up and headed to the door.

"You know, Chris...you're the first person who's ever told me that youth night sucks. But I've thought the same thing for a long time...just with a softer vernacular."

"Yeah, I'm sorry, I can be a little rough around the edges still. My wife reminds me of that frequently. Well, have fun at the bank," Chris said before leaving the pastor to go to the bank.

****

Later
At the bank

"Myers?" a bank representative called out in the lobby of the bank. Myers stood up and followed the rep into his office.

"How can I help you?" the rep asked.

"Yeah, I'm interested in the old community center down on Ivy St.," responded Myers.

The rep glanced at the pastor in disbelief. "That hollowed-out piece of junk in the center of Brick Town?"

"Yeah, that would be the one."

"Can I ask what your interest in it is?"

"Absolutely. I'm the pastor of Hope Community Church, and the idea of expanding our youth ministry has recently come up. We would like to use that building for that purpose," Myers explained.

"Okay. I'm sure we can work something out. How are you planning on paying?"

"Cash," Myers said.

"Really. How much are you offering?" Pastor Myers then dug out the cash from his pocket, though a bit hesitantly, and sat it on the rep's desk.

The rep counted it. "Sir, this is sixty dollars." Myers nodded. "I know the building is in bad shape, but it still sits on about four acres."

"Just out of curiosity," Myers interjected, "how many offers have you had on the property since you've repossessed it?" The rep sat silently in his chair indicative of receiving Myers's point. Then the branch manager knocked on the door.

"Come in," the rep said.

"Sorry to interrupt, just a reminder we have a meeting before we close up shop today."

"I'll be there after I'm done here," the rep said. "Hey, boss!"

"Yeah."

"This gentleman wants to buy the old community center for his church...for a youth-group-type thing."

"The one we've been carrying down in Brick Town on Ivy?"

"Yeah, that's the one."

"How much is he offering?"

"Sixty dollars," the rep informed.

"*Sixty dollars*?!"

****

"Hey, hunny," Katrina said in front of the stove, cooking dinner. Chris was under the kitchen sink fixing the leak.

"Yeah," he responded.

"I'm gonna go check out that fashion place tomorrow. I want to pick up something new for our date."

"Nice!" he responded. Then there was a knock on their front door. Katrina answered it. It was Pastor Myers.

"Hey, Pastor, come in," she said.

"Thanks, I have some news from the bank." Chris crawled out from under the sink, got up, and turned on the water—the faucet was fixed.

"What kind of news?" Chris asked. The pastor handed him his sixty dollars back. "Well, it was worth a shot at least."

"It was a good one. Because they gave it to us," Myers revealed.

"What! That's amazing!" Chris said excitedly.

"Wait, what's going on?" Katrina interjected. "Who gave us what?"

"The bank gave us the community center," Chris simply explained.

"I didn't know we wanted it. What are we going to use it for?" she further inquired.

"For the youth. It can be an expanded part of our outreach," Chris further explained.

"So when we're you going to tell me about this?" Katrina asked.

"Didn't I tell you?" Chris thought to himself, to which Katrina simply shook her head.

"I think I'll leave now," Myers said, sensing a slight controversy. "Have a good evening, you two. Whatever you're making, Katrina, smells great."

"Thank you, Pastor, have a good evening too," Katrina responded.

"Sorry, babe, it just came to me so fast. The community center was repossessed by the bank after some guy who ran it died. But most of the kids in the area flock to this place."

"It sounds like this Joshua Nickel fella does too. This better not cause problems," she reminded Chris.

"No problems. In fact, I think the Lord wants me to connect with that kid."

"How do you know?"

"I just feel like that's what he wants me to do. Plus, he's afraid of me."

"Did you give him a reason to?"

"No. I'm not sure why, but he is."

"I hope you're right."

CHAPTER

7

A COUPON FROM GOD

It was mid-morning. Katrina had left to visit the Sassy Fashion Store, armed with her fifty-percent coupon, to find something new to wear for her and her husband's date later that evening. On the way, she stopped at two traffic lights, and at both lights, there was a billboard within view. Both billboards featured the same model but advertised different products; one was makeup and the other lingerie. Normally billboards never drew her attention, especially ones featuring a lacy woman. But she found herself drawn to the model's face both times.

As she pulled into the parking lot of the fashion store, the picture of the woman on the billboards was annoyingly in the front of her mind but soon took a back seat as the sense of being out of place became a prominent thought. Even her car, though clean and not very old, couldn't compare to the mostly Porsches, corvettes, Lexus, etc. outside the fashion store. She debated with herself about possibly ditching the fifty-percent coupon and going to a different store, closer to her income level, but then said to herself, "Surely something in there is under a hundred dollars," then proceeded into the store.

Inside, every item was high-quality and not to mention high in cost. She walked around row after row, occasionally stopping to look at a dress that was pretty. "Three hundred dollars? For what? A silk rag with a string on it?" she would say to herself before moving on.

"Oh good, a clearance rack," she said, thinking surely she could find something. As she rummaged through the shirts, which weren't as prestigious as the majority of the clothes, she looked up and saw a woman trying on lipstick at the makeup counter just across the aisle from her. Next to her was a cart with three dresses in it. After every lipstick trial, she would hand it back to the associate lady tending the counter who would then hand her a different color. Something about the red hair reminded her of someone but wasn't sure who. At one point the woman turned and looked in Katrina's direction for just a split second before saying something to the associate then throwing the lipstick in the cart and moving on. Immediately the woman's face from the billboard came back to mind—that was her. She then felt a prompting to follow her, but she fought against it thinking it was a ridiculous idea, but becoming annoyed at the prompting she randomly grabbed a shirt off the rack next to her, threw it in her cart, and went over to the makeup counter to talk to the associate.

"I'm sorry, but was that—"

"Tiffany Love?" the retail associate responded.

"Tiffany Love?" Katrina wasn't all that familiar with the name.

"The model, Tiffany Love," the retail further explained.

"The girl on the billboards by—"

"Yep, that's her. She's in here five or six times a month," the associate added.

"Oh, so you must know her pretty well then, I take it."

"Not really. She doesn't say much. She smiles a lot though. But I have to say, sometimes I'm not convinced those are her smiles," the associate further explained.

"Oh really, that doesn't sound good."

"Right, I guess being the sexiest woman in America, doesn't equate to happiness. At least from my perspective."

"That's a good perspective. Thank you for that."

"No problem. Hey, we're having a flash sale. Twenty percent off lipstick."

"Sure, how much?"

"Seventy-six dollars."

"SEVENTY-SIX DOLLARS!?"

Katrina complained out loud to herself, within the comfort of her own car of course, about the cost of the shirt that she bought, which she never even unfolded to see what was on it. "Forty dollars for a t-shirt even with a fifty-percent coupon. I'm crazy."

She came to a stop at a red light. Shortly thereafter, a convertible pulled up in the lane next to her. She glanced over and saw Tiffany. Immediately, she again felt prompted to follow her. But she argued with the prompting once again. After the light turned green, the annoying feeling caused her to change lanes, two cars behind Tiffany, and soon turned into a wealthy suburban housing development. Katrina kept her distance, and when she saw Tiffany pull into a cul-de-sac, which only three small mansions occupied, she stopped along a curb just outside.

"I'm pretty sure this is stalking, Lord. And there are laws against it, especially in this city," she informed God. After a few minutes, she finally drove into the cul-de-sac nervously and up the driveway. The wide driveway was long and led to a three-car garage that attached to the house. The garage door was still up with only one vehicle in the garage—the convertible. The driveway also split and curved leading to the front of the house, which Katrina followed. She got out again nervously, and looked around.

The house was a very luxurious building. Opposite the house in a section of the yard was a concrete fountain. But it looked as though it hadn't run in a few years. Several flower beds lined both sides of the drive, and though there were some plants, it looked as though whoever took care of them was fairly amateur in the field of horticulture.

She then walked up the large steps to the front door, which was lined with decorative glass. As she approached, she noticed the door was half-open. She knocked on it and said, "Hello?" No answer. She took a couple of steps inside and again, with a little more force, said, "Hello?" She looked around the large formal room. Not much was in it other than a couple of couches on a beautiful hardwood floor though needed sweeping, and of course lined with wine bottles. Near the door was a fireplace, which also needed to be cleaned.

There were framed pictures on the mantle above the fireplace, all face down except one. "Hello? Ms. Love?" she again said. Her curiosity drew her to the pictures on the mantle, and thus she walked all the way in and over to the fireplace. The one standing was of an older gentleman's face close-up, brown hair, and silver eyes. She then began standing up the other pictures. One was obviously a family picture—an older couple, and three teenagers; two girls and a boy. Another picture had a little redhead girl and an older man who appeared to be playing with the child. Other pictures were obviously of a romantic or married couple. Katrina assumed the pictures were of Tiffany's family. She got lost in thought as she studied the photos, until, "Why are you following me?" a stern voice from the doorway startled Katrina. She quickly turned to see Tiffany—her eyes wide open, her mouth tightly closed. She had on a provocative dress, the same one Katrina saw her in at the store. Immediately a negative feeling engulfed the environment.

"Oh my goodness! You startled me. I'm sorry. The door was open. I knocked, and well, I'm sorry. I'm leaving," Katrina said, grasping for words.

"What do you want?" Tiffany said, again in a stern tone.

At this, Katrina closed her eyes and took a breath considering her words carefully, then responded, "I just wanted to know that you're okay."

"I'm okay," Tiffany un-hesitantly responded. She never moved from her position in the doorway, which was Katrina's only way out of course; in fact, Tiffany stood stiff as a board.

"Oh, okay. That's, good. I really didn't mean to intrude—"

"Who are you?" Tiffany cut her off.

"I'm sorry, I'm Katrina Belvu, and I'm actually part of a minis try that—"

"Katrina?" Tiffany again cut her off.

"Yes."

At that, Tiffany's shoulders dropped, her breathing changed, and her hostile expression vanished. "That was my mom's name."

"Your mother's name was Katrina?" Tiffany simply nodded. Katrina then turned to the pictures and pointed to the redheaded lady in them. "Is this your mom?"

"Yeah."

"Is this you?" Katrina pointed to one of the teenagers in the family picture.

"Yeah. And my brother and sister." "I'm guessing this is your father." Katrina referred to the picture of the gentleman close-up, to which Tiffany nodded. Tiffany then walked over to that same picture and put her hand on top of it. Katrina considered her next statement carefully and then said, "Can I ask a question? And if you don't want to answer, that's fine...I guess I'm just curious."

Tiffany turned, holding the picture close to her chest, and answered, "Yeah."

"What happened to your family?"

Tiffany didn't answer immediately. Her eyes moved, as if trying to remember the answer to a multiple-choice question, then responded, "They're dead." The answer was what Katrina feared.

"Can I ask what happened?"

Tiffany slowly put back the picture of her father, then grabbed the family picture and stared at it for a moment, again, as if searching for the memory. "My daddy owns...I mean, he owned a company. So he has...he had a private plane. There was a family vacation. I couldn't go because I had to finish a term paper for college. On their way back from Cancun, something went wrong on the plane and it crashed." Tiffany slowly put the picture back on the mantle then stared at it.

Katrina teared up and put a hand over her mouth. "Oh my goodness, child. Are you okay?"

Tiffany turned around, almost like a robot, completely emotionless, but then responded, "I...miss...them."

At that, Katrina slung her arms around Tiffany and pulled her close. "You're not alone, Tiffany." An expression of shock took over Tiffany's face as if this type of embrace was completely foreign to her. She stood there stiff as a board still with Katrina's arms wrapped around her. Then, a single tear fell from an eye, bringing with it some of her eyeliner. Her face then sunk onto Katrina's shoulder and her arms, likewise, wrapped around Katrina's back before she began sobbing.

"Shhh, it's okay, it's okay," Katrina consoled her for several minutes. "Do you live here all alone?" Tiffany nodded. "Would you like to come with me and stay with us for a couple of days so you won't be so alone?"

"I can't."

"Why not?"

"I have a photoshoot this afternoon."

"Can you reschedule it?"

"No. That's why I had to buy some new dresses. I always have to be pretty," Tiffany explained without much enthusiasm.

"Sweetheart, you look gorgeous in what you have on now. To be honest, you could cover up a little more."

"I have to be prettier than everyone else—all the time."

"But why?"

Tiffany wrapped her arms around herself and looked at the floor before responding. "People own me." The statement immediately aroused a sense of aggression within Katrina.

"What do you mean *people own you? Who does*?" Katrina said with a firmer voice.

"You know, I used to be smart. I have degrees and certificates. I was getting my master's degree in physics. After the accident, I inherited the company. But I didn't know what to do. I made some mistakes. And the stocks fell. The board of directors locked me out, but it couldn't recover, so they liquidated my shares and the company was taken over by the other company. *I lost my daddy's business*," Tiffany continued explaining while tears flowed down her face. "Five million dollars sounds like a lot of money. But my daddy's house is really expensive and just the property taxes, in a year, took all the money. I got an attorney to file bankruptcy. The attorney said he found a way I could keep my daddy's house. So I signed things. I found out later that Glamour Entertainment was one of my attorney's clients too. They said they'd pay off my daddy's house for me, and I can still keep it. All I would have to do is have some pictures taken every once in a while. It sounded okay; I was desperate. Now I have to show up at venues and dance a little...if you want to call stretching and shaking things dancing," Tiffany shamefully explained.

Katrina listened intently while also considering ways to help her out of her obviously negative situation. "I have to ask, do they make you do anything?"

"Sexually?" Tiffany assumed.

"Yeah."

"No. I was at least smart enough to get that in the contracts. But in the industry, you meet really cute guys. And they're nice, *really nice*...in the beginning," Tiffany expressed more shame as she continued. "And I get really attached. I don't know why. But I bring guys home sometimes thinking, if I make them happy, maybe they'll stay, and then I'll be happy, I guess? But they always go away. Except for Brett. He stayed."

"Brett?" Katrina asked.

"Brett Karmal was an MMA fighter. He was good for my image. But when he lost to Joshua Nickel, he lost his sponsors and everything," Tiffany further explained.

"Joshua Nickel?" Katrina recognized that name immediately.

"Yeah. Do you know him?"

"My husband ran into him the other day" was all Katrina said about Joshua, for one, she simply didn't know him and, two, she noticed the mere mention of his name appeared to have an arousing effect on Tiffany.

"Oh, okay," Tiffany said, then continued, "but Brett, he was always angry. And he never had very good hygiene," Tiffany admitted. "Me, I like to be clean. I take a lot of showers. Which is weird."

"What's weird?"

"I take showers after showers. Sometimes I'll stay in the shower all day. But I never feel clean. Sometimes I wish I could take off my skin." She then looked at Katrina as the fact that she was a complete stranger in her house dawned on her. "Why am I telling you all this? I don't even know you."

Katrina grabbed her hand as a sign of comfort and support. "I think God is letting you know that you can trust me."

"God?" Tiffany said as if the word was somewhat foreign to her. "How come he didn't take me with them?"

The question further tugged at Katrina's heart, "Maybe we can search for that answer together."

Tiffany smiled—the smile was definitely hers—then looking at a clock on the wall, said, "I need to start getting ready."

"Of course. Thanks for sharing," Katrina said, then grabbed a piece of paper and pen out of her purse. "Here's my number, call me for any reason any time, okay?" She handed Tiffany the piece of paper then backed up toward the door.

"Okay. I will." Tiffany stood in the doorway watching Katrina leave. They waved at each other as Katrina drove off, then she closed the door to prepare for her photoshoot.

****

"Chris!" Katrina said after getting back home.

"What's up?" he responded, eating a bowl of cereal.

"You won't believe what happened today?! I ran into Tiffany Love!" Katrina put her purse down and the bag containing the high-priced shirt on the table.

Chris's eyes went back and forth trying to compute who that was. "Hmmm, sorry, babe, not quite ringing a bell."

"Tiffany Love is a supermodel."

"Okay?"

"I saw her at Sassy Fashion."

"Did you talk to her?"

"Well, I followed her to her house, and—"

"Babe, that's stalking."

"*I know*, that's what I said to the Lord, but I kept feeling like he wanted me to follow her."

"Really?"

"It was kinda creepy in the beginning. For a minute I thought I was about to be part of a *Slasher* movie." Chris gave her a concerned look at that statement. "Oh, don't look at me like that, you were part of a *Slasher* movie," she said rhetorically.

"Okay, so what happened?" Then Katrina began telling him what transpired.

"Oh, and she knows Joshua Nickel."

"Really? Like, she knows Joshua Nickel, or does she *know* Joshua Nickel?"

"Well, we didn't get much further into that part of the discussion, but she mentioned his name, and I thought out loud, hmmm, my husband met a Joshua Nickel. When she heard that, her estrogen level went through the roof."

"How do you figure that?"

"Babe, I'm a woman, I can tell when another woman's in heat, especially for someone specific."

"Fair enough," Chris simply responded and then, being nosy, went to see what she bought from the fashion store, while Katrina got on her phone to search for a connection between Joshua and Tiffany. Chris pulled out the shirt and simply unfolded the first half. It was a t-shirt with a silhouette of a cowgirl. He turned to Katrina with the shirt, which the bottom was still folded, with a questioned look on his face.

"Is this for you? Or for me?"

"Oh, goodness gracious," she said out loud. "I guess for you."

Chris then unfolded the rest of it. It was a triple extra-large. "Hmmm, I don't think so," he responded as the length of the shirt ended at his kneecaps.

"Well, I guess I needed a new nightgown," she concluded, to which they laugh. Then she found what she was looking for on her phone and showed Chris. It was the highly publicized exotic interaction from Joshua's first, and thus far last, professional fight.

"Woah," Chris said. "How come you never kiss me like that?" he sarcastically commented.

"How come you don't give me a reason to?" she replied with a flirtatious smile and then kissed him on the lips.

"Hmmm. Maybe we can skip the date and—"

"Oh, I don't think so," Katrina quickly responded.

BUILDING HOPE

Early the following Monday morning, Katrina woke up with tears, hearing the scream of an infant. The dream of the child in a black abyss lingered in her thoughts for a moment. Her breathing was fast. She sobbed as silently as she could to not wake her husband next to her. She then got out of the bed and went into the living room in which the only light was from a dim night light next to the couch where she knelt down at the foot of in intense prayer. Chris woke up hearing the sobbing. It wasn't the first time she woke up from the dream of a screaming infant, but they had become less random. He stayed in bed and prayed for her. Then after a few minutes, he came out, knelt down next to her, and put his hand on her shoulder. She then fully embraced him, crying on his shoulder, stuttering the words "I'm sorry, I'm so, so, so sorry" over and over again, but the phrases weren't directed to Chris. This scene went on for some time.

****

Later that same morning, after daybreak, Chris, being the athletic junky, went for his daily run. However, his destination was the community center. Pastor Myers had given Chris the deed to the property, and Chris carried it with him on his jog. On his route, he came across an older black man having trouble with his truck.

"Need some help?" Chris said as he approached.

At first, the individual was hesitant but then responded, "I don't know if you can help. I've been having problems with this piece of junk for a while. I think it may have finally kicked the bucket."

"Do you mind if I take a look?"

"If you want to waste your time on it, be my guest." He handed Chris the keys, who attempted to start it, but it only made a noise, though one he was familiar with.

"Do you have a hammer?"

The old man fetched an old wooden handled hammer. "Here you go," he handed it to Chris. "Are you going to beat the engine to make sure it's dead?" he said sarcastically.

"Ha ha ha. Believe it or not, sometimes the ol' banging on stuff works." Chris then got on the ground, looked under the vehicle, found the starter, and tapped on it a few times. He then got back in the truck, and the engine started. "Well, the good news is, it's just your starter. The bad news is, it's your starter."

"Ha ha ha," the old man laughed.

"I can probably get you one, but I would most likely need yours. Do you need the truck right now?"

"I have a doctor's appointment in a bit."

"I can give you a ride—"

"Nah, I don't want to be a burden."

"It's no burden. I just live down the block, in the parish."

"Well, thank you—"

"Chris is my name."

"Thank you, Chris. My name is Jerry. I think I'll just try my luck with this hunk."

"All right. Let me pray for you first real fast." "Sure." Chris then put his arm around Jerry and prayed for protection over him and that his truck would get him where he needed to go and back.

This was the beginning of a new hope in the area as Chris continued on his jog stopping to greet and pray for everyone he saw on his way to the community center where he began cleaning, taking out the trash, fixing fixtures, and remodeling. There was a boxing ring in the center of the building; it had some tears in the mat and some of the ropes had been cut. He repaired, to the best of his jerry-rigging ability, the tattered fabric and ropes.

Another smaller room contained some weights and a bench. Dust covered them all. He dusted and organized the weight room. The bathroom plumbing had a few issues, which he also fixed. He spent the majority of the day in the community center. Katrina came down and brought him lunch, and he showed her around. She still had mixed feelings about it. Katrina, though having more faith in God than most Christians, still tended to veer on the side of practicality more than Chris who had no problem stepping out on faith in any circumstance; thus, the couple balanced each other out very well. What Katrina would see as merely a tree stump, Chris saw a platform to share his faith in Jesus.

It was approaching midafternoon. About the time for the kids around the neighborhood to begin their descent onto the property, Chris was mowing in the front of the building when the first few kids showed up.

"Hey! You're that guy that was here a couple of days ago," they said.

"I *am* that guy," Chris responded. These kids appeared to range in age from ten to fifteen.

"Joshua's not going to be happy that you're here."

"Why's that?"

"Didn't you hear what he told you? He said it's not your playground."

Chris smiled, then pulled out a folded piece of paper. "You know what this is?"

"It says deed on it," they responded.

"This is the deed to this entire four-acre lot, including the community center. The bank that owned this place gave it to the church I belong to. And I'm in charge of taking care of it now."

More kids from the area began walking up onto the property. Now they ranged in age from nine to nineteen. They began encircling Chris to hear what he had to say.

"What are you going to do with the place?" they further asked.

"Come in and see." Chris then led them into the community center. Many of the older kids had been in the center, but it had been before the bank repossessed it and locked it up after Cad had passed away.

"Woah!" Many of them were excited, especially the younger ones who'd never seen a boxing ring in real life before. The place still needed a lot of work—cracks in the paint, the windows still had boards on them because the glass was busted out in most of them. Yet others expressed that exact sentiment to Chris. "This place looks like a dump."

"I'm working on it. There's a lot to do, though. I could use the help. Any volunteers?"

Many of them liked the idea of being a part of the project. Still, others weren't all that enthusiastic about it. One such couple was in a corner making out. That was one of the other activities many of the area young people would use the community center for—promiscuity. Drugs and alcohol had been used on the property as well. Chris spotted the two in the corner and said, "Hey, you two?" They looked over at him. "Do one of you need an ambulance?" he said rhetorically. They looked at him cockeyed and responded in the negative. "Let me see your hands," Chris then said. They held their hands up.

"I don't see any rings on those hands." They got the hint and backed away from each other though disapproving of Chris's statement.

One of the older kids, who happened to be a friend of Joshua, took a picture of Chris with his phone and texted the picture to Joshua with the text, '*Look whose back.*'

Chris divided all who volunteered to help transform the community center into groups. Some were trimming the overgrown bushes around the center; others were pulling grass and weeds out of the cracks in the basketball court. Some worked inside puttying the walls, and still, others painted.

"That looks great," Chris would comment on the work as he passed the different crews on different projects.

The sun was getting low in the western sky, so Chris knew it was time for the kids to be heading to their homes—though, many didn't want to go home as they came from varying degrees of dysfunctional families. "Great job today. There will be more to do tomorrow afternoon if anyone wants to come back. But before you all leave, I'm going to pray over you all real quick."

Now, that was something almost every single one of these kids—which numbered at least fifty—never heard. Again some of the older/young adults of the group thought it was kind of embarrassing. Many of the younger kids were enthusiastic about it though. "Okay, grab a hand from someone next to you!" Again, the young enthusiastic kids quickly grabbed a hand. One of the older kids crossed his arms in defiance until a little girl looked up at him and asked, "Can you hold my hand?" to which he did, though hesitantly.

Chris then began his prayer. It lasted several minutes. His prayer projected so all could hear, even some of the homeowners across the street from the community center stepped outside to see what was going on. When they heard that it was a prayer, many of them even came out and joined the group. Chris prayed for the protection of each individual. He prayed for the community center and the work to be done there. He prayed that God through the Holy Spirit would stir the hearts and minds of all those in attendance to seek God. He prayed for many more things before ending the prayer, "In Jesus's name, Amen." And a choir of voices repeated him, "AMEN!"

After the prayer, the kids began disbanding. Some of the parents from across the street who had witnessed Chris and joined in the prayer stayed to talk to him about how bad things had gotten and how wonderful it was to see what he was doing. But the evening wasn't going to necessarily end on a happy octave, as a big four-by four began speeding down the street toward the community center blaring heavy metal music.

"Uh-oh. Here comes Josh," some of the remaining kids said.

Some of the younger kids began punching the air in anticipation of a physical conflict. Chris shook his head, disappointed at the obviously learned behavior. Joshua jumped out of his truck and came toward Chris with a look of hostility. The remaining kids parted to avoid getting in his way. Chris, however, remained cool, calm, and collected.

"Maybe you can't hear, but I said—"

"I heard what you said. And I respect what you said," Chris quickly interjected.

"Respect? That's funny considering I told you to not show up on my playground again."

"You did tell me that. But the problem is, this isn't your playground."

"What!" Joshua shouted.

Then one of the kids spoke up saying, "He's got a deed."

"A deed? To what?" Joshua continued.

Chris showed him the deed to the property. Joshua looked at it then back at Chris in disgust. "But you know what the difference between you and me is? You can be on my playground. As long as you follow the rules."

"This is bull—"

"FIRST!" Chris cut Joshua off before he could finish his profanity, "...rule. No *cursing* on my playground." Joshua's look of hostility was still present, but his understanding of property ownership laws compelled him to lightly nod, then slowly backed up, got in his truck, and peeled out.

"Oh man," another kid said. "I for sure thought he was going to UFC your butt."

Chris looked at the young kid and said, "Shouldn't you be heading home?"

"Yeah, but my parents are always yelling. They don't even know when I'm gone."

The statement broke Chris's heart. He then knelt down to his level and talked to him for a few minutes about love and the importance of respecting your parents. After the young kid affirmed that he wasn't in any physical danger, Chris encouraged him to go home. After a while, only one kid remained—the oldest who had taken the picture and sent it to Joshua.

"I don't pray much," the kid said. "Honestly I don't pray at all. But I have to admit, that was pretty cool."

"I think praying is pretty cool too," Chris responded with humor.

"I told Josh you were here," he then admitted.

"Well, I appreciate that."

"Do you?"

"Of course. The start of a new relationship, I think."

"If you say so, man. He's one of the few guys that you probably don't want a close relationship with. In fact, I didn't know if I wanted him to come down to see *his* butt get bit, or *yours*."

Chris smiled and nodded. "Which way you headed?"

"I live down that way."

"I'm going in that direction myself. Mind if I walk with you?"

"Yeah, if you want." Then the two of them began walking down the street talking.

"Do you know a whole lot about Josh?"

"It depends. I don't know a whole lot about his background, but he's from around here. He and his mom used to live in some crack house apartments about a twenty-minute walk from here. Actually, this area here is paradise compared to where he lived. I think I was nine when I first met him. He's six years older than me. I used to think he was so cool. He was tough and mean. But for some reason, us younger kids, he was fairly easy with. In fact, some guy tried picking up my sister one day—she was like seven—and Josh hurt that guy real bad. So I guess you can say he's a double-edged sword. But, his mom apparently got married to some big tycoon executive fella, and they ended up mov'n to *Richville*."

"Richville?"

"The Heights. I doubt you can walk on the sidewalk around that development unless you're worth half-a-mil a year." Chris chuckled at the rhetorical statement. "After that, he still came by every once in a while, but I don't think his mom liked him coming back down here. There was an incident apparently, something that happened to his mom. He didn't tell me what happened, but whatever it was I guess affected him pretty bad. That happened before I knew him. But he's a smart dude. He's a mechanic and owns his own business. Other than that, he's always been really reserved...unless he's mad. You just didn't want to get on his bad side. For whatever reason, he would go from okay nice to hulk out in a split second. He just snaps."

"He seems to have a temper on him," Chris agreed.

"Which is weird, why he didn't come after you the other night... or tonight. I don't know, maybe he's finally growing up. Ha ha ha."

"Speaking of the other night, what's the deal with him and Trevor?"

"Ha ha ha! I'll just say that I'd be surprised if there's a chick anywhere in the city between twenty and thirty who hasn't gotten to know Joshua...if you *know* what I'm saying. Trevor's just one of the few that actually has the balls to attempt to stand up to him."

"Well, that's a good thing."

"I guess."

"How long has he been a professional fighter?"

"That's a whole other story. What you're doing here with this place, another guy did the same thing a few years ago. This place was a dump...basically like it is now...and this guy Cad Arris leased this place and somewhat made it nice. He didn't invest too much into it, but he opened it up for the kids in the area. He didn't pray though."

"Cad Arris? That sounds familiar," Chris said. "Wasn't he a wrestler or something like twenty years ago?"

"Nah, man. He was a retired boxer. Another wealthy cat. Ha ha. Cad put that boxing ring in there, and when Joshua saw it, it's like he got addicted to it. That's when Joshua really started getting into fights. Normally Cad didn't come by; he just made sure the place was open. But one evening he did just in time to watch Josh take down three dudes in a row. One of them he put in a coma. It was said that those dudes were physically abusive to their ladies, and that's what set Joshua off. But he did get in a lot of legal trouble for that. From what I'd heard, Cad promised Josh he could make him into a professional fighter on the condition that he didn't get into any more fights outside of the ring. Of course, he was on parole for the guy who he put in a coma, but after that, Cad was good to his word. It just sucks that the old man overdosed before Josh could fight again. The community center got taken by the bank and closed. They tried to keep kids off the property for a while, but they quit trying. A little over a month ago Josh had his first MMA fight. And that was a heck of a fight. It's still being talked about. But after Cad passed and potential sponsors pulled support for his connection to Cad, Josh started losing it again. He's only been off parole for about seven months, and two busted-up guys got dropped off at the hospital in the past month."

"Are they sure it's Josh?"

"Those guys aren't saying. So it's not for sure. But it wouldn't surprise me."

"Sounds like he misses being in the ring," Chris determined.

"Could be, he told me being in the ring helped channel his aggression. Well, this is my house."

"All right, man, thanks for the info on Josh."

"You're welcome. But whatever you're thinking about Josh, think it through carefully."

"I will. Have a good night," Chris concluded.

"You too."

DEVINE PURPOSE IN DEBAUCHERY

"Morning, Snuggles," Tiffany said as she woke up with the usual depression and anxiety. She again medicated herself with the anxiety medicine and wine which she held in her arms. However, the wine didn't seem to have the same positive effect on her it normally has. Since Katrina's unexpected visit last weekend, her emotions appeared to be harder to push down with mere prescription drugs and alcohol. It had been a few weeks since her erotic encounter with Joshua. She had done her best to forget his eyes, and her interpretation of Joshua protecting her from Brett Karmel made it even harder to forget about him. The last person to ever protect her from anything was her deceased father, over four years ago.

Then she remembered Katrina and her words: *Call me if you need anything, anytime.* The idea of calling her conflicted with her physical desire, which she continuously confused with love. She didn't have Joshua's number but knew he had an auto service center. So she looked up the address. The thought of Katrina continued to annoy her, but she subdued it with more passionate fantasies of Joshua. After the usual several hours of getting ready, in the most provocative apparel she had—most of her clothing was provocative—she left for Joshua's shop.

The auto-shop was busy. Every bay had a vehicle in it. Apparently business was good, but then, Joshua was known to be one of the best mechanics in the area, which balanced out his more negative attributes—that is, pummeling people with his fists and his way with women.

The customer service door opened, which was also part of the garage. Immediately work stopped as all the men saw Tiffany walk in. She went to the counter and leaned over it glancing up at the counter rep and softly asked, "Is Joshua in today?"

He was just as speechless as the rest of the mechanics. But then replied, "Um, yeah. He's in his office."

"Thank you," she said and then stood back up and walked around the counter to the office door.

"Knock-knock."

"It's open," Joshua said.

Joshua was busy crunching numbers on his computer when the door opened and then closed. "Yeah, what's up...holy pink flamingo!" he responded as he turned to the surprise of Tiffany's presence—and appearance.

"Hi, Josh," she said seductively.

"Hi-i-i-i-i. It's, um, been a while. Is that...um...a new dress?"

"Yeah. Do you like it?" She then walked over to him, then sat on his desk directly in front of him.

"Yeah. You...um...look nice."

She smiled at the comment and then replied, "So do you."

"Thanks," he responded, looking down at his oil-stained mechanics uniform.

Meanwhile, Brody walked into the shop and headed toward Joshua's office.

"Joshua's kinda busy," the rep told him, but Brody ignored him. The office door opened. "Get out!" Joshua shouted.

"Sorry," Brody quickly said then slammed the door shut. He then walked over to the counter rep, leaned on the counter, and asked, "Just out of curiosity, was that—"

"Yep," the rep replied. Brody just nodded.

"I'm guessing he'll be taking the rest of the afternoon off."

"Probably," the rep agreed.

"Well, tell him to call me when he gets free time."

"Sure."

Back in the office, Tiffany continued her flirtatious visitation by asking, "Whatcha thinking about?" To which Joshua couldn't answer. "You want to know what I've been thinking about?"

"Yeah," he said, believing it to be something exotic.

She then leaned forward some and whispered, "Your eyes."

"My eyes?" he responded, surprised by the answer.

"Uh-huh." She finally slid down onto his lap then asked him, "What do you want right now?"

The whole situation was set up from the start to get Joshua to come back home with her, and thus far seemed to be succeeding, which was evident by his slow yet emphatic response: "Yo-o-u-u." The answer lifted Tiffany up.

"Really?" She brightly smiled then leaned in to kiss him, but then moved her mouth to his ear and whispered, "Dinner's at 6:00 p.m. I know you know where I live." She then got up and headed to the door. Seeing his wallet on the counter next to the door, she picked it up and added, "Just a little collateral...see ya at six." She then left the office, closing the door behind her.

"Wait!" Joshua shot up out of the chair after watching her leave with his wallet, but then quickly sat back down to let his hormones relax. "Oh man. Freak'n women."

****

Joshua was on time for dinner at Tiffany's house. She had the formal dining room set for the two of them. A candle was the centerpiece of the elongated table. The atmosphere was a lot different in Tiffany's home than when she was at his office. In fact, it was different from the first time he was there. Joshua stared at his plate of food—salmon, with a few vegetables.

"Do you like it?" she asked.

"Um, yeah. It's great," he fibbed. The salmon was burnt on the outside and not quite fully cooked on the inside. The vegetables were a bit runnier than he was used to as well. The glass of wine was good though. Tiffany watched intently how he was reacting to her attempt to be romantic.

"You're lying."

"Huh?" He looked up at her. She had an upset expression. The feeling of not wanting to be there welled up in him as he felt more embarrassed for her than anything. "No, it's...it's fine."

"You're not eating it." "Yeah, well, to be honest, I'm not all that hungry," he responded. She then jumped up out of her seat, went to the freezer, and said, "I can cook chicken, or some steak?" she began listing all the food in her freezer in an attempt to salvage her failure to impress Joshua enough to be with her.

"Can I ask you a question?" he said.

"Yeah."

"Have you ever cooked before?"

"Of course!" But then she realized that her cooking skills were limited to microwavable oatmeal and cereal primarily. "Okay, maybe not stuff like this. But I can figure it out. Please give me a chance."

"Look, it's been a nice evening...sort of, but I should be getting home," he said, getting up from the table.

"Wait!" Then out of desperation to keep him there by the only way she knows how, she ran up and threw herself onto him, licking his neck and kissing him. Her plan B was a relative success; after all, Joshua couldn't pass up a sexual encounter—too easily, that is. And soon they were both in Tiffany's bedroom.

****

Meanwhile, since the Nickel vs. Karmel fight, Brett had indeed lost everything. Over the past several weeks since the fight he's been living down in Canyon Park, brewing with vengeance against both Tiffany and Joshua, though Tiffany was more on his mind than Joshua. Brett's increasing hostility toward Tiffany led him toward Tiffany's development heading to her house. At the time he wasn't expecting anyone but Tiffany to be home. As he crossed her front lawn, he spotted a truck in the driveway but didn't know whose it was. He approached the front door. It was unlocked, and upon opening it, he heard the sounds of fornication from the upstairs. The pleasurable sounds intensified his feeling for vengeance. He slowly crept upstairs, pulling out a gun from the back of his pants. He then slowly walked into the room. The lust-filled couple wasn't paying attention until "Well, well, two birds at once," Brett said.

"AHH!" Tiffany screamed. Joshua, out of reflex, seeing the gun, tossed Tiffany aside and stood on the bed between her and the gun; though anticipating being shot, a surge of fear ran through his body. And then...nothing. The bullet got jammed and the gun didn't go off. Immediately Joshua seized the opportunity and grabbed Brett's arm, twisting it, which released the gun. Then Joshua began pelting Brett's face with his fists until he was on the ground. Joshua grabbed the gun, released the clip, and then as Brett started to get on his feet, Joshua hit Brett with the handle of the gun as hard as he could across the side of his face, cracking his skull right above his left temple. Blood poured from the gashing wound. Brett was dazed having not anticipated a physical fight, as he was expecting to simply shoot the fornicating couple. Tiffany, seeing that Brett was no longer a threat ran over to him, and began shouting at the top of her lungs in his ear as he crawled to the door, "LOSER! LOSER! LOSER! GET OUT OF MY HOUSE YOU STUPID UGLY LOSER!!"

Brett crawled out of the bedroom then got up and stumbled his way down the stairs and out of the house. The incident not only aroused Tiffany a hundred times more, in which she flung herself back onto Joshua to continue in their immoral acts that night, but Tiffany's infatuation for Joshua was now permanent as she saw him as her protector.

FAITH IN DEAD BRANCHES

Tiffany woke the next day with a smile. The fact that Joshua protected her a second time from Brett surely meant that he had a deep love for her—or so she thought until she rolled over and opened her eyes to an empty bed. "No-no-no-no-no," she said to herself over again. The feeling of life, again, drained out of her instantly. She grabbed the pills and the wine. When they didn't feel like they were working she jumped out of bed. She ran to her parents' room with a deranged hope that her parents were miraculously in their bed. As she entered the room she morphed into her younger self—running into the room as fast as seven-year-old feet can run and jumped on the bed. Her father woke up to the myriad of little Tiffany kisses before sitting up and tickling her. Her older brother and sister suddenly ran into the room as well and jumped on the bed laughing.

Tiffany was laughing hysterically until tears came running out. She then opened her eyes to find herself laying on her parents' empty bed. The tears were no longer joy-filled but of desperate grief, as she cried for Daddy. She ran to the bathroom and stared in the mirror. Her hair was more curly than usual—having just woken up not long before, not to mention the excitement that night added some additional characteristics to the matted red mess. She took a few deep breaths and collected herself. She wiped the mascara-filled tears off her face then began talking to her reflection to artificially lift herself up while pushing the grief back down.

"Why are you crying, Tiffany? You're Tiffany Love, and everyone *loves* Tiffany Love. You're the sexiest chick in the country, and sexy chicks don't cry. You get what you want, remember? Everyone turns their head when they see your body. That's right, Tiffany Love doesn't cry. She doesn't cry. You don't cry." Every phrase seemed to become more aggressive, the tears were difficult to keep back, which enhanced her aggression toward her reflection. "You can't cry, Tiffany. Stop crying, Tiffany. Stop crying! Stooop crying!" Finally, she grabbed a hairdryer on the counter and with a shout, "*stoooop cryyying*!" she slammed the hairdryer into her reflection, shattering both the mirror and the hairdryer.

A small piece of glass flew out and nicked a small area on her neck. A drop of blood rose out of her skin. She dabbed a finger in the drop of blood and stared at it. A piece of the shattered mirror laid in the sink, and she turned her gaze from the blood on her finger to the sharp edges of the piece of broken glass. For a brief moment, a vivid idea of how to see her family again passed through her mind. But then her phone started going off, which broke her out of her self-destructive conglomeration. She went back to her bedroom and grabbed her phone off the nightstand and answered it; it was a wrong number, however. But after hanging up, she saw a text message alert. She clicked on it. It simply said, "Unless you have a car problem, don't ever come to my shop again. Thanks. Josh N." The message took her breath away, stirring up her emotions she had just left in the bathroom and amplified them exponentially. But then, Katrina's words came back to mind: *Call me for anything, any time.*

Finally, she went to her contacts of which there were only Sandra, Kara, and the newest addition, Katrina, and tapped on her name. She let the phone ring just a few times before hanging up without an answer. "No, you don't need her," she again said to herself. But then her phone rang; it's Katrina.

"Hello?" Tiffany said.

"Hi, someone just called me from this number."

"Yeah, I did," Tiffany responded.

"Is this Tiffany?"

"Yeah."

Katrina was glad to hear from Tiffany as she was thinking about her and praying for her continuously since their first meeting. "Hey, sweetie, I'm glad you called. What's on your mind? You sound upset."

"Um, I...um...I need...someone," Tiffany replied, not really knowing why she tried to call in the first place.

"I'm free. Do you want to get together?"

"Yeah, I think I do."

"Sure, I can meet you for lunch. Do you have a favorite place?"

That perked Tiffany up as her favorite restaurant came to mind. "Yeah."

They then made arrangements to meet for lunch, in which Tiffany went through her many rituals of getting ready.

****

"Hey, Josh!" said the counter rep walking into Joshua's office. "There's a guy here with a car part he needs replacing."

"Okay? What does he want me to do with it?" he asked, which the rep shrugged his shoulders. Joshua left his office and to his annoying surprise stood the new community center owner. "Oh, you got to be kidding me!"

"Wow, that doesn't sound like very good customer service to me. I may have to write up a negative online review," Chris said, though sarcastically.

Joshua lightly nodded at the comment then asked, "*What can I do for you?*"

"I need to replace this starter for a friend of mine."

"Right. As you can see...*sir*...this isn't a *parts store*. It's a *service center.*"

"I know. I hear you can get some pretty cheap parts. Or did I hear wrong?"

"Depends, who's your friend?" Joshua asked rhetorically, not expecting an answer that was familiar to him.

"My good friend Jerry. He lives down the block from my house."

Well, the name did ring a bell, but it couldn't be the same Jerry. "Jerry? Is he an old black dude with an old ugly truck?"

"Yeah, do you know him?"

"I know just about everyone in that neighborhood."

"Did you know he needed a new starter?"

"Man, I've fixed his truck a few times...for free. What he needs is a new truck."

"That's for sure," Chris agreed. "But are you going to buy it for him? 'Cause just between you and me, I can only afford the starter," Chris responded with humor. Finally, Joshua chuckled a bit. For the first time, Joshua appeared to relax in Chris's presence. "Can we talk for a minute? I think we got off on the wrong foot."

Joshua nodded then walked him back to his office where he sat, slouching in his chair, still not too fond of the guy but, at the moment, seemed to tolerate his presence. "I watched the replay of your fight with Karmel. You ever gonna get in the cage again?"

"Is that what this is about?"

"Just a question, man."

"My only sponsor backed out when my old trainer was found dead from overdosing on black ice. Two other potentials ran for the hills. I tried crawling through every hoop to get them back. But they didn't want anything to do with someone who was connected to a drug trafficker."

"Did you know that he was doing that?"

"I knew he was selling something from time to time...or so I thought. I had no clue he was trafficking kilos of drugs," he replied then looked down at his desk. "Someone I thought I could actually admire and look up to...but just another disappointment. Just like almost everyone in my life."

"Except for your dad, I'm sure."

Joshua didn't say anything at first, then slowly nodded, then responded, "My *dad* taught me how to work on cars. He was one of the best mechanics in the area."

"He *was* one of the best? He retired now?"

Again, Joshua delayed in the response, then answered bluntly; "My dad's dead."

"Man, I'm sorry. I didn't know."

"I know you didn't. But you're asking a lot of questions. You're not like an undercover cop or something, are you?"

"Ha ha ha, I'm no undercover cop, man. My wife and I are the outreach pastors at Hope Community Church."

The title drew a look of shock across Joshua's face. "You? A pastor?"

"Yeah, I get that a lot. I'm an honorary pastor with lots of experience basically. My wife...she's the smart one. She's got the experience and the degree."

"You sure weren't acting like no pastor the other night."

"You mean, when I said no cursing? Or when I stopped a fight? Look, if you want to get back in the cage, I'll be at the community center this evening," Chris explained. "But I still need a starter."

Joshua got out of his seat, took the old starter from Chris, and said, "You know what? I have a date with my girlfriend tonight. But what I will do is, go get a new starter...for *Jerry*. Then I'm going to go install it...for *Jerry*."

"Man, thanks. I might make it home by dinner time then."

"Make it home by dinner? It's only three o'clock?"

"I know, but I walked here...for *Jerry*," Chris returned the rhetorical emphasis, to which Joshua smirked and nodded. "So you're in a committed relationship?" Chris further inquired, which Joshua again nodded—lying. "That's awesome, man. What's her name?"

"Dude, you ask a lot of questions."

"It's just a question."

Joshua disapprovingly nodded but then answered, "Jennifer."

"Cool, well, have fun on your date with Jennifer. And thanks for taking care of Jerry's truck for me," Chris said as he headed to the exit.

"You don't have a car?" he asked.

Chris explained, "My wife's using it today. She's out mentoring a young lady."

****

At a really expensive restaurant

"*Twenty dollars for a salad?*" Katrina thought to herself reading the menu. She then got a text from her husband informing her that Joshua had a girlfriend named Jennifer. And finally, after sitting there for what seemed like hours, she looked up and saw Tiffany walking toward her table. Katrina's eyes widened at her overly provocative appearance of which if she was her mother, she would not have let her out of the house in.

"Sorry, I'm late. I had to get dressed," Tiffany said as she sat down across from Katrina.

"Well, it's a good thing you took the time to dress up...for lunch, though it's almost dinnertime. This is quite a restaurant."

"They have yummy breadsticks," Tiffany said.

"Well, I'll have to try the breadsticks then," Katrina responded, noticing they weren't much cheaper than the salad. After giving the waiter their order, breadsticks and water for Katrina and wine for Tiffany, they began talking.

"So, Tiffany, how was the photoshoot?"

"It was okay, same as usual. Except for different colors."

"Different color clothes?"

"Yeah."

"So you sounded a little sad when I talked to you this morning."

"I did?" Tiffany said as if ashamed that Katrina could tell.

"Tiffany, it's okay to feel sad about things sometimes. What was making you sad?" Katrina assumed that it had everything to do with her deceased family.

"I, um—" She didn't want to explain to Katrina what actually took place the night before, which was what provoked her emotional distress that morning, so she recalled a dream she had about her family a few nights earlier.

"I had a dream about my family."

"Was it a good dream?"

"Yeah, it was my birthday. I forgot how old I was though. I have the dream every once in a while."

"So it's a reoccurring dream."

"Yeah."

After a few minutes, the waiter brought the breadsticks, water, and wine out.

"I'm going to say grace if that's okay."

"Yeah, that's okay." Tiffany watched Katrina put her hands together and bow her head. She followed suit but in a way that suggested that praying was foreign to her. Tiffany bowed her head, but her eyes stayed opened as she listened and watched Katrina pray, which included a prayer for Tiffany as well.

"Amen," Katrina concluded.

"Amen," Tiffany repeated. Then they both dove into the breadsticks.

"Wow, you're right, these are good breadsticks," Katrina added, "though not worth fifteen dollars in my book still." Tiffany chuckled at Katrina's comment.

"My husband, Chris, and I were discussing your situation this morning, from what you told me. And we felt that if your concern about leaving this Glamour Entertainment Company was for not having a place to live, we decided you can stay with us to help you get on your feet."

"If I leave, they'll take my daddy's house though."

"So it's not that you're worried about being destitute, you don't want to lose your daddy's house." Tiffany nodded in response. "Tiffany, sweetie, you know that your daddy's house isn't your daddy, right?"

"He built it though."

"You know, I know how you feel. My parents built their house too when I was a little girl. And when my dad passed away and my mom had to go into a nursing home, we had to sell my parents' house. And it was sad for a little while. But, sweetie, I'm afraid that you might be projecting the idea or character of your daddy onto his house," Katrina explained, to which Tiffany expressed a look of con fusion. "Okay, in other words, you're equating your dad's house to your dad. So in your mind somehow, you think since your dad built the house, that the house is your dad."

"That's silly, I know the house isn't my dad," Tiffany responded with a serious tone.

"I know that you know, rationally and logically, it's not, but..." Katrina could tell by Tiffany's expression that she was seemingly offended by the comment "...okay, I was just making an observation. And perhaps it was an inaccurate one." Katrina then reached into her purse and pulled out a pocket-size New Testament. "I thought maybe I could share some Bible verses with you, would that be okay?" Tiffany nodded, but in a way that suggested she wasn't too interested in the subject. After just a few moments of listening to Katrina read scripture, which she began in John 1:1, her eyes began wandering around the restaurant.

"Are you okay?" asked Katrina.

"Honestly, I kinda don't want to talk about the Bible," Tiffany said timidly.

"Okay, that's fine. What would you like to talk about?" Katrina then put the Bible back in her purse.

Tiffany bit her lip then responded, "Joshua."

"Joshua, Nickel?"

"Yeah," Tiffany responded, both verbally and bodily, suggesting the thought of Joshua was arousing to her but depressing to her as well. That same response, however, indicated to Katrina that Tiffany had an infatuation that could be a potentially dangerous mix combined with her other emotional instabilities.

"Well, he's a handsome young man, isn't he?" Katrina added, to further the conversation.

"Oh yeah, he's yummy."

Katrina chuckled, but more out of respect than that it was actually funny. "So what about Joshua attracts you to him?"

"I think it's his eyes. They're gorgeous."

"Okay, so just his eyes?"

"Well, he's pretty ripped too, but his eyes, there's just something about them."

"Not to get too personal, but have you two...been together?"

Tiffany put her head down a little then answered, "Yeees."

Katrina nodded, knowing this is going to be a more difficult quest than originally thought. "My husband told me that he has a girlfriend."

The statement made a noticeable change in Tiffany's demeanor, like someone about to hyperventilate. "Tiffany, are you okay?" Katrina asked, concerned.

Tiffany then pulled herself together, smiled, then asked, "What's her name?"

"Jennifer, I believe." If jealousy was a skin condition, Katrina could tell Tiffany had a severe case of it. Then, Tiffany grabbed her glass of wine, of which she had only taken a sip, then chugged the glass. She then signaled for the waiter.

"More wine please," Tiffany said to the waiter, holding up her glass. He filled it and was about to leave the table, but Tiffany grabbed his arm to keep him where he was while she chugged the whole glass of wine in front of him, to the shock of Katrina, who's jaw dropped and was slightly speechless. "More," Tiffany again said to the waiter. He again filled the glass and again she chugged it. She then grabbed the bottle from the waiter, which she then proceeded drinking directly from, all the while clasping the waiter's arm. Katrina was finally getting annoyed at her and grabbed the bottle from her.

"Young lady! That's enough." Katrina's firm tone got Tiffany's attention.

"Um, can I have my arm back please?" the waiter said.

Tiffany then looked up at his face and smiled, then asked him through the obvious influence of the alcohol, "Do you think I'm hot?"

"Um"—the waiter witnessed Katrina glancing up at the ceiling shaking her head, not as much embarrassed as she was righteously aggravated—"you...are...very attractive...*very, very* attractive." Tiffany's face lit up at hearing that.

"Keep stroking her ego, my friend," Katrina said to the waiter sarcastically, having slouched back in her seat and crossed her arms.

"Want to marry me?" Tiffany nonsensically blurted out just loud enough that a few other guests could hear.

"Is this going to affect my tip at all?" the waiter asked Katrina, who then leaned over the table and smiled at him.

"Tell her the truth, and I'll make sure you still get a tip. In fact the blunter it is, the better it will be," Katrina said.

"Well then, um, Ms. Love, I am deeply flattered that you would see me as someone you'd like to marry, but unfortunately, or should I say, fortunately, I'm already married..." Tiffany's smile began sinking, "...to someone who doesn't have a drinking problem..." her face sank further and her grip on his arm tightened, "...and *isn't* violent."

"Well said," Katrina commended the waiter, who continued describing Tiffany.

"And who hasn't slept with every guy in—"

"Okay, that's enough," Katrina stopped the waiter.

"You said to be blunt," the waiter reminded her.

"That I did. And you hit the nail right on the head," Katrina then rummaged through her purse and grabbed some money. "And for that, here's a crisp ten-dollar bill," to which the waiter looked at her funny. "What's wrong?"

"Ten dollars?" he said as if she had given him a penny.

"Okay, what would constitute a good tip?"

"Um, thirty bucks at least?"

"What? The breadsticks were only fifteen dollars," Katrina responded.

"The bottle of wine was three hundred dollars, ma'am." Katrina picked up the bottle and looked through the red-tinted glass, then noticed that Tiffany was successful at drinking nearly the whole bottle. "Also, could I get my arm back please?"

"Tiffany, let go of him." The command had a reverse effect as her hand squeezed tighter allowing her nails to dig in.

"Ouch!" he said.

"Tiffany!" Katrina reached over and slapped her hand, then she let go. Then Katrina ordered, "Now, let's see your credit card," with her hand out. Tiffany, obviously drunk, unzipped her little purse and handed the credit card to Katrina who in turn handed it to the waiter.

"Why'd you give him my card?" Tiffany slurred.

"Sweetheart, I might be a Christian, but rarely do I pay for other's stupidity," Katrina said with a smile. Tiffany just stared at her with a puss face. Shortly the manager came out to return the card as the waiter who had earlier served them refused to return to the table.

"Here's the credit card," the manager said, handing it to Katrina.

"Thank you."

"And if you don't mind, please get her out of here," the manager added.

"Excuse me?" Katrina responded.

"She bruised my server's arm. And she's obviously drunk," he explained. Katrina nodded, accepting the manager's request.

"I apologize, I'm trying to help her," said Katrina.

"Here's a little advice for you. She frequents this restaurant fairly often, and don't get me wrong, she will drop a few hundred dollars at a time, but she's the last person you want a relationship with."

Katrina smiled at the comment, then observed Tiffany who was in a drunken stupor staring at her fingernails and responded, "I'm not going anywhere."

"It's your life," the manager rhetorically responded, "just get her out of my restaurant."

Katrina took Tiffany's arm and walked her out of the restaurant and to her Toyota.

"My car is over there," Tiffany slurred.

"You're not driving. You're drunk," Katrina responded.

"You're not...my mom."

"Call me a concerned citizen." Katrina got her in the passenger seat and shut the door. She looked up and saw the manager in front of the restaurant waving at her; she left Tiffany's credit card on the table, so she walked back to the restaurant.

"Thanks for that," Katrina said, but the manager's eyes were about to bulge out of his head, to which she turned to the shock of seeing Tiffany having gotten out of the car laying on the hood provocatively. "Oh. My. Gosh!" Katrina exclaimed as a customer then came out of the restaurant and, also seeing the event, said, "What I'd like to do to that—"

SLAP! Katrina's hand contacted his face, then immediately said, "She's unavailable!" Then she marched to the vehicle like a mother intending on whooping a child. The manager shook his head and went back inside.

"Get back in that car, young lady!"

She got Tiffany back in the car and then set the child lock on the door before taking her back to her *daddy's* house.

****

Later that same afternoon, Joshua, having said he was going on a date with Jennifer, in order to convert his lie into an honest comment or at least a partially honest one, called the one woman who could possibly bring him to his knees, which is why he had avoided calling her for so long.

"Hello?" Jennifer answered.

"Hey, Jennifer?"

"Yeah?"

"Hey, it's Joshua."

She moved the phone away from her face, looked up at the ceiling, and silently mouthed "Yes!" then put the phone back to her ear.

"Jennifer? You there?"

"Yeah, sorry, I dropped the phone. Joshua who?" she said, deciding to play hard to get.

"Joshua Nickel?"

"Hmmm, the name rings a bell." Joshua at this point felt insulted. She really didn't know who Joshua Nickel was? "Do I know you?"

"Wow, um. You were at my after-fight party a month ago. We had a couple of beers together?" he reminded her.

"Oh, Josh Nickel. Yeah, now I remember. I dragged your drunken butt inside. That was romantic."

Joshua dropped his head and let out a sigh. This was definitely not the conversation he was expecting. "Right. Sorry about that."

"Eh, it's okay. So what can I do for you, *Joshua Nickel*?"

"I was wondering if you'd like to go out this evening."

"Hmmm, let me check my calendar real quick." Then, she laid on her bed, pretending to look at the calendar on her phone, "Nope, tonight I have a date with Tony." Joshua expressed shock at hearing that, but Jennifer continued, "Tomorrow, I have a date with Steve. The day after, I'm going out with Brandon. It looks like I'm booked all the way through next Friday. Wait, never mind. I have a date with a guy from my trigonometry class...he wants me to help him solve for X. I'm sure you're familiar with that, right, hunk? So I guess I can put you down for next month. How's that sound?"

"Um...okay?"

"Great. I have you down. Don't be late. Too-da-loo!" Then she hung up. He stared at his phone attempting to determine whether or not that conversation actually happened. He then grabbed a beer and began drinking when his phone rang again. It was Jennifer.

"Hello?"

"Josh, I'm sorry. I really don't have any dates. I don't want you to think I'm a slut like my roommates."

"We heard that," they said in the background.

"The thing is, you made me wait six weeks before you called me. So you're going to wait six weeks before you're *privileged* to take this gal out. That being said, do you still want to go out with me?"

After all that, Joshua thought, No way. But his vocal cords didn't get the message. "Yeah, I do."

"Okay. I expect you to call me every evening and keep a conversation. And in six weeks, you can come to pick me up for dinner. Oh, and, Josh, don't even *think* about touching anyone while you're waiting."

"All right."

"Well, I'm in the middle of doing psychology homework. So I got to let you go."

"Okay, have a good—" The phone hung up. "Night?" He went and sat in his living room. The TV was on which the news was reporting: "*This morning a terrorist plot on an FDA admin building in DC was thwarted by TID.*" Then he got a text from Jennifer. It was a picture of her, prominently displaying her permed brown hair and brown eyes. You'd think she knew his weakness. "Oh, crap."

CHAPTER

11

IRRATIONAL LOVE

Tiffany rambled on stuttering drunken words the entire ride back to her house. Katrina's experience with Tiffany, however, was beneficial in understanding her mentality. Once back at Tiffany's home, she assisted Tiffany into the house and sat her on one of the couches in the formal living room. After dropping Tiffany on the couch, Katrina straightened up and stretched—even a hundred and twenty-pound woman isn't that light for her. She turned around catching her breath just for a moment. And in that time, Tiffany managed to grab another bottle of wine that happened to be sitting next to the couch since wine bottles were obviously all over the house.

"Tiffany!" she shouted, seeing her chug another opened bottle of wine. Katrina grabbed it from her and took it to the kitchen and threw it in the trash. When Katrina returned to the living room, she saw Tiffany hanging off the opposite arm of the couch where another open wine bottle was, chugging that one as well. Katrina went and grabbed that one out of her hands too. "That's enough, young lady!"

"You're...not...my...mom," Tiffany stammered, wobbling back and forth in the couch seat—obviously her equilibrium was now affected by the alcohol.

"Would your mother let you drink like this?" Katrina asked. Tiffany broadly shook her head indicating that her mother would not have approved of Tiffany's behavior any more than Katrina approved of it. "Then consider me the ghost of your mother."

"*O-o-o-o-o-h...ghost...spooky*," Tiffany slurred rhetorically then fell over face-first onto the couch cushion out cold from intoxication. Katrina stood there, shaking her head. Then, with the bottle of wine in her hand, she took a drink. "Hmmm, not bad," she said.

Katrina managed to get Tiffany over her shoulder and slowly carried her up the many stairs to where the bedrooms were. One bedroom door was open and she went in. Then seeing a multitude of wine bottles all over the floor and that the bedding was covered in stains, evidence of her promiscuous lifestyle, she opened a door down the hall to a bedroom that looked like it hadn't been slept in in years. The air was stale, but not like the mustiness as what lingered in Tiffany's bedroom. This was Tiffany's parents' bedroom. Katrina laid Tiffany in the bed and pulled the sheets and blanket over her. Once she was covered up, Tiffany, in her sleep, maneuvered instinctively into her normal comfortable sleeping position. Katrina watched her curl up, and she smiled. She then sat next to her and prayed over her before finding a clear spot on her cheek from hair and kissed her with a motherly kiss. Katrina got up and opened a window to let some fresh air in the room. Then she left the room, closing the door most of the way but leaving it cracked.

Katrina considered leaving, but then she passed Tiffany's bedroom and decided to clean her room some by picking up all the wine bottles. The empty ones she put in the dumpster and the full ones she sat on the island in the kitchen. Then pulling the bedding off, she went looking for the washing machine.

She eventually ended up downstairs. However, upon entering the basement, a negative depressive feeling overcame her, enough so, she placed her hand on her chest. She saw the piles of upside-down pictures on the floor next to the walls where they once hung. Boxes of things such as Christmas decorations and other holiday or festive décor sat in random areas around the room. Several family-made DVDs sat on the floor in front of the large TV. She turned on the TV and pressed the play button on the DVD player. A video of Tiffany's family resumed. It was her birthday party. She let it play as she walked around the basement listening to it. Certain key phrases stuck out in the video.

"You have pretty eyes, Daddy."

"You're strong, Daddy."

"You protected me, Daddy."

"Anything for you, sweetheart."

"You're the prettiest little girl in the world."

At hearing these phrases, Katrina began considering that Tiffany's promiscuous lifestyle may not necessarily be an attempt to find a man for the sake of a relationship or even for the physical pleasure of sex.

Katrina found the room where the washing machine and dryer were. It was also the wine cellar where a collection of what seemed like an endless supply of wine was stored. Piles of clothes lined the floor. It almost appeared as if Tiffany had never done laundry, which explains why she always had a new outfit. She found the detergent, which had been bought four years ago—probably her parents bought it. She started the machine and put the bedding in the washer, with the detergent and as many clothes that she could fit in with the bedding that was on the floor.

While the washing machine was going, Katrina continued exploring the large house. The thought of one young lady maintaining such a huge mansion was overwhelming. She eventually made it to the desk in the back of the basement. She nearly passed it by when the top page of one of the two packs of papers in the cubby of the desk caught her eye: "Glamour." She then pulled the packs of paper out of the cubby. They were the Glamour Entertainment contracts. She started flipping through the pages, though her lack of legal terminology made it difficult to understand the majority of the contracts. Not to mention the length of each contract was easily over a hundred pages long. However, this prompted Katrina with an idea that could possibly help get Tiffany out of her situation. While she was flipping through the pages, she was startled by knocking on the front door and then, "Hello? Tiffany? It's us. Kara and Sandra!"

Katrina raced upstairs to meet them. "Hi, I'm Katrina. Tiffany's asleep," she said.

"Katrina?" they repeated as the name was familiar.

"Yeah."

"Tiffany told us about you."

"Oh, really?"

"Yeah. She said some lady just showed up in her house one day."

"Is that what she said?"

"Yeah. But she said you reminded her of her mom."

"Did you two know her parents?" Katrina asked.

"No. We only knew Tiffany from college. We remember the day she found out her parents died though."

"What happened?"

"She went pretty crazy. It was sad. She was at the top of the class. She was actually pretty dorky in a way. Her glasses made her eyes big. But she attempted suicide and was admitted to a hospital. She was there for a week I think. I know she missed their funeral even because of it. And then she moved back in here. She worked for her dad's company for a few months. I don't know what all happened there, but I guess it didn't work out. But then she, out of nowhere, got this modeling gig. I guess it works out for her, but she's not a happy person," they explained.

The three of them spent much of the evening talking and getting to know each other. They had migrated to the kitchen and sat at the island. Eventually, the topic came to boys, primarily prompted by Kara and Sandra due to their lustful nature. Katrina simply listened to them.

"I was thirteen when I got my first boyfriend," Kara said.

"Wow, that's young," Katrina responded.

"Not as young as Sandra," Kara added.

"I lost count how many boyfriends I had by that age," Sandra informed. Sandra and Kara laughed. Katrina on the other hand lightly grinned at the comment.

"So, just out of curiosity, were you two sexually active at those ages?" Katrina further inquired, to which they both acknowledged in the affirmative. "Why? If you don't mind me asking?"

The two of them looked at each other trying to think of an answer. "I don't know why. I just remember that I wanted my first boyfriend to perform certain acts on me and he couldn't, so I dumped him," Kara responded to the humor of herself and Sandra.

"How did you know about the act you wanted him to perform?" Katrina pressed. She felt that the two girls may have had something tragic happen to them but possibly suppressed. Kara thought harder and, at first, her answer was in the negative, but then, "Oh wait, I remember seeing that act at my aunt's house. She had some dirty magazines with couples performing different sex acts." After Kara said that, it then dawned on her. "You mean all my sex-crazed mentality spawns from one little magazine I saw one time?"

"I think so," Katrina said.

"Wow. I guess the whole 'A picture's worth a thousand words' is pretty accurate, huh," said Kara. "Sandra though, she's a porn addict...big time."

"Would you shut up," Sandra said in retaliation. "Besides, I was having sex before I ever seen naked pictures of anyone...in magazines or otherwise. Plus, pictures, aren't anything. I'd rather have it than look at it, if you know what I mean." Sandra laughed at her own statement, but that time neither Katrina nor Kara laughed with her. "Okay, so my uncle when I was like nine would get frisky with me. But it happens all the time, right? Besides, it was a long time ago. So no harm, no foul...it's okay, right?"

Kara and Katrina both glanced at Sandra with consoling expressions, then Katrina bluntly responded, "No, sweetie, it's not okay." Immediately tears welled up in Sandra's eyes. Katrina rushed around the island where she and Kara both embraced Sandra as she began sobbing. Soon all three were sobbing.

After several minutes, Sandra then looked at Katrina, smiled through her tears, and said, "Okay, it's your turn. Do you have a story?"

To which Katrina replied, "Yes."

The sun had set and the girls had to leave. They all hugged each other in the driveway with plans to meet again, and Kara and Sandra went back to their dorm. Katrina was considering leaving as well, but as she stood in the driveway after waving goodbye at Kara and Sandra, she could hear weeping coming from an upstairs window. She then went back into the house and up to the room. Tiffany was sobbingly muttering words in her sleep. Katrina then called Chris to inform him that she was going to stay with Tiffany that night, which Chris then decided to work on the community center later into the evening as he was anxious to get it ready for Friday evenings youth group.

It was around seven when he heard a truck approaching the front of the building. Chris headed to the front as Joshua stormed in through the front doors.

"Joshua," Chris greeted him. "How was your date?"

The look on Joshua's face was still that of someone vehemently disapproving of Chris taking over the center. "Something came up," he responded.

"Hmmm, that's convenient."

"You think I'm a liar?" Joshua responded. Then to keep his story straight, he showed Chris the picture of Jennifer as evidence that he—supposedly—had a girlfriend.

"Josh, I didn't call you a liar," Chris reassured him that he couldn't read his mind. "Pretty girl though. Treat her good," Chris advised. "So what brings you to my playground this evening?" Chris rhetorically inquired as he went to a wall and hung a large canvas of the Ten Commandments on it.

"You don't remember what you said this afternoon?" Joshua responded.

"I remember, but I want to hear it from your heart."

"My heart? What does that have anything to do with getting back in the ring?"

"Because, if I do this, I'm not going to be training you to fight so much as teaching you discipline."

"Discipline? I am disciplined."

"Oh, really? Tell me about the three guys that got dropped off at the hospital in the last month with their faces beat in."

Joshua lightly nodded his head, then hesitantly answered, "Those sons-of—"

"*First* rule!" Chris interjected him.

"Those *guys* like to beat their ladies. They got what they deserved. And they signed up to fight me. Besides, what makes you think it was me anyway?"

"Honestly, I didn't. But you just now told me you did," Chris responded, to which Joshua was dumbfounded at his own admission. "And I take it you can't pass up a set of fluttering eyes," Chris added.

"What?"

"For someone who *didn't* go on a date with the *girl he's committed to*, that's one bold paint job on your neck there."

Joshua wiped the area Chris was referencing with his hand, and some of the lipstick rubbed off. "Yeah, well, um—"

"Josh, if you're going to lie to me, you better have an amazing memory. So here's the deal, if you want to do this, you're gonna follow my rules."

"You know what, *Pastor*? You can *eat* your rules!" Then Joshua stormed out. Chris shook his head in disappointment. But Chris barely moved from where he stood when Joshua came storming back in.

"What rules?" Joshua emphatically asked.

"You already know my first rule. Second rule: no fighting unless it's in this ring here and I'm present." Joshua slowly nodded his head.

"Third rule—and this one will be tough: hands off the ladies."

"What?" Joshua again said in retaliation.

"You heard me," Chris simply responded. Joshua lightly nodded as Jennifer's words then rang in his head: *Don't even think about touching anyone while you're waiting.* "Last, but not least, Tuesday evenings, I go to a men's group."

"Are you serious?" Joshua responded. "Six o'clock at Hope Community Church."

"You want me to do all this stuff, but how do I know you're going to do what you said you're going to do?"

"That's a fair question. You don't know me very well. So I'll tell you what. If I don't follow through at the end of six months you're off the hook."

"Six months? That's a long time!" Joshua exclaimed.

Chris then put a hand out about shoulder-high. "Let's see your roundhouse," he said.

"Psh. Roundhouse?"

"That's what I said."

Joshua nodded then admitted, "I don't know what that is."

"You don't know what a roundhouse is? And you're supposed to be doing professional martial arts? Can you kick at all?"

"Well, yeah." Joshua then kicked but couldn't get his leg up to Chris's hand. Chris was shocked. Chris then lowered his hand. Then Joshua kicked and made contact, sort of.

"What was that?" Chris said insultingly.

"That was a kick."

"That wasn't a kick."

"Yeah, it was."

"My five-foot-tall grandmother can kick harder than that...and she's dead. If my eyes were closed, I would have thought a feather touched my palm."

The two of them looked at each for a moment, then Joshua began laughing. Chris smiled seeing Joshua's hostility subside. "You should probably give me eight months," Chris then added.

"Eight months?"

"It will probably take me that long to teach you to kick."

Joshua chuckled at the sarcasm again then responded, "Six months."

"You got it, six months. It's getting late, we start tomorrow night, good?" Joshua agreed, then left.

CHAPTER

12

HORROR STORIES & DELUSIONS

A series of mumbled words protruded from Tiffany accompanied with her normal morning tears as she began coming out of her sleep. She felt a hand stroking the side of her face, accompanied by the words "It's okay. I'm here."

"Mom, I miss you," she said through the tears.

"I'm here" again was said.

Then, as she became more cognizant, Tiffany realized that the short phrase wasn't from a dream or her imagination. Her eyes opened wide. "*MOM?*" She then lifted her head off of Katrina's lap expecting to miraculously see her mother. "Katrina?" she said.

"Yeah, it's me."

"You're not my mom."

Katrina lightly nodded with a consoling grin. "You're right."

"Why are you doing this?"

"Because I love you."

"But why do you love me? No one does."

"Jesus does. And your friends do too."

"No, they don't. They don't really know me. They just use my stuff."

"Well"—Katrina sat up from leaning against the wooden headboard of the bed all night and stretches—"it's almost eleven o'clock, my back's aching, and I'm hungry. I think I'm going to use your kitchen."

The two of them meandered to the kitchen, where Katrina rummaged through the cabinets and fridge finding food to cook for the two of them. Some of the unopened containers were a few years old. Katrina made some omelets for the two of them. At one point Tiffany grabbed a bottle of wine and was about to drink out of it when Katrina, without saying a word, grabbed it out of her hand, put it on the counter, then handed her a glass of water instead. Tiffany stared at the glass of water as if determining what it was for a moment before taking it to the island and sitting down. Katrina sat two plates on the island, both with an omelet and a piece of toast. Then she sat across from Tiffany, tipped her head, and prayed out loud. Tiffany bowed her head as well but mostly watched Katrina pray.

"In Jesus's name, Amen," Katrina concluded.

"Amen," Tiffany repeated, then they ate.

The stories of Tiffany's friends from the night before were on Katrina's mind, and she wondered whether or not something similar happened to Tiffany—that would surely explain a few more things. "Can I ask you a few more questions, Tiffany?"

"Okay," she replied.

"What do you think of pornography?"

"What? That stuff is disgusting. And my parents would have gone ape if they caught us with anything like that."

The answer was not what Katrina had expected. "Oh, really? I agree with you and your parents. It's horrible stuff. When did you start having sex?"

"Wow, Katrina, these are pretty personal questions."

"I'm sorry. I'm just trying to get to know you better and have a better understanding of your situation. But if you don't want to answer, that's completely fine."

Tiffany hesitated at first, but then told her, "When I first started working for Glamour Entertainment, one of the photographers was really nice. He would tell me things so I wouldn't be anxious. At one point he started buying me flowers. And then we started dating, and sex followed...he was my first. After a month, he had got a new photography job. He said he'd be gone for a week. Well, during that week, a woman called me, threatening me. It was his wife. I never felt so disgusting...and angry. I was sooo angry. So much so that there was another cute guy, who also flirted with me all the time, in more of a goofy way though, because he was married—no secret about that, and he talked about his wife quite a bit. I don't know what came over me, but I went to his house one evening and managed to get him to have sex with me."

"So you caused him do commit adultery?"

"I worked it out so that his wife would show up in the process. It worked."

"Oh my gosh, Tiffany!"

"I know it was horrible. I felt awful about it. But seeing the look on his face, I felt vindicated for what the first guy did to me. However, I got it back. His wife left him then we began dating and I fell in love with him. Then he left me two months later. He said he was waiting for me to get attached to him so he could hurt me. But that's how it started. Now I want it all the time. But I always feel filthy and disgusting. Everyone I meet says they can see a future with me...or something like that. But then they're gone. Anyway, that's my horror story."

"We're you ever forced to do anything against your will?"

"Well, no, not really. My first, over time, would make *suggestions*, and I did them...but I loved him. I'm messed up, aren't I?"

"Well, sometimes people don't think and instead act on impulse. But I won't bother you with any more questions like that. Okay?"

"All right." They then continued eating.

"Oh, I did, however, do some laundry for you yesterday."

"You did?" Tiffany was shocked.

"I did. I washed your bedding and about one-twentieth of the clothes you had piled up in your laundry room." Tiffany partly smiled, but out of embarrassment. "It's been a while since you did laundry it looked like."

"I kinda don't know how."

"You don't know how to do laundry?"

"I tried once. But nothing came out the same. There was a lady that did that stuff for us, so we never had to."

"Well, you have some clean clothes and sheets for your bed. Oh, and while I was doing that, I watched some of your home videos downstairs."

"You watched my movies?" Tiffany said disapprovingly.

"Yeah. You had a nice family. Were you homeschooled?"

"No. My sister and I went to a private girls' school. My brother went to a boys' school."

"That's nice. Not too many are privileged to be able to go to a private school."

"Have you ever—"

"You know what?" Tiffany interrupted, beginning to get annoyed at the onslaught of questions, then leaned forward and said antagonistically to Katrina, "Let's talk about something else."

"All right, what do you want to talk about?"

"You." Tiffany then leaned back in her chair with an antagonistic glance.

"That's fair. I have asked you a lot of questions. What would you like to know about me?"

"Hmmm. You radiate with *perfection*. You go to *church*, you're *married*...I bet he's hot too—"

"Oh yeah, he is. And off-limits," Katrina affirmed.

"The only thing missing is your quadruplets of kids you people are all about."

"Wow! I radiate perfection and am worthy of having quadruplets of kids," she responded rhetorically.

"I *surmise* you don't even have a pinprick of a negative moment in your life."

"Oh, sweetheart, I'm far from perfect."

"But you're supposed to say that, right? 'Cause it helps your appearance of being able to relate to us who've had screwed-up lives."

Tiffany's comments revealed to Katrina that Tiffany believed herself to be more of a victim than she actually was, which began to annoy Katrina, thus she asked, "Okay, so you want a story?"

Tiffany then leaned in on the island again resting her face on her hands. Every additional statement heightened her antagonism. "Actually, I want a *horror story*."

Katrina smiled then responded, "You want a horror story, huh? You got it...*Princess Jasmine*!" she retorted. "My father was the associate pastor of our church growing up."

"Ms. *Perfect*," Tiffany interjected.

Katrina ignored the comment and continued, "Which means, my parents had set standards of how we were to dress. I was seventeen. There was a boy I went to high school with that I was really into."

"Was he hot?"

"Oh yeah. I was totally infatuated with him...but so were a lot of girls though too. I was invited to a party at his house. So as to not look like such a goody-goody church girl, I took other clothes to school with me and changed. Then I went to the party afterward."

"Did you guys do it?"

"Well, I got what I asked for to say the least. They were doing beer bongs. I had *never* drank alcohol in my life. I basically *inhaled* two beers. I was immediately sloshed. I woke up the next morning *not a virgin* and next to a toilet in my own vomit. Talk about embarrassing. And *beyond* ashamed. I had to clean my own vomit at that guy's house. It wasn't until the following Monday before I was told of all the graphic things that he did to me...while I was intoxicated."

Tiffany's expression immediately changed upon hearing Katrina's story; it made hers pale in comparison not to mention it seemed like something completely uncharacteristic for a Christian girl to do. And for Tiffany, that was indeed a horrific event. "Oh my gosh. I'm so sorry," Tiffany said, having expected that to be the horror story.

"Oh, sweetheart," Katrina said condescendingly, "that's not the *horror* of the story. That's the opening credits. Two weeks later I was getting sick every morning. I was pregnant. I didn't tell anyone. Not my parents, my friends, *or* that guy. But after three months, it was starting to get noticeable. So I decided I needed to tell the dad. I remember I was kind of hoping that in a sense, if he found out that he knocked me up, then he'd stick around. Nope. He, instead, was *livid*. He antagonized me every day until finally I caved and had my innocent, unborn baby *torn apart—limb from limb—*and *ripped* out of me!" She emphatically described her abortion.

Tiffany's expression was as Katrina hoped, that of shock. "Is that horror enough for you, sweetheart?" Tiffany nodded. "Oh really? Well, guess what, that's still not all of it. During the *murder* of my baby, they screwed up. And I had to be taken to the hospital, where my uterus had to be removed. So I can never have *quadruplets* of kids, *dear*." Tears then welled up in Katrina's eyes as she aggressively lectured Tiffany. "So, Tiffany, I had my *baby murdered*! And though I have hope that I'll see my baby again, and I know Jesus forgave me of my *egregious* sin, even after almost thirty years I *still* wake up at night to the *screams* of a child and *dreams of a bloody baby*! You act like you're the world's biggest victim. Yet I *surmise* you don't even know what your friends have been through. Did you know Sandra was raped when she was nine years old?" Tiffany shook her head, disturbed by that new-found knowledge as well. "*SO STOP CRYING TO ME ABOUT HOW HORRIBLE YOUR LIFE IS WHEN YOU CAN CHANGE IT IN A SPLIT SECOND...MS. PERFECT*!"

Katrina's story concluded with both of them in tears. Tiffany then greatly regretted asking for the horror story. "I'm sorry," Tiffany mumbled.

Katrina closed her eyes and collected herself then said, "No, it's not your fault. I'm sorry I yelled." She sat back down at the island across from Tiffany and took her hands and smiled. "I created my circumstances. And they're irreversible. You've created circumstances too in many ways. But they are *reversible*. You haven't done anything yet where you can't change your course. That being said, I want to ask you something very important."

"Okay," Tiffany responded.

"You know I talk a lot about God and Jesus." Tiffany nodded. "Can I tell you why?" Again, Tiffany nodded. "You know, it's a misnomer that children of *righteous* and *faithful* Christian parents, especially those that are part of the pastoral team, are *perfect*, *godly* offspring—*immune* from the influence and attractions of the material world. I kept all that I had done to myself for a long time. But the thing about living in a smaller community, word eventually gets around. Not to mention, my normal positive, optimistic attitude had changed. I isolated myself from everyone, even from my family and the church. But that's what the devil likes to do—get you by yourself. Because, really, he's a big chicken." Tiffany chuckled at that comment.

"My parents finally confronted me about it, and I told them. But the fear of them being outraged and the idea that I was going to be rejected by everyone...well, it didn't happen. They didn't get angry or hostile. They were a bit disappointed that I didn't tell them what happened from the start, but they, instead, embraced me...my entire church did. And through the love and grace that they showed me, I knew Jesus had that for me too. That's when I accepted Jesus and made a commitment to follow him, no matter what. He saved me and forgave me—even for murdering my baby. And, Tiffany, he can save you too. If you let him. So my question is, would you be willing to receive him?"

Tiffany thought about it for a moment. There was something about Katrina that was enticing about her, even from the first time the two met, and she knew she needed that. But her physical desires and troubles (though many of which were self-inflicted) in her mind were too big for something or someone she couldn't see, hear, or touch to save her from. However, not wanting to upset Katrina, she simply responded, "Can I receive him later?"

Katrina was a bit disappointed, though prepared for some answer in the negative. After all, Tiffany wasn't the first young lady Katrina mentored by far. "Tiffany, you can ask Jesus to save you whenever you want. But until then, I want to have a relationship with you. If that's okay?"

"Yes. I want that too," Tiffany admitted. Katrina smiled at hearing that at least. Then Katrina brought to Tiffany's attention that she had found the Glamour Entertainment contracts.

"Oh, and I didn't mean to be snooping, but I came across your contracts with Glamour Entertainment. Would it, by chance, be okay if I took them with me?"

"What are you going to do with them?"

"Besides the fact that I would love to burn them...if it would do any good"—Tiffany grinned at the comment, as there have been times she thought the same thing—"I would like to read through them, and maybe I can find a legal way to help you out of your situation...maybe even without losing your daddy's house. I can't guarantee anything of course, but I thought it would at least be worth a shot."

Hearing that, Tiffany lit up. "Okay, you can take them with you," she said, nodding her head.

"Great! But first, I'm going to show you how to do the laundry...and fry an egg." Tiffany smiled at the comment—and it was her smile.

CHAPTER

13

RENOVATING A HEART

Katrina brought sandwiches to the community center to eat lunch with her husband. *Hope Community Youth Center* was painted in big colorful letters on the wall behind the boxing ring and was prominently noticeable immediately after walking through the front doors. He showed her around excitedly. She was impressed by how much he had accomplished, though still on the fence about the whole project.

"How was your night at Tiffany's?" Chris asked as they sat together on the floor eating.

"It was interesting," she responded. She told Chris all that had happened that night including meeting Kara and Sandra. "But I kinda blew up on her this morning though."

"Really? What for?"

"Between her home movies of her family and all that she shared with me, you'd think she was the world's most privileged woman. Growing up, she had everything and had everything done for her. I had to show her how to do laundry this morning and taught her how to make eggs. Yet she feels that she's the world's biggest *victim*. So I shared my story with her."

"How'd she respond to that?"

"She was shocked."

"Well, sometimes a reality check is a good thing."

"Yeah. But then I googled her when I got home. Being in the public eye can have its benefits sometimes. So now I feel a little convicted over my outburst."

"What did you find?"

"After her parents passed, she had quite the nervous break-down. She was in the hospital for about a week then immediately was in charge of her father's company. Her father apparently left her with everything—even the company he ran. In fact, if her siblings had survived, she would have still gotten nearly everything."

"Talk about a daddy's girl," Chris interjected.

"No kidding. But she made a lot of mistakes in a short time too. She ran up millions in company expenses, and several vendors filed motions for breach of contracts. She tried to pull off a merger with another company, but instead, that company used her to absorb Skyward Industries. The board of directors locked her out after that, and she was essentially out of a job."

"Then she got the modeling gig?" Chris assumed.

"Basically. While she was filing bankruptcy, this entertainment company shows up promising to take care of her. Since then, she's engaged in a few emotionally erratic affairs and has had quite the lineup of men...but I think it's because she's never grieved for the death of her family. It's just been one thing after another from the moment her family died. She even missed their funeral."

"And she still doesn't want to leave that house?"

"She's *severely* attached to it. I've known many ladies to come out of a tragedy and obsessively cling to an inanimate object like a doll, or even a note from someone they lost, but I've never dealt with a woman who's this excessively obsessed with something, especially a house.

"Well, house is home; she grew up there. I can see why she would have a difficult time letting her house go."

"But that's just it. It's not *her* house. It's her *daddy's* house. She never considers it her house. In fact, from what I can see, she's never changed anything in the house. Except that she's removed all the pictures...well, sort of. They're either turned around or piled up where they used to hang or sit. It's like she wants them there, but doesn't want to look at them. It's possible she has a personality disorder. People with personality disorders can have an excruciating time accepting change...especially when it comes to loss. I've been praying that God gets her out of that house and out of this company she got involved with no matter what."

"*No matter what* is a scary phrase to pray, babe."

"Yeah, I know. But the path she's currently on is scary too. I think this company is grooming her. She went from goody-goody virgin with no interest in boys, to all she can think about are guys."

"Was her family really religious?"

"There's no indication that religion played any part in their lives. They had strict morals though. Probably because of their status in public. Actually I found an article about her father saying that he twice had an affair. But they were all into science big time. Her father was into aeronautical type of stuff. Her mother was a science teacher, her brother and sister had chemistry degrees, and Tiffany was closing in on getting her masters in physics...when the accident happened."

"Wow! I can't remember middle school algebra," Chris responded.

"Yeah, well, either can she...now. She did, however, give me permission to take her two contracts with Glamour Entertainment."

"What are you going to do with those?" "I called Pastor Myers to see if he knew an attorney that might be willing to comb through 'em and see if there's a legal way for her to get out of this whole thing. She really doesn't like what she's doing in this company. She takes medication to numb herself before photoshoots or doing shows."

"Does the pastor know of any?"

"Apparently there's one who goes to the church. I'm going up to meet with him after lunch."

"Sweet! Is there anything you need me to do?" he asked.

"Unless you can decipher legal terms, probably not at this moment," she responded sarcastically.

"Yeah, that's well above my pay grade." Katrina kissed her husband then got up to leave. "Oh, and I'm going to be here a little late this evening," Chris added.

"Fixing more stuff in here?" she assumed.

"Actually, I'm meeting Josh here around six."

"Josh Nickel?"

"Yeah," Chris hesitantly responded.

"You know, I googled him too. He's dangerous."

"He showed up last night. We had a good discussion."

"And what are you meeting with him for?"

Chris was somewhat hoping she hadn't asked that question, but then answered, with his mouth full of food, "Training."

"Did you say training?" she asked sternly.

"Uh-huh."

"For?"

"A UFC fight?" he further answered, nervously.

"Chris, are you crazy? He's already known for bludgeoning people for no reason! And *you* can't get into a fight!"

Chris then got off the floor to calm her down. "Babe, trust me. Fighting is his outlet. I'm just trying to get him to contain it...to the ring. And really, I'm teaching him to be self-disciplined."

"I hope you're also teaching him to keep his hands off girls! Especially Tiffany, because she is ridiculously infatuated with him big time. I'm not sure why really, but I think she might also have obsessive love disorder. Which, if she does, could be dangerous for even *Joshua*. So I wouldn't bring her up to him, unless it's to tell him to avoid her at all costs."

"He's already promised not to get into fights outside of my presence and also, believe it or not, to keep his groping reserved to his girlfriend."

"I bet," Katrina responded suspiciously. "Okay, Chris. I hope you know what you're doing."

"I do. I've been praying about this constantly."

"Well, I need to go talk to the attorney. I'll see you later. Love you."

"Love you too," Chris responded, then Katrina left. "Whew."

****

Later at the attorney's office

"Hi, Katrina, come on in and have a seat," the attorney, Joel Dynsk, greeted.

"Thanks for meeting with me so quickly."

"Thank you for what you and your husband are doing."

"Well, hopefully, we'll be a benefit to the community."

"It sounds like you already are. So what can I do for you?"

Katrina then handed him the contracts. "I was hoping you might be able to look through these, they belong to a young lady, Tiffany Love."

"Tiffany Love...that sounds familiar."

"She's a model. She's on some billboards and some magazines that I *wouldn't* recommend."

"Ah, okay, I think I know who you're talking about." Katrina then explained everything that she knew about Tiffany Love and her situation to him. "The way you describe it, it sounds like how sex traffickers find victims. This company must have been eyeballing her for some time."

"I know. I'm familiar with that as well. I've worked with many young girls who had gone through those experiences in the past. However, this is more of an extreme case than I've encountered. I've never seen contracts involved in sexual exploitation...at least nothing like these."

"It's not entirely unheard of. But I have to tell you that I'm a criminal defense attorney. Contracts aren't necessarily my area of expertise. But I do have an attorney friend that heads up the American Center on Sexual Exploitation. They specialize in this kind of thing. They're based in DC and promote a lot of policy and legislative recommendations to Congress. They also go after, and publicize, companies who promote pornographic material."

"I'm familiar with them."

"I'll get in touch with them and see what they think about these contracts."

"How long do you think this will take?"

"It's hard to say. But I'll definitely keep you up-to-date. Is she being forced to do anything illegal?"

"Not that I know of. She has semi-exotic photoshoots for magazines and that sort of thing, but she said nothing completely revealing. She also makes appearances at venues on occasion. But those things are, apparently, in these contracts that she signed."

"Okay, Katrina, I'll get on this. Thanks for bringing this up," he concluded. Katrina then left his office after their discussion.

****

That evening, Joshua was on time at the community center. Chris had set up a steel-framed manikin with multiple extensions protruding out to the sides. It was covered in thick padding. Chris was teaching him how to kick.

"That's a little better," Chris would say. Joshua so far could only kick about waist-high. Chris then explained to him how to do a roundhouse. When Joshua attempted it, he was way off target and then lost his balance and fell. Chris laughed.

"Not funny," Joshua said, taking Chris's hand to help him up.

"Oh yeah, it is. We'll work on your roundhouse another time it looks like. It's about eight-thirty, so do one more sidekick as high as you can get it, and we'll call it a night," Chris said.

Joshua kicked but then felt something stretch more than what was comfortable. "Ouch!" he exclaimed.

"You all right?" Chris asked.

"Does it look like it?"

"Yeah, you're all right. You want some ice for that?" Chris asked jokingly.

"Whatever, man."

"I'm going to get a bottle of water, you want one?"

"Yeah," Joshua responded, holding himself while sitting on the edge of the boxing ring.

"All right. While you're sitting there, read the Ten Commandments off that wall," he ordered as he left the room to get the water.

Joshua shook his head to himself then began reading out loud. "You shall have no other gods before me. You shall make no idols—"

"I can't hear you!" Chris shouted from another room.

Joshua rolled his eyes then continued, a little louder, "*You shall not take the name of the Lord your God in vain!*" A small sense of guilt crept up in him at that commandment, as it was common for him to violate it. "*Keep the Sabbath day holy! Honor your father and your mother*!" That one also pricked him as well. "*You shall not murder*! *You shall not commit adultery*!" Ouch, that one really stung. "*You shall not steal*! *You shall not bear false witness against your neighbor*! *You shall not covet*!" Chris then reentered the atrium and handed Joshua his bottle of water.

"Good. You coming to opening youth night tomorrow night?" Chris asked, as tomorrow was Friday and was going to do his first youth sermon in the community center that night.

"No offense, *Pastor*, but I'm probably going to stay home," he said, somewhat rhetorically.

"All right. Monday then, six-o'clock," Chris said then he put a hand on Joshua's shoulder, who looked at him confused at first, but then Chris began praying over him for protection and conviction. "In Jesus's name, amen."

"Right, amen," Joshua responded again rhetorically. "See you Monday," Joshua said as he left the center.

CHAPTER

14

CHANGING SEASONS

It was afternoon and many of the neighborhood kids, as usual, descended onto the community center. Some were lifting weights, others were playfully wrestling in the boxing ring and the basketball court was full as well. As Chris walked around watching many of the kids having a good time in the—somewhat—newly renovated community center (many of the windows were still busted out, thus were still boarded up), he saw the usual teenage couple attempting to make out in a corner, to which he again showed them his hands, and they got the hint and moved apart. Another kid had snuck a bottle of alcohol on the property, but Chris confiscated it, saying, "If you want to destroy your liver, do it at your house." Other than a few issues he had to resolve with a couple of individuals, the evening started out pretty well. Besides, it's not like Chris was going to change the hearts and minds of the neighborhood in one week—or one Friday night.

Chris blew a whistle as he walked back through the center on his way to the atrium that had the boxing ring. As he did, he shouted, "Everyone, up front!" The kids didn't know what was going on but did as he said and gathered around the boxing ring which Chris climbed into so that everyone could see him. He had a little podium with a Bible on it in the center of the ring as well. Just as he was about to speak, one of the kids shouted, "Joshua Nickel's here!"

As Joshua came in, the kids' attention shifted to him. Then Chris greeted Joshua by saying, "Josh! You should show them your roundhouse!" He smiled, but Joshua looked at him fearfully, knowing full well that he couldn't pull off a roundhouse. But the kids began shouting, "Roundhouse! Roundhouse! Roundhouse!" Then Chris gestured for him to come up in the ring, which he did. Chris had a bottle of water and sat it on one of the corner posts of the ring and gestured to Joshua to kick it off, but Joshua refused. Since the kids were anxious to see a roundhouse, Chris then leaped off the mat, turned in the air, and kicked the bottle of water off the post. The kids cheered and Joshua was amazed, for he had assumed Chris was mostly just talk and appearance than action.

Chris then leaned into Joshua and said, "Don't tell my wife I did that." Joshua simply nodded.

Meanwhile, the youth pastor at Hope Community Church walked into Pastor Myers's office and sat down. "Aren't you supposed to be leading youth group tonight?" Pastor Myers said.

"Only one kid showed up."

"Only one? There's usually more than that."

"Right. But he got a text about something going on at the community center, then left."

That got Myers's attention. "Really?" Then Myers felt led to check out the community center.

When Pastor Myers showed up at the community center, he saw the inside packed with kids from under ten to twenty years old. He stood in the back listening to Chris speak to the kids.

"Since we're talking about roundhouses and fights, what would be something that you would bring to a conflict?" Chris asked the crowd.

"Mr. Righty and Mr. Lefty! Pow! Pow!" one of the younger kids shouted, punching the air.

"Okay, so an eye for an eye and a tooth for a tooth then?" Chris responded.

"Yeah!" they shouted.

"You know what Jesus said? '*You heard it said; an eye for an eye and a tooth for a tooth, but I tell you if someone strikes your cheek, offer your other cheek too—*'"

"Man! You're saying if someone hits me, I'm just supposed to let him hit me again?" another kid said.

"Not at all. There's a time for self-defense, but let's break down what Jesus said in the context of that day and apply it to today. First of all, a strike across the face was an insult. Anyone here ever ticked a girl off and she smacked him?" Chris looked around the room; no one raised a hand, but it was obvious that they were familiar with the illustration. He then glanced at Joshua who said, "Maybe." Chris smiled then continued, "That's what it basically means. Today most insults are done through words. How many of you have been in a fight before?" Many hands rose to that question. "All right, how many of those fights started simply because someone said something insulting to you, or maybe you said something insulting to that other person?" Nearly the same hands rose.

"But people say mean things, and it makes me mad," another younger kid responded.

"Yes, people say mean things and do mean things. But the reason for that is one of two things. They are mean just because they want to be antagonistic, or two, they're mean because they are dispelling some of their own hurt from their lives in a negative way."

"So if someone comes and says your mother's a, fill in the blank, what would you do?"

"Well, I'd probably get angry at first. But I would be curious to know why that person thought that in the first place. So knowing me, I would ask, *why do you say that*? It's easy to get riled up sometimes, but when you're in the heat of anger, that's when you need to ask Jesus for strength. Think of everything he went through—physically—and he never laid a hand on anyone. So what I say you should bring to a conflict are three things: love, grace, and forgiveness." Chris continued talking for a while. Many of the kids were inspired by what he had to say. A few others left during his talk though. Even Joshua was a bit stirred by Chris's words. Many of which were actually familiar to him.

After talking to the youth, Chris was approached by Pastor Myers to articulate his thoughts on what he witnessed—he was very impressed. Not to mention it was the first time setting foot inside the community center since it was given to the church. Then Chris introduced him to Joshua. Joshua simply shook Pastor Myers's hand without saying anything. "The boxer?" Pastor Myers assumed, as he wasn't all that familiar with the different fighting sports.

"MMA," Joshua corrected him, to which Chris added, "If you want to call it that." Joshua rolled his eyes at the comment in obvious reference to the fact that Joshua didn't really know much in the way of martial arts. They talked for several minutes while Chris showed Myers around the facility. Joshua just followed quietly. After some time, all the kids had left for the evening followed by Joshua, Pastor Myers, and Chris.

But as Joshua was driving home, he decided to stop at the liquor store he routinely frequents. He went straight for his usual alcohol then took it to the register. "Hey, Josh," Stacy said, who was running the register.

"Hey, Stacy."

"Twice in a week, huh. Either you have an alcohol problem, or you like spending time with me," she said, winking at him then leaning over the counter provocatively.

"Yeah, well, it's been a weird week, to say the least," he responded, pulling out his wallet.

"So no funsies with me tonight?" she said with big fluttering eyes.

"Um," needless to say, Joshua was speechless. Any other night, they would've already been engrossed in their open fornication session in the utility room, but Joshua was inundated with conflicting feelings as both Jennifer's voice and Chris's words came forth.

"It's been slow tonight...as you can see." But then a couple of customers entered the store. "Too late now. That will be forty dollars." Joshua then paid her and left with the alcohol.

"*What is wrong with me?*" he thought to himself on the way home where he would get drunk and pass out—the usual on a Friday night, minus a girl.

****

A noticeable difference in the community began taking place over the following weeks. Chris would go on his daily jogs and over time noticed many of the neighborhood residence talking with each other and waving at him as he passed. Many times Chris would stop to pray for people, and after a while, he noticed the residents of the community stopping to pray with each other without Chris—though he would join them if he saw them. Of course, on occasion there was still a tragedy in the area, fights still broke out from time to time, but there was a noticeable positive mood rising in the center of Brick Town. More kids began attending youth group on Friday nights, and not just youth, but many adults as well. This overflowed into Hope Community Church as the attendance began slowly increasing Sunday mornings.

Three to four evenings a week and some Saturdays, Joshua was training with Chris. His kicks were slowly getting better, but still, nothing compared to what he witnessed Chris do *once*. Katrina would bring snacks down for them to eat, and a close relationship began between Joshua and Chris as a result. Tuesday evenings, as promised, Joshua went to the men's group, where many of the men further encouraged Joshua, though he never spoke; he just sat in a chair within the circle and listened with his arms crossed —like someone forced to be in a family function in which they had no interest in being at. However, he wasn't always good to his word on not lying to Chris, especially with the girls. For as much as he legitimately attempted to keep himself strictly for Jennifer as he promised, he caved a few times. Alcohol was usually involved of course. He was, however, good to his word regarding staying away from fights outside the ring. Even though Brody would still find willing participants to take him on for money, he said no.

After a month and a half of following through with the training and the men's group, a question arose from one of the men in the class: "How many of us had negative experiences with their father?" Most of the class rose their hands. Joshua didn't however. But for the first time, he spoke in the class, saying, "I had a good dad." He added, "He taught me to work on cars."

Chris nodded and smiled at him, but he could tell that it was not a true statement. However, Joshua's answer prompted him to learn a little more about his background specifically regarding his late father and their relationship, thus the idea to visit his mother and her husband was on his mind.

DATE NIGHT WITH JENNIFER

Jennifer was completing her hair for her date with Joshua. She had a complexion that needed very little enhancements. There was a knock on the dorm door, and one of her roommates answered.

"Hey, Josh," they said playfully. He had a bouquet of flowers, and he was dressed impressively. Sandra and Kara were fairly shocked at the flowers and nice clothes as they weren't typical of Joshua when picking up a woman—or for any reason for that matter. He walked in and the door was closed behind him. "Wow! How come you never brought us flowers?" they commented. He just lightly smiled at the sarcastic comment.

"We're just kidding," the other said. "We know, you're off-limits now...at least tentatively, right?" they added with a wink.

"Do you girls even know what that means?" he rhetorically responded. They were aghast at the comment.

"You know, we're not as dumb and ditzy as you think."

Jennifer stepped out into the small living room, having finished her hair in time to hear the comment, and interjected her opinion, "That's why you two are getting a master's in botany."

"Hey, without plants, we'd all be dead. Someone's gotta take care of 'em," they responded, to which they all laughed.

"Wow, you look great...and not like a teacher this time," Joshua commented on Jennifer's appearance.

"Thanks," she responded. "I like the flowers too. And no t-shirt and jeans? I would have never guessed you owned anything else."

"I just bought them," he admitted.

"Aw, now I really feel special. That's more impressive than the flowers." Jennifer took the flowers to the kitchenette to put them in water, and while doing so, her roommates antagonistically made hearts with their hands while fluttering their eyes at Joshua, to which he rolled his eyes at them in embarrassment.

"Okay, don't wait up for me, ladies," Jennifer said to her roommates as she grabbed her purse and headed to the door with Joshua behind.

"When do we ever do that?" they respond.

"We're going to a concert tonight anyway," Kara informed.

"For free even," Sandra added.

"Whatever, have fun," Jennifer responded as she closed to the door.

"You're getting in for free?" Kara said to Sandra.

"Hmmm, sort of."

"Slut."

"Gold digger."

Joshua took Jennifer to a fancy restaurant where he had a reservation. The restaurant was even more out of character for Joshua than his casual dress clothes. Inside, the waiters were all dressed in tuxedos. They were seated and began looking at the menu. Jennifer could tell that the setting was slightly uncomfortable for

Joshua as he was even having trouble pronouncing the dishes on the menu.

"You eat here much?" she asked him.

"Actually, I think this is my first time. But you're a classy chick, I thought you'd like a classy restaurant," he responded.

"You thought so, huh," she said, laughing on the inside as she received the thought positively, but she wasn't that impressed with the restaurant. "You know what sounds really good? Mexican."

"I think this is some kind of enchilada on the bottom here," he said, trying to discern the fancy words on the menu. Jennifer then pulled his menu from in front of his face and leaned in toward him. "Mexican, as in burritos, baskets of chips, and salsa, tacos," she explained in detail.

"I do know of a really good authentic Mexican joint. But it's a hole-in-the-wall type of place in the middle of Brick Town—"

"Perfect, let's go," she immediately responded, leaving her seat.

"Nice," Joshua said to himself, then followed her out of the restaurant just before the server showed up with a bottle of wine that was originally ordered, but finding the table empty.

The Mexican restaurant was a fairly small old brick building. The two of them were laughing when the server came to their table.

"What can I get you guys?" she asked, not enthusiastic at all. Jennifer was giving her order to the server when the server dropped her ordering pad. The server was an attractive young woman, and Joshua did his level best not to make it noticeable that he thought so. However, when she bent down to pick the ordering pad up, the bottom of her shirt lifted just enough to where he noticed a fairly large welt just above her hip. The sight triggered him to look for other indications supporting the immediate thought that she may have been beaten up recently. When she turned to take his order, he noticed on her cheek a thickened layer of foundation. A memory of watching his late father put his hand in a wall near his mother raced through his mind.

"Josh!" Jennifer said, as his zoned-out stare on the server's face was longer than usual for someone about to order food. "Are you going to order something?" she added with a firmer voice.

"Um, yeah. I'll have the number two Mexican combo." The server jotted it down then left the table. Joshua's eyes followed her around the table until his eyes met Jennifer's, which were staring back at him expressing a little anger. At that, he snapped out of his fantasy of running his fist into whoever caused the bruises on the server's body.

"You know, I'm sitting right here," Jennifer said, upset. "I haven't seen you look at me that intently tonight?"

"Wait, it's not what you think—"

"Is it because I'm not wearing a noticeable pushup bra?" she continued.

"No, it's just—"

"Or maybe my pants aren't so tight that—"

"Would you listen? Someone beat her up."

"What? How could you tell?"

"I'm just familiar with that kind of thing. She has a bruised up welt on her side and her cheek is swollen."

"Maybe she fell," Jennifer responded, feeling more at ease that Joshua's reason for staring at the server as he did wasn't for lust—though, that's not a foreign reason for him to stare at a woman.

"She didn't fall."

"How do you know?"

"As I said, I'm very familiar with domestic violence."

"Oh, I'm sorry."

"Look, there's an awful lot you don't know about me. Honestly, a chick like you wouldn't be sitting across the table from me if you knew my life. I live in a nice house, I own my own business, and I got money in the bank. I've accomplished quite a bit, and I'm only twenty-five. My mom's married to the president of a multimillion-dollar manufacturing company, and they live in the heights outside of town. But life hasn't always been nice. In fact, I grew up right around here. Well, for a while, we lived with my grandparents out in the country until my grandfather passed away and my grandmother was put into a retirement home," as he revealed a brief summary of his childhood, he stared at the table. But then it dawned on him that he was even revealing any of it at all. "Wow!"

"What is it?" she responded in a more comforting tone.

"I've never told anyone this stuff."

She then took his hands, smiled, and responded, "You can tell me anything. I want to know everything about you. Besides, there's a lot about *this chick you're sitting across the table from* that you don't know." Joshua grinned at the comment. "Like the fact that I don't like fancy restaurants."

Their food was brought out, and they spent the rest of the evening eating and talking. Every once in a while Joshua would spot their server clearing a table or taking other customers' orders and think about the welt and swollen cheekbone, but didn't make it noticeable to Jennifer. After eating, Joshua threw an above-average tip on the table and left to take Jennifer back to her college dorm.

The first few minutes of the drive back to the college campus was quiet, which was unusual for even if there was no passenger to converse with, he normally would be blaring his heavy metal music. Finally, Jennifer broke the silence.

"Thanks for dinner," she said.

"Oh, you're welcome. It was nice."

"Is it Marcy?" she asked, having an intuitive feeling that Joshua was thinking about their server at the Mexican restaurant.

"Marcy?" he responded, having not gotten her name.

"The server at the restaurant. Her badge said Marcy on it."

"Oh, I didn't see her badge."

"Of course you didn't," she responded.

"Jennifer, I wasn't ogling her. I swear."

"I'm not saying you were. But I don't want you to feel like you have to do anything about it. It's not your problem."

"Compassionate much?" Joshua responded rhetorically.

"Excuse me? Um, compassionate in that I don't want to see you go to jail. Isn't that why you were on probation for two years? Beating some womanizer into a coma?" she said, revealing that she knew a little more about him than he thought she did.

"I see you did some reading up on me." "How about I'm room-mates with two of your former flings, and they know *a lot* about you?"

"Oh, right."

"More than I wish they did, to be honest. But then, you obvi-ously know a lot about them," she rhetorically added, referring to his past sexual relationships with Kara and Sandra.

"Actually I don't know anything about them...outside of... well, we won't go there. In fact, let's change the subject."

"Okay. I'm sorry, I didn't really mean to cause any tension between us." She then scooted closer to him and put her hand around his arm. The feeling of her touch eased the tension.

"If I may ask, where's your dad?"

"Huh?" the question caught him off guard.

"You said your mother married the president of a manufac-turing company. I'm assuming that's not your dad, or you would have just said *your dad was the president of a manufacturing com-pany*. I'm analytical...sorry."

"I guess so. My father passed away when I was seventeen," he explained.

"Oh my, I'm sorry to hear that."

"It's okay. I'm over it."

"Are you?" she further inquired, not fully convinced of it.

"Well, yeah. That was eight years ago."

"Okay. What did he die from? If you don't mind me asking."

"Cirrhosis of the liver."

"Oh, wow. Did he drink a lot?"

"Um, he drank a little bit," he responded, unwilling to re-member his father for the alcoholic, womanizing, violent, family-neglecting individual that he was. They arrived at the campus and parked in front of her dorm room entrance. The silence came back as the questions prompted his memories to retrieve painful events from long ago. Then a single tear fell, though his reaction assumed it to be a foreign action when he quickly wiped it off and regained his composure. But Jennifer saw the single tear which drew her closer to him. She gently pulled his face to hers, and they kissed for a moment.

"It'll be okay," she said, consoling. "Want to walk me to my door?"

"Yeah, of course." He then hopped out of the truck, walked around, and opened the passenger door for her then they walked to her door. She unlocked the door and cracked it open before turning around to Joshua to tell him, "I did have fun. Sometimes it's nice just to talk and get to know each other through conver-sation...isn't it?"

"Yeah, you're right. Although I still don't know that much about you," he said with a chuckle, "other than you don't like fancy restaurants." They both laughed at the comment. "Well, have a good night," he said, then as he was turning to leave, Jennifer spontaneously grabbed his arm, spun him back around, and pulled him by his shirt into the dorm. She moved her face to-ward his to kiss him again, but then pulled away with a grin and said, "I want you to know me." She again brought her face close to kiss him, but again pulled back and said, "I don't share."

"Okay" was his only response.

She did it a third time, then asked, "Do you dream of Tiffany?"

"Who?" he said, having, for the most part, forgotten all about Tiffany Love. His thoughts were obviously fully and completely on Jennifer. The response brought a huge smile to Jennifer's face as the answer aroused her, compelling her to risk bringing Joshua into her bedroom for the night.

CHAPTER 16

A VICTORY FOR THE DEVIL

It was late in the morning of the following day when Jennifer woke up. Rolling over in bed, she found that Joshua wasn't there. She had partly anticipated it as she knew what kind of guy she was getting involved with. After a brief moment of disappointment, she got out of bed, threw a robe on, and meandered into the living area where Kara and Sandra were watching TV. Her two roommates glanced at her with a smirk then went back to watching their show.

Then the door opened. It was Joshua. He had a large paper bag.

"Hey, I was hoping to be back before you woke up," he said.

She smiled as the feeling of victory welled up in her. "It's rare when I sleep past noon," she responded. She then glanced at her roommates with a smirk of her own and rubbed her fingers together at them to which they each pulled out some bills and threw them on the floor. Jennifer picked them up and said, "Thank you, ladies."

The action perplexed Joshua. "What's that for?" he asked while pulling out some Styrofoam boxes out of the brown bag. They each had eggs and pancakes in them.

Jennifer was slightly hesitant to explain but then admitted, "They didn't believe you were going to be here this morning."

"So I was a bet?" he asked.

"Yeah, that sounds horrible, doesn't it? Sorry." She then leaned over the small counter toward him in a provocative manner.

"I'm both flattered and insulted at that," he responded sarcastically.

"More flattered or more insulted?" she inquired.

"More flattered I suppose," he answered.

"That sucks, I was hoping you'd been more insulted...then maybe I could have made it up to you later," she added flirtatiously.

He chuckled at the idea. "Sounds fun," he responded as they sat down and ate. "But I do have a few things to get done today."

"Like what?"

"Mostly training. You can come if you want."

"And watch you do what? Hit a punching bag for a couple of hours?"

"Right. There's a little more to it than that though."

"I know, but it kinda sounds boring for me."

"It probably would be. And then I'm going to a life group with Chris after that."

"Chris, your trainer? That's kind of an odd combo—fighting and religion," she commented.

"Yeah. I know you don't like it—"

"Which, the fighting? Or religion?"

"The fighting, I thought."

"Oh, I don't know. I think I could get used to watching you pummel people with your shirt off."

"So it's the religion you have a problem with?" he then assumed.

"I've just never needed it. I'm not really bragging, but I really had about as perfect of a life as you can get. Other than my parents being divorced, I have a great relationship with both sets of my parents. They put me in private schools, I was head cheerleader for a time, and I was a team leader for my school's baseball and volleyball teams. I was prom queen both my junior and senior year. So I guess if there is a god, I really never needed him," she responded somewhat egotistically.

"Wow!" Josh simply responded. "We are definitely *opposites*, aren't we?"

"That's why I didn't bring that up last night. After sharing your past, I didn't want you to get the wrong idea about me. So I can see god being for you more than me."

"Thanks," Joshua responded, feeling a bit more insulted over that comment than being a bet. "I think."

"Can I ask you a somewhat personal question?" she then asked.

"Sure."

"Do you ever talk to Tiffany Love?" The question revealed a slight insecurity within her.

"Seriously?"

"Well, she's a rich, hot, redheaded model. And I told you I don't share. Nor do I compete," she explained.

"Listen, I haven't talked to her in a couple of months. I haven't even thought of her. Until you just now mentioned her. There's a lot of rich redheads, rich blondes. And if you ask me, the richer they are, the more they cost...and the more graveling they require. Besides, it kind of takes a lot for me to get attached to someone."

"Brown hair and brown eyes?" she inquired.

Joshua looked at her awkwardly as if his secret identity had just been revealed. "Where'd you hear that from?"

Nervously she responded, "Not to bring up the past, but after you didn't call me the day after our first night together, I was a little anxious to know why. So since I knew where Cad Arris lived, I went there and asked if he knew what you thought of me."

"What he say?"

"Besides sharing that you get attached to brunettes with brown eyes, he told me to be patient, which admittedly, sometimes I'm not as patient as I should be."

"Either am I," he also admitted.

"By the way, do you know that you talk in your sleep?" she added with a grin.

"Really? What did I say?"

"Wouldn't you like to know?"

"Um, yeah, kinda."

After a long conversation, Joshua left to meet Chris for another round of off-schedule training. Jennifer was difficult to get off his mind as he drove. But on his way to the community center, he passed the small Mexican restaurant that he and Jennifer ate at the night before. Immediately the thought of the server and her bruised side and swollen cheek inundated his thoughts, which relit the emotion that welled up in him when he first observed it.

"Jenny's right, it's not your problem," he said to himself. But the thought of the possible situation Marcy was in began swarming his imagination, which ignited his temper.

He then turned around and parked behind the building. He grabbed a hoody from behind his seat and slipped it on then went inside. After he determined that Marcy was there, he sat in a booth in the corner with his hood on. A server, that wasn't Marcy, stopped by his table to take his order, which he simply requested a soda. He only left the booth to get a refill on his soda every so often. After about an hour, he observed Marcy appearing though she was getting ready to leave. At that, he then quickly left the small restaurant and waited outside nonchalantly against the brick building for her to pass by, and when she did, he followed her from a distance.

Meanwhile, after it appeared to Chris that Joshua was later than usual arriving at the community center, he called him.

"Hello?" a woman's voice answered.

"I'm sorry I must have dialed the wrong number," he thought.

"Are you looking for Joshua?" she said.

"Yes, ma'am. This is Chris."

"Oh hi, Chris. This is Josh's girlfriend, Jennifer. He left his phone here."

"Oh, do you know where he is by chance?"

"He said he was heading to the community center to train with you actually. But that was about an hour ago when he left."

"Really. He hasn't shown up yet. Well, thanks, Jennifer."

After the call ended, Jennifer's concern for Joshua prompted her to go look for him. After roughly three quarters of an hour passed, Chris got the impression that Joshua was going to be a no-show. Concerned that Joshua would be in any danger was an obvious non-issue, so his desire to understand more of Joshua's background then compelled Chris to finally go visit his mother in the heights.

WOUNDS OF MEMORIES

Ding-dong!

17 A young lady, around Joshua's age, opened the double doors to the extravagant home. "Yeah?" she said to Chris. She wasn't used to such a rough-looking individual coming to the house as was expressed by her glance at him.

"Hi, I'm Chris," he introduced himself. "I was hoping to speak with Trisha, Joshua Nickel's mother."

"I bet you are," she said suspiciously, then shouted back into the house, "Dad! There's a strange guy at the door who wants to talk to your wife!" She then turned back to Chris and added, "Just a minute," then closed the door.

"Strange guy?" Chris said to himself, then looking at his clothes—a tank top and jeans. "Katrina's right, you need a new ward robe." Shortly after, an older gentleman came to the door.

"I'm Trisha's husband, can I help you?"

"Hi, I'm Chris. I'm an outreach pastor from Hope Community Church," he said with his hand out to shake. Trisha's husband,

Frank, shook it hesitantly, as Chris didn't resemble any pastor that he's ever seen. "I'm trying to get a little more background information on Joshua Nickel."

"Ah, you know Joshua. Trisha mentioned that he had started attending some church group during the week. I'm assuming you're responsible for that?"

"I'd say the Lord's more responsible for that...but I'll definitely take *some* credit," Chris responded using a little humor to break the ice. Frank chuckled at the comment, which relieved any suspicion he had of Chris do to his appearance.

"Here, come in. I'll get Trisha. She obviously could tell you more about Joshua than I." Chris entered the house, and Frank led him to the kitchen. "He never did open up to me, as much as I tried getting him to," Frank explained then left him in the kitchen to get his wife. The young lady who answered the door was sitting at the island playing on her phone.

"You must be Josh's stepsister."

"Yeah, I'm Janice. Sorry for my rudeness...pastor, huh?" she said with a grin in reference to his appearance.

"Yeah, I get that a lot."

Frank and Trisha then descended the stairs and entered the kitchen.

"Hi, Chris," Trisha introduced herself. +

"Frank said you're looking for information on my son."

"Yes, I am."

"What's this for?" she inquired with an idea that he might be in trouble.

"Chris is the community outreach pastor for Hope Community Church," Frank told Trisha, who looked at him awkwardly attempting to unite the title with the tattoos, piercings, and tank top.

"In my defense, I did just come from the community center in Brick Town. Joshua was supposed to meet me for training, but he was a no-show. Since my schedule obviously opened up, I felt led to introduce myself to you."

"Training, for what?"

"He has a bit of a temper, and he did admit to me that professional fighting helped to channel some of that. Since his previous trainer is deceased, I made him a deal that I would get him back in the ring if he followed some rules...including attending the men's group every week."

"He said he was going to a Bible study. It was great to hear that. I didn't know about the training thing though."

"Yeah, it's definitely not my standard way of reaching people. Not to mention finding a sponsor for him has been tough with some of his baggage. But I noticed that he has a pretty big influence over the kids around town. I honestly believe that the Lord can use this man in a huge way...that's why I've taken an interest in mentoring him."

"Well, that would definitely be a miracle," Trisha rhetorically remarked. "I mean I love my son with all my heart, and we pray for him all the time, but we've never been able to get through to him."

Frank softly rebuked his wife's pessimism by responding, "Trisha, maybe this is an answer to prayer. He's going to a Bible study now at least," to which she nodded in agreement.

"You know, my wife and I have mentored hundreds of kids over the years, and some of his temperament resembles those who didn't have much a father figure growing up," Chris delicately commented, "and maybe a little on the physical side?" A blind gaze came over Trisha as his comment nailed the issue on the head. "If it's a sore subject, we don't have to talk about it. I'm just trying to—"

"No, it's fine. You definitely do your homework, don't you?" Trisha observed. "Not to relieve his father of his sins, but I was pretty rebellious at the time he and I got together. Temperament and personal habits were the last things on my mind when I thought about guys, which was all the time. Muscles were my thing." Frank squeezed his biceps when his wife mentioned muscles, and Janice saw it and rolled her eyes. "When I was seventeen, there were several boys who wanted to take me to homecoming my senior year." She put her hand over half her face in embarrassment as she recalled the past. "I was indecisive, so I said whoever gets to my house first could take me. Well, the first guy there took me...but not to homecoming. Instead, I got pregnant. And essentially my life, and Joshua's, was a living hell for the next sixteen or so years...until I met Frank. But then his life was hell for a while," she explained with sarcasm.

"Trisha," Frank rebuked again.

"I'm just saying you married a basket case of a woman who had a basket case of a son."

"I married a daughter of the King, not a basket case," Frank corrected. Chris smiled at the comment, then asked,

"So how did you two meet? If you don't mind me asking?"

"Joshua and I lived in a studio apartment at the Landing apartment complex. Most just called them the crack apartments—for obvious reasons—I couldn't afford anything else. Once a week I'd go next door to the laundry mat. One day I went and they had raised the price for the mini-boxes of detergent twenty-five cents...you've heard the term 'counting pennies,' well, that was literal. Anyway, I had two baskets of clothes, and only enough money to either buy the detergent, and one cycle of laundry *or* one cycle in the dryer. I just broke down. So embarrassing. Then a lady came over and put her arm around me and talked to me. She and another couple of ladies came from a church just to pay for people to have their laundry done. When I asked why they were doing this, they said they were doing it to tell people about Jesus. I hadn't thought about God in years up to this point. My parents were religious, but, as I said, I was rebellious. I guess it would be pertinent to the story to explain that I left Josh's dad when Josh was five. We lived with my parents in the country until my father passed and then my mother had to be put into a senior home because of health problems. She passed shortly after that. But that's when I moved Josh and me to Brick Town...I think Josh was about eight or so at that time. But the lady at the laundry matt, Dorothy, talked to me about Jesus. I didn't accept him at the time, but she convinced me and Joshua to go to church, and we did. After a while, I finally accepted Jesus and met Frank shortly after that. We got married a year later."

"That's amazing how you accepted Christ after all that. I've known so many people that continue to reject him based on their continued negative circumstances."

"Yeah, Joshua was one of them. Well, maybe he would have been more open to it if it wasn't for his father," Trisha added.

"Oh, so his father was still around then?" Chris further inquired.

"Joshua saw him every so often. You know it's funny because Josh really looked up to my dad for a while. But once he passed away, Josh began idolizing his father. When we lived in Brick Town, Josh was within walking distance to his father's shop— he worked on cars—the only positive trait that Joshua inherited from his father. He's an amazing mechanic. He was always jerry-rigging my old Toyota to get it to run. The odometer had stopped at nine hundred ninety-nine thousand nine hundred ninety-nine miles a few years before that. He would occasionally go see him. But his father was always trying to get back with me. I felt so horrible for Josh because his father didn't really want anything to do with him, just me. But two particular days I'll never forget. One of them was when Joshua came home after having visited his dad's shop one day. He's all excited telling me that his father is a Christian and is reading the Bible now. And based on that, he was trying to convince me to take him back. I thought it was pretty odd how quickly after I started attending church, that he became so religious. So I, being skeptical, decided to meet him for lunch one day. He had his little Bible and was reading completely irrelevant passages. Not to mention he didn't address any of his root issues. But basically, it came out that he had watched me go to church a couple of times. When I called his bluff about being saved and changed...yada, yada, yada...he got irate and chased me to the parking lot, but didn't touch me—he never did physically harm me, just intimidated me. It broke my heart to see Josh's reaction when I told him that his dad was lying. He said he hated me and he wanted to go live with his dad. Of course, I wouldn't let him go live with his dad, nor did his dad really want him around. Joshua was his father's only way to me. After that, he basically tuned church and everything related to it off."

"So his father never hit you. Just intimidated you though. Did Joshua ever see that?"

"No, not that I recall."

"I've never known anyone who has a fetish for primarily going after womanizers before. That's why I had assumed that maybe there was an incident."

"Oh, yeah. That was day number two, that I'll never forget," Trisha ashamedly revealed.

"If it's too much—"

"No, it's just that I was so, so stupid. I got fired from just about every convenience and food store job in the area because I had to leave so often to take care of Joshua. He got in fights a lot at school. So after I couldn't find work, I...tried to"—she couldn't even say the degrading word—"you know what I'm saying. But on this day, Joshua got suspended from school...talk about irony. Josh showed up just before the guy did anything, but Josh heard him call me a few things I won't repeat, and Joshua attacked him thinking he was assaulting me. The man was a lot bigger than Joshua and threw him across the room. I had my dad's gun under the pillow, in case things got too out of hand. I grabbed it, threw his money back at him, and yelled at him to leave...and he did. So I didn't get hurt, but Joshua did. He cried...the last time I ever remember him crying, to be honest. I was crying too and apologizing. He had a bloody nose from getting hit. I don't know how many times, after that, I've woke up to Joshua just sitting in the corner on a chair having stayed up all night watching over me. What kind of mother am I?" Trisha began crying at this point. Frank put his arm around her.

Janice walked over and put her arms around Trisha as well. "You've been a great mom to me. My real mom would be happy you took the job," she said, for her biological mother passed away five years before Trisha and Frank got married. Janice then said to Chris, "Joshua really isn't bad in every sense. He just loses control. I tried to be his friend. Our lockers were in the same hallway in high school. One morning some jocks were trying to make a pass at me. Josh saw it. I mean, yeah, what that jock did was offensive to me, but Josh, he wouldn't stop. He just kept hitting him. I've never seen that much blood on a person's face in my life. It took three guys—bigger than him—to get him to stop. I had nightmares about it for a while."

"And his father passed away that same year...liver failure. So that was another rough twelve months for him," Trisha further added.

"How'd he take that?" Chris asked.

"It's hard to say, to be honest. He accepted it rather quickly. When I took him to see his dad at the hospital, he didn't even look at Josh once—not once! Josh kept asking how he was feeling. But his dad just stared at me the whole time. Then the heart monitor flat-lined and he was gone. Joshua asked, 'Is that it?' I didn't know what to say, then Josh left the room like it was nothing. No emotions, nothing. No one was home...soul wise. I've never seen anything like it...someone so checked out."

"He said he calls you every week though."

"Yeah, he calls me, like clockwork...every weekend. He doesn't talk to Frank or Janice though. Just me. Although, after he got expelled from high school, he got his GED, he wanted to get some mechanic degree or certification, but before he left he said to Frank he trusted him, right, hunny?"

"Yeah, one day he walked in the house—I was the only one here—and said to me, 'I trust you with my mom now, thanks for taking care of her.' Then he left. I tried to get him to stay and talk... that was the closest I've ever gotten to have a conversation with him. He said he had an interview to go to though. He got a job at an auto service center. Although, that is one of his better traits—punctuality. He's rarely late or absent for a scheduled event."

"I've noticed that, even on Tuesday evenings, he's at church usually a few minutes early. I've been quite impressed with that," Chris commented.

"Yeah, which if he didn't show up for you today, there's usually one of two reasons why he didn't and not tell you. One, he's with a girl, or two"—Trisha sighed—"he's venting."

Janice then added, "And since it's the middle of the afternoon, probably the latter."

"When he *vents*, does he go anywhere in particular?"

"He at one point had a restraining order to stay away from Brick Town. I don't know if they could ever enforce it because it was a pretty broad order. That was after he put a guy in a coma which got him a few days in jail and received two years parole. He used to get into fights all the time down there. That's where he and I lived until Frank and I got married. Just an idea."

"Well, I appreciate the info about your son. I'll do my best with him. Oh, did he tell you he's in a committed relationship now?"

Trisha and Frank glanced at each other with concerned looks at hearing that. "No?" Trisha replied.

Janice then loudly asked, "Is he with Tiffany Love, the super-model?"

"Um, no," Chris responded.

"Oh, okay."

"Oh, good," Trisha said with a sigh of relief. "We saw how she latched onto him after his first professional fight."

"You saw them?"

"Actually we were there. Although I might as well not have been. I sat the whole time facing the floor praying," Trisha explained.

"I watched it, I even rooted for him," Frank interjected.

"Frank likes that kind of stuff."

"I like to watch it. Fighting, I mean. I was on the college wrestling team...back when I had muscles," Frank added with humor.

"Just out of curiosity, since you mentioned Tiffany Love, do you know much about her?" Chris further inquired.

"She's crazy," Janice again interjected. "But her makeup line is pretty awesome...just saying." Her comment drew an awkward glance from Trisha. "You know, I'm going to go downstairs and watch a movie." Janice left the kitchen at that point.

"I asked because she pretty much fell into my wife's lap. And she and Joshua did have a one-nighter from what I was told, unfortunately," Chris informed them. Trisha shook her head and sighed again.

"My company used to have a contract with Skyward Industries. We manufactured some of the components for their planes. I knew her father, professionally. When her family passed away, she became the CEO immediately. Obviously, I don't know all the internals of what exactly happened, but within about six months another company took it over and she was gone. There were multiple breaches in contracts during that time from dozens of their vendors, including my company," Frank explained.

"In a way it was sad. Locally it was pretty big news. But then she, like, fell off the earth. That was about four years ago. Then roughly a year later, she's showing up on billboards and maga-zines half-naked," Trisha added.

"It's possible she might be caught up in a pretty bad situation. My wife found some contracts that belonged to the modeling company that Tiffany signed. She's having an attorney go over them. It's possible they're taking advantage of her," Chris further explained. Trisha made a look that expressed little compassion for the model, to which Chris expressed confusion over.

"I guess you're wife is a lot more compassionate than I am. You have to understand my concern is for my son. I mean, not that I'd wish for her or anyone to be exploited, but she's falsely accused two men of sexually assaulting her."

"It was actually big news...for about two days, then you didn't hear anything more about it," Frank added.

"That's why I got a little worried when you said Joshua was seeing someone."

"Well, with all that in mind, I can definitely understand your concerns," Chris responded.

"So my son is finally committed to a girl, huh."

"Well, I'm not sure how committed, but apparently committed enough to leave his cell phone at her place," Chris responded with humor.

"What does she look like?" Trisha nosily asked, with a smile. That's when Chris noticed Trisha's hair and eye color.

"You, actually...I mean she has brown hair and brown eyes."

They continued conversing for a while longer—over lighter topics though. Finally, Chris left the house. Before entering his vehicle, however, Frank came out to talk to him about one more thing.

"Chris, exactly how confident are you in your pursuit to reach Josh?"

"That's a loaded question, to be honest. I've mentored kids who got it...they were on fire for the Lord. Then a year or two later, back on drugs, or worse. On the other hand, I've seen kids walk away from me cussing my name in vain along with Jesus's, but a year or five later, they're leading Sunday school classes and pointing others to the Lord. So I obviously can't promise anything. But the Lord has laid it on my heart to do all that I can to point him to Jesus. And that's all I can promise you," Chris explained. Frank nodded and smiled seeing the passion in Chris for his stepson.

"Real quick, can you tell me more about the type of sponsorship you're looking for?"

CHAPTER

18

REASONING OF THE FLESH

While Chris was meeting Joshua's family, Joshua had been following Marcy from a distance. He kept his hood up and walked casually behind. After several blocks, she turned off into an apartment complex—one that was indeed familiar to him, though he didn't pay much attention to the familiarity of the building. He walked on passed it as not to look like a stalker, but after she headed up the stairs he then quickly turned back and ran under the breezeway to the stairs. His head barely popped up over the warped wood planking of the top-floor apartments from the stairwell, just enough to see what apartment she went into.

He quickly ran up the rest of the stairs and to the apartment door. He put his hand on the knob, but then Jennifer's words came to mind: It's not your problem. His temper subsided enough to think rationally about what he was about to do. He then let go of the knob and then turned to leave. He only got a couple of steps away from the door when he heard a smack from inside, followed by a scream then a toddler's cry. Immediately his rage plumed, dispelling everything that Jennifer said to him as well as Chris's rule about not fighting outside the ring. He grabbed the doorknob again. It was unlocked. He opened it. The living room was a mess. The carpet was covered in stains, dust on the furniture, and drug paraphernalia was everywhere. There was a mustiness to the small apartment as well.

The living room was absent of people, but a bedroom door was open off of the living room. He then heard a man's voice yelling about someone not bringing home enough money. There was a child in the room crying. As he approached the open door, Marcy walked out of the room backward, afraid, with a bloody lip. The crying child in a pull up ran out after her followed by a large man with his hand raised toward Marcy. She saw Joshua and was startled, though she didn't recognize him with his hood up. Joshua grabbed the abuser's arm before he could strike her again. The abuser turned and shouted at Joshua, "Who the hell are you?" Joshua then threw him back in the bedroom and began beating him, though the man was rounder and taller than Joshua.

"HELP! HELP! the abuser shouted. The neighbors in the apartment next door were friends of his. After Joshua was finished with the man, or so he thought, he exited the bedroom. Marcy was curled up in the corner of the living room terrified clenching her son who was crying. Joshua was about to leave when two of the neighbors showed up in the doorway.

"Dan! What's going on?" they shouted. Dan, the abuser, then limped out of the bedroom behind Joshua, with a bloody nose and mouth.

"This *cat* just walked into my apartment and attacked me!" he explained furiously.

"Oh, is that so!" Dan's neighbors replied. They balled their fists ready to fight Joshua, and since they were between him and the door, Joshua quickly began analyzing their physiques. One of the neighbors was bigger than Joshua, as was Dan. But the other neighbor was roughly the same size as Joshua, thus might be more of a challenge for him. The neighbors approached Joshua, then Dan pushed him into the neighbors, and the fight was on as fists flew connecting with faces. Joshua took several hits, but he was also more of a challenge to the three of them than they had anticipated.

At one point the neighbors had Joshua in a chokehold with his hands behind him, but Joshua refused to be put on the floor. Dan came up to hit Joshua while he was seemingly incapacitated, but then Joshua pushed off the ground and, as Chris had been training him, jump-kicked Dan in the face sending Dan falling over the couch while the force of the kick propelled him with the neighbors back ward smashing them against the wall, which caused them to release Joshua. He then began attacking them with even more rage—swinging his fists and now his legs—until they were unconscious. Then Joshua, having lost all control of his anger, grabbed Dan's hair with one hand and began slamming his other fist into Dan's face—again, and again, and again. Each hit intensified Marcy's terrified scream as well as the child's. Finally, Joshua calked his fist back for another punch, but his forearm was stopped by someone else's hand. Joshua quickly turned. It was Chris with a scowl across his face like Joshua had never seen.

"Get. In. The. Car," Chris said through his clenched teeth. Joshua's expression of rage immediately changed at the sight of Chris to that of someone waking up from a dream. "NOW!" Chris then commanded with a shout. Joshua then left without even observing the scene he created in the apartment. Chris looked around. The amount of drug paraphernalia in the apartment caused Chris to believe they were drug lords of some sort. Other items were also spread out across the living room floor along with overturned tables and other objects. He knelt down to examine the apparent victims' injuries. They were banged up and dazed, but alive, though Dan might as well not have been as it was obvious his jaw was dislocated and his nose was pointing due east. Hearing the crying of the woman and child, he stood up and looked over in the corner at the two.

"Are you okay?" Chris asked. Marcy just stared at him. "Do you need help?"

"Just leave us alone," she timidly said. Chris nodded in respect of her request, then turned and left the apartment.

Joshua had gotten into Chris's car as was directed. He saw Chris on his phone as he approached the driver side door. He hung up just before getting behind the wheel.

"Did you call the cops on me?" Joshua anticipated.

Chris didn't answer right away. He started the car first then put his seatbelt on and began driving. "No. That was DCF. *Although, I'd like to hear a really good reason why I shouldn't* drive your butt to the police station *right now*!"

Joshua thought for the answer, and when he didn't have a valid one, he simply said, "I don't have one."

"Really?" Chris responded, surprised. "That's a first." There was another silent pause. "Nice lip," Chris then commented on Joshua's swollen and bleeding lip.

"The little guy...he was pretty tough," Joshua explained.

"Little?" Chris inquired as the little guy appeared to be the same size as Joshua. However, the statement explained to him why Joshua was afraid as him. "Is that why you're afraid of me?"

"Afraid of you?" Joshua replied with a cockeyed look, but then looked out the window.

"The bigger they are the slower they are...generally...even if it's half a second slower," Chris concluded.

There was another pause of silence during which time Chris could tell that Joshua was anxious about the possibility of being in trouble. Then Chris spoke again. "They were drug dealers. Odds are they won't be calling the cops either." Joshua relaxed a little more upon hearing that. "*What were you thinking*?"

"I wasn't."

"That's for sure. You know, she didn't even leave the apartment," Chris explained.

"Who didn't leave what apartment?"

"The girl, whose man you nearly killed for hitting her."

"Okay?" Joshua didn't understand the point.

"Joshua, that woman had the chance to leave. It's her choice to be in that situation. I don't like hearing about that kind of thing happening either, but if the heart doesn't change the person doesn't change. That lady needs to come to terms with herself about her life. If you want to help people like that, there are other ways to go about it. But still, statistically speaking, a lot of girls end up going back to that kind of environment. Praying for them is one way."

"*Prayer*? *Really*? Do they even work?" Joshua cynically asked.

"*Ya they do*," Chris matter-of-factly replied.

"How come *God* wasn't there for me and my mother?" Joshua added to his cynicism.

"Well, Josh, personally *I'd* be asking, why wasn't your *father* there for you and your mother?"

"He was busy working," Joshua simply responded.

"Okay, fair enough. But since your father was *busy working*, thus he wasn't at home to protect his family, God *was* there. You don't see it, because you don't want to, Josh."

"Well, it's hard to believe in something you can't see, touch, or feel."

"There's some truth to that. But would you believe me if I said I got you a *sponsor*?"

Joshua quickly looked at Chris in disbelief. "Are you serious? *You got me a sponsor*?"

"Hold on. So you *believe* that I got you a sponsor? The funny thing is, I didn't even say I got you a sponsor and you believe that I got you one."

"Well, why would you bring that up if you didn't?"

"I don't know, you tell me."

"So *did you?* Or did you *not* get a sponsor for me?"

"I tell you the truth, I absolutely did." Joshua's face lit up. "Wait, I don't have any evidence that I got you a sponsor. This sponsor didn't even write up a contract, he just said *I'll sponsor him.* So all you have to go on that I *got you a sponsor* is me *telling you* that you have a sponsor. So how come you *believe* me?"

"Because I trust you. You've never lied to me before. Plus you're *here...now.* It's hard to take to heart what a man who lived two thou sand years ago said."

"I agree with that...in part."

"Which part is that?"

"If a man said that he'll never leave me or forsake me, but he lived two thousand years ago...it would indeed be difficult to take that to heart. But if that man who lived two thousand years ago was *still alive*, well then, I think I could put some trust into that person."

"Why?"

"Let's just say I have a personal, unwritten policy to believe everything a man says if he rose from the dead."

"Yeah, I guess that would be a good reason to believe...*if* he rose from the dead. I have a difficult time believing in the reanimation of a dead body. I guess it goes against everything I've been taught in school."

"Really? According to your mother, half the time you were either suspended or expelled. I'm surprised you remember anything from school." Joshua gave him a look indicative of disapproval that Chris talked to his mother about him. Chris then continued, "There's been a ton of research done on the resurrection. Believe it or not, there's more historical evidence that supports the resurrection of Jesus Christ than we have evidence for the existence of Aristotle, Plato, and Socrates. And there is *plenty* of evidence to support their past existence. In contrast, there's zero conclusive evidence of a common origin of all life."

Joshua was somewhat intrigued by the information. However, the compounding annoyance of Chris's continuing to dive into his life began to overflow into words.

"You know, Chris, you know an awful lot about me. Apparently, you're talking to kids that know me, googling me on the Internet, now you say you went and talked to my family about me...to get some dirt on me. But I don't know anything about you, homie. You just showed up a month and a half ago taking over the community center. Preaching about God all the time. I mean, you're training me to fight, *which I already know how to do*. So how come you don't tell me about your life? What God has done for you? And I don't mean, *every breath I take is from God*, or *I lost my job and the rent was coming due when a check for the exact amount of money miraculously showed up in the mailbox*."

"First off, you never asked me anything. Secondly, your family loves you more than you know. And I *just* came from talking to your mother. That's how I knew where to find you. What do you think would have happened if I didn't stop you? You would have probably killed that man. So you might want to *thank God* I did go talk to your mother." Joshua accepted the latter part of Chris's statement.

There was another round of silence for a moment while Chris organized his thoughts before revealing his testimony, then began by saying, "I never even knew my parents. I was in an orphanage until my mid-teens. Then I went from foster home to foster home. I had a lot of aggression and took it out on many of the other foster kids. When I was eighteen I was out of the system and onto the streets. Sometimes I picked fights with people just so I could go to jail...because at least there, I got some food and a bed for a night. One night I was in a holding cell with a few other guys. One man thought he'd get smart and said something I didn't like, so I beat him up, right in front of the other cellmates. One of which was a member of a local gang. I was put in solitary for a few hours, but after I was released, that gang member found me under an overpass and said, 'You're pretty tough.' Then he asked, 'You want a real home?' I said yeah. He said, 'It costs to get in, but once you're in, you're in for life.' I agreed."

"Okay, so you joined a gang. You obviously got out," Joshua reasoned.

"Yeah, I did. But I'll tell you it costs a lot more to get out than to get in. In fact, I wouldn't have even considered it until I ran into my wife at a store one day. We were in the same aisle. Man, she was hot." Joshua laughed at that comment silently. "But not in a sleazy exotic dressed way. There was just something about her that drew me to her. I couldn't even tell you what it was at the time. But it was her relationship with Jesus that got me. It just radiated from her. Now, I shacked up with my share of loose chicks —in a gang, they're easy to find. When I first joined the gang, I had to get a tattoo of our gang logo. It's that one on my arm there, with the cross over it now. But everyone in town basically knew what that was. I tried talking to her. She saw that tattoo, and she said, 'I ain't gonna be with no dude in a gang...unless it's Jesus's gang.' Ha ha, that was the oddest rejection line I'd ever heard."

"Yeah, I would say so," Joshua agreed.

"I'd see her around every so often. We'd talk for a minute. She would basically tell me the same thing every time. I got a Bible one day and began reading it. I saw her again and asked her if I left the gang if she would be with me."

"Of course she said yes," Joshua assumed.

"Nope. She said I should get out of the gang anyway, but even if so, there wasn't any guarantee. Her first priority was to the Lord. I kept reading the Bible. Romans 8:28 stuck with me. '*All things work together for those who love God and are called according to his purpose.*' I honestly took that as if I followed God, then maybe

I'd get the girl. Kind of a goofy translation, but I had begun feeling deep conviction about what I was doing in the gang. Beating people up, stealing, and worse. Next thing I knew I was trying to stop my bros in the gang from beating people up. Finally, they gave me an ultimatum: get with their program or leave. And to leave, as I said, costs more than to get in."

"So what happened?"

"We usually hung out in this old abandoned warehouse on the edge of town. They opened a door for me, threw my Bible outside, and then told me to go get it. I had to go through ten guys to get to the door. I remember the first two stabs. After that, I woke up in the hospital."

"Where'd they stab you?"

"Well, I don't remember which ones were the first two now. The surgeon said they stopped counting at fifty though."

That got Joshua's attention. "You were stabbed over fifty times?"

"Yep."

"Is it weird that I kinda want to see the scars?"

"Ha ha. No, it's not. Remember, Thomas didn't believe Jesus rose from the dead until he saw the scars."

"So after you got out of the hospital, Katrina obviously got with you," Joshua again incorrectly assumed.

"Nope. She was at the hospital though when I woke up. Pastor Wesley was there too. He took me in. I started doing odd jobs for money. But it wasn't until one day I ran into a couple of old bros from the old gang who were beating up some guy for his wallet. I just lit with rage and I tore them both up. They ended up in the hospital—one in critical condition. I sustained a broken nose and a busted tooth...and a jail sentence for a year. Jail wasn't necessarily unfamiliar to me like I said. I would sometimes do things to purposefully go to jail, for like a night or two...a week tops. But a whole year in the slammer...man, I hated it. Pastor Wesley and Katrina came to visit me every week. I'll never forget what she said one day. 'I'm afraid you're not going to get through this without God.' That same day, I was sitting in my cell, on the bed. I could hear the other inmates cussing and talking perversely like always. I knew I didn't want to be like these guys. I got on my knees and basically told God that exact thing. I said whatever you want me to do, just get me out of here."

"Did they release you?"

"Nope. I did my *whole* sentence. But they had a chapel, and I eventually got permission to help in the chapel. I read the Bible every day. I remember this new kid showed up. Man, he was scrawny, but he hated life. I felt led to talk to him about God, and after some time, he accepted Jesus. Man, it was *awesome*. I knew what God was going to have me do when I got out. I was finally released and had to do some parole time, but anytime I saw a kid walking the street or wherever, I would run up to them and tell them about Jesus. Honestly, I think I freaked some of them out the first couple of times I did it... you know, skin-headed, pierced-up tattooed dude running at you." Joshua laughed at that comment too.

"But Katrina saw that God had become my first priority and then, then...that's when she said, 'I guess I can tolerate spending the rest of my life with you.'"

"Ha ha ha," Joshua again laughed.

"So, Josh, that's my story."

"Man, I thought I had it rough."

"You'll find that there's always someone out there that has it or *has* had it tougher than you."

Joshua nodded at the comment, not something he's necessarily thought about before. They began pulling up to the community center, and as they did, there was a single car in the parking lot and a woman sitting on the trunk.

"Who's that?" Chris asked.

Then as they parked, Joshua said, "That's Jennifer." They got out of the car, and Jennifer slid off the trunk of hers.

"Did you forget something?" she said to Joshua, then held up his phone and his wallet. He quickly checked his pockets, which all he had were the keys to his truck. She had a face that was neither happy nor angry—but indifferent.

"Jennifer," Joshua said, walking toward her.

"I thought you had training to do. Or was that a lie to do something else?"

"It wasn't a lie."

She then noticed the welt on his cheekbone and a cut on his lip. "What happened?" she asked.

Joshua glanced at Chris who simply responded, "Don't look at me."

"I saw your truck behind the Mexican restaurant," she revealed.

"I was heading here. As I was driving by the restaurant it all came back. I lost control," he admitted.

She then gently placed her hand on the side of his face and looked into his eyes with a forgiving expression, then asked, "Who am I?"

"Who are you?"

"I thought I meant something to you. I thought we were, maybe, an item?"

"You do. We are. I want that," he replied, revealing his intention to make a real commitment.

She smiled at his comment. Then as fast as her smile appeared, it fled as she took her hand off his cheek and smacked him across it. "Then that's for not listening to your *girlfriend.*"

"This is the best training session we've had," Chris said to himself.

"I have high standards for my man. So if you want to keep me, you better meet them." Joshua nodded. "Actually, now that I'm thinking about it, I don't think you can meet them. Lose my number please so I don't have to block you," she said as she turned to go back to her car and leave.

"*WHAT?*" Joshua shouted as his heart sunk. He hadn't felt something like that in years. "Jennifer, wait!" She stopped and crossed her arms. She continued facing away from him to hide her manipulative grin as this was a test; she had no real intention of breaking up with him. Besides, he was a popular successful man, who was tough—everything she wanted in a guy. Though tolerable was his police record, she knew she could still flaunt him.

"I'm s-s-s-o-o-o-o-r-r-r-y," he struggled to say.

She pulled her smile down and turned around with an expression of disapproval. "What was that?"

"I said I'm sorry. I'm very sorry I didn't listen to you."

She then walked back up to him. "I can walk away just as easy as you do."

"Right," Joshua affirmed her statement.

"You used your *one* and *only* strike. You're not getting another." She then kissed him on his lips. "And you're lucky that I don't make you *gravel*," she added, then turned to go back to her car. As she backed out she rolled her window down and concluded the conversation with, "and you're coming over tonight by the way—*just* to watch a movie though. It's a *real* tear-jerker. And it's *really* long."

"Why?" he inquired.

"Because I'm your *girlfriend*, and *I said so*. See you later," she said, waving then driving off.

Joshua turned to Chris who had been silently sitting on the hood of *his* car watching the two. "*What* just happened?" Joshua said to him.

"She just busted you in half and wrapped you around her finger...like all of her fingers."

"No, she did not."

"Dude, she turned you into a yoyo," Chris continued.

"A yoyo?" he responded, insulted.

"I lost count of how many cracks of the whip I heard."

"I'm not whipped."

"It was awesome!" Chris concluded. They looked at each other then laughed.

"You're right. She got me good," Joshua finally admitted.

"Don't sweat it, man. Commitment is a good thing. And I'm not just talking about a commitment to a woman, but being committed to anything you do. If you commit to God, he'll commit to you. That's a promise even." Chris then walked over and put his hand on Joshua's shoulder. "Josh, I'll make you a deal. If you listen to everything I say...do everything I tell you, I promise, as God as my witness, I promise to be whatever you need me to be for you." The statement almost drew a tear as that's what he had once longed for from his own father. He smiled then nodded. "But you have to listen to me and do everything I say."

"All right. I will."

"Do you trust me?" Chris asked.

"I do."

"Good. Now go in there and get me a bottle of water."

"Why?"

"Because I'm thirsty...and I told you to." Joshua laughed then ran into the center to get a bottle of water for Chris, as he was told to do.

****

Their relationship grew exponentially as Joshua more and more looked to Chris as a father figure than that of a trainer or even some youth pastor. Everything Chris told Joshua to do, Joshua rarely hesitated. And to that effect, Chris *never* asked him to do anything inconsequential, as everything had a purpose. For if Joshua could become obedient to Chris, he could be obedient to

God. Joshua also began opening up at the men's group on Tuesday evening's regarding some, though not all, of his upbringing. As a result, he also began developing relationships with the other men of the group as well.

Unfortunately, Joshua still drank, though his drinking began decreasing and his visits to the liquor store became less frequent, plus the less he went, the less he would be tempted by Stacy, the evening liquor store associate.

Paralleling Joshua and Chris's relationship was Tiffany and Katrina's relationship. Katrina spent many daylight hours with her and even stayed over some nights on occasion. Katrina routinely did things around her house for her and showed her how to be more efficient in many ways, besides simply doing laundry and making eggs. Though Tiffany still bought plenty of new outfits. A few times Katrina helped do her makeup before she had to leave for a photoshoot, and if a venue that Tiffany was required to perform at was within driving distance, Katrina went—though most of her time there was spent running off guys, to which Tiffany had mixed feelings about.

Since it was common for Kara and Sandra to visit Tiffany in the afternoons, it became routine for the four of them to play games together, go to the movies together, and do various other activities together. As a result, Kara and Sandra also began developing a relationship with Katrina and occasionally they met together even without Tiffany, for sometimes Tiffany still brought a guy over and had an excuse to not be available for Katrina and/ or her friends. As far as Kara and Sandra, it could be assumed that their *perfect* roommate may have had something to do with them needing a reason to get away from the dorm on a regular basis. Nevertheless, Katrina's presence had a positive impact on them as was evident when on one particular weekend Jennifer commented on the fact they hadn't had guys over for an entire forty-eight hours.

And speaking of Jennifer, her and Joshua's relationship also grew. However, Jennifer had become addicted to the popularity she was obtaining through her relationship with Joshua Nickel—especially as advertisements of his next fight began broadcasting locally. Her social media was inundated with pictures of her and Joshua, but with her more prominently displayed in the photos. The two of them still slept together from time to time as well, something that Chris did not approve of and occasionally brought to Joshua's attention.

SKIN DEEP

Joshua's MMA match was fast approaching. His training had become more intense as he advanced in other fighting techniques. Also, his left hook was getting stronger, and his kicks were getting higher and more powerful. Then on the last training session before his fight arrived, Chris put a bottle of water on a stand that stood about shoulder high.

"All right, let's see a roundhouse," Chris said. Joshua spun around with his leg high in the air and with his foot, kicked the bottle off of the stand, and without pulling anything. Chris smiled and clapped, then the two knuckle-bumped. "Excellent!"

The next evening was youth night—though, there were many others than just youth as seemingly the entire neighborhood had become regular attenders to the Friday night gathering. After the normal time of playing and fellowship, Chris blew his whistle and instinctively the crowd headed to the atrium where, as usual, Chris would get into the boxing ring and preach. This was a special youth night too, as the next day was Joshua's second MMA fight. Halfway through his sermon Chris had Joshua step into the center of the boxing ring.

"Kneel," Chris told Joshua, and he did. "Everyone, come on up here!" Chris told the crowd. Then as many kids that could fit in the boxing ring climbed in, and those who couldn't, gathered around the ring placing their hands on Joshua or holding their hands out toward Joshua as Chris prayed for his protection, perseverance, stamina, and guidance for the upcoming competition. "In Jesus's Name, Amen!" Chris concluded the prayer.

"Amen!" the crowd in unison repeated.

"So! Who can tell me three things you bring to a conflict?" Chris then asked the crowd, to which, in a shout, they all replied in unison, "*Love! Grace! And forgiveness!*"

****

The next day, Chris, Joshua, and Jennifer arrived at the participants' entrance of the coliseum. They were escorted down a walkway—lined with cameras, journalists, bouncers, and fans that paid extra to see the fighters outside the ring, by security. Once they entered the auditorium, the crowds roared, shouting, "Ni-ckel! Ni-ckel! Ni-ckel!" High-definition screens all over the coliseum displayed spectacular graphics in conjunction with Joshua Nickel's return to the octagon. It was quite the welcoming mat that Joshua hadn't anywhere near expected. "Whoa! This is all for me?"

Chris turned back to him and said, "Your sponsor's a big fan."

"When do I get to meet him?" Joshua responded. Chris simply smiled then looked onward. The atmosphere was arousing to Jennifer as she grabbed Joshua's arm and threw it in the air, to which the crowd then shouted even louder. Based on Jennifer's reaction, you would have thought that she was the center of attention. Chris then led them down the aisle way to the octagon.

After settling into their area outside the ring, Chris spoke to Joshua about tactics, while Jennifer continued absorbing the atmosphere as this was an adrenaline rush to her.

"Now remember, this guy has most likely studied your moves from your last fight just as you have his, so don't anticipate him to follow the same pattern. If he doesn't start swinging soon, that's a good indication he knows your defensive tactics and you'll need to lead him. You got a kick now, use it. You have a reputation for not kicking, so that will be your secret weapon tonight." Joshua listened intently, nodding in acceptance of Chris's advice as he gave it. "All right, let's pray," Chris concluded. Joshua had since become accustomed to Chris praying over him and accepted it. "You want to join us?" Chris invited Jennifer.

"No. That's your guys' thing," she responded, backing up from them, as the idea of praying seemed beneath her. So Chris put his hand on Joshua's shoulder, and they both tilted their heads to the ground as Chris prayed for him.

As Chris and Joshua were praying, an unexpected salutation in Jennifer's ear startled her. "Hi." Jennifer quickly turned around to see a woman's unfamiliar face somewhat covered by the hood of a zipped-up hoodie. That same woman then said, "Want some tips?"

The question was perplexing to Jennifer, which was evident by her expression. "I'm sorry, I don't understand." The woman then removed her hood as if revealing a secret identity. Jennifer was struck by the woman's beautiful appearance. However, it wasn't until a monitor behind the woman within Jennifer's view flashed a make-up advertisement that featured the same woman's face that Jennifer realized she was face-to-face with Tiffany Love.

Immediately, Jennifer's hidden insecurities surrounding Joshua's past relationship with the model, which was greatly exaggerated in her own imagination, vanished. Tiffany then placed her hood back over her head. "Wow," Jennifer responded to her beautiful complex ion. "I have to admit, you are gorgeous. I thought those photos were airbrushed, to be honest." The comment enhanced Tiffany's grin as well as her inner pride, but she didn't respond.

"Listen, sweetie, I don't want to fight," Jennifer admitted, however, Tiffany remained silent, but her intense gaze was, in itself, antagonistic toward Jennifer. "Okay, I see how this is going to be. So as far as your tips go, look where I am and look where you are." For a barricade divided the limited-access area around the ring, in which Jennifer was privileged to, from the spectators, where Tiffany was.

The comment caused Tiffany's grin to slip some, which in turn bolstered Jennifer's confidence thus encouraging her to add to the insult by saying, "And, sweetie, he doesn't even think about you. You're like a paper cup when someone wants a quick drink...when they're done, they throw it away"—Jennifer then leaned toward Tiffany's ear and whispered—"because you're trash."

The insult heightened Tiffany's inner hostility, and if it wasn't for the bouncers lining the limited-access side of the barricade, she would have attacked her. But just then the announcer, to hype the crowd up more, ran highlights of Joshua's previous victory over Brett Karmel, which also included Tiffany and Joshua's hormonally induced lip-locking conclusion to the first competition. The decibels of the crowd went off the charts at the rerun being displayed on the video cube.

However, Joshua, who was standing on the steps to the entrance of the ring, glanced down at Chris with an apologetic and embarrassed expression. Chris simply shrugged his shoulders, indicating the scene wasn't a surprise to him but also observing that Joshua felt some shame over the particular moment as the past couldn't be changed, just revisited. Joshua then looked back where Jennifer was, expecting a negative expression over the replay. However, her back was turned to him as she was talking to someone, but he couldn't see who it was.

The replay brought back Tiffany's grin, which then prompted Jennifer to respond, "You know, sweetie, I don't like to compete," she admitted, "but in this atmosphere, I'm kinda feeling it." At that, Jennifer turned as the fighters had entered the octagon. She ran up the steps into the ring, grabbed Joshua, threw her arms around his neck, and began kissing him intensely. The cameras were rolling, and the scene was live, in which the MC responded through the PA system throughout the coliseum and the streaming simulcast, "It looks like Tiffany Love is old news." Tiffany watched the romantic display on the video cube in horror as it was comparable to a thousand blades plunging into her body.

Jennifer looked back toward the barricade just as she witnessed the hooded woman turn and disappear into the crowd. The whole incident perplexed Chris, as he felt an odd tension arise that he couldn't quite pinpoint the source of. Jennifer's spontaneous action also surprised Joshua as it seemed out of character for someone as *supposedly* ethical and classy as she was. "Wow, what was that for?" he asked.

"I just wanted to give you my good luck." She then kissed him again then added, "I feel on top of the world."

"Just don't fall...it's a long way down," he responded.

"I never fall." She then left the ring and stood next to Chris and smiled, before looking once again back at where she and her rival were previously conversing with a grin that could have circled the Earth. Chris then looked back to see what Jennifer was seemingly enthralled with, but nothing, in particular, stood out to him. Chris still didn't know what to think about Jennifer, only that he knew what drew Joshua to her. Jennifer then turned her attention to her prize in the ring as the fight began.

"Round one!"

****

Tiffany flew home in her convertible, running red lights, yield signs, and almost wrecked several times. As she was pulling into her development, Katrina spotted her as she had just left Tiffany's house, to which she quickly made a U-turn and followed Tiffany home. Tiffany pulled into her driveway without slowing down and nearly ran into her garage door. Katrina pulled into her driveway behind her, not quite as fast though. However, she could easily determine something was wrong.

Katrina quickly exited her car and ran to Tiffany who just sat in her driver seat looking straight ahead in the spaced-out gaze that most were accustomed to seeing.

"Tiffany, what's wrong?" she said, running up to her. Tiffany had a grip on her steering wheel with both hands. The engine was still running and the gear was still in drive. After Tiffany didn't answer her, Katrina's concern grew. Fearing that she was about to do something stupid, she reached over Tiffany's arms and shut the engine off. That got Tiffany's attention, and she finally looked up at Katrina. Her eyes were wide. They looked like they could shed a river full of tears at any moment, but nothing came out.

"I waited for you. We were going to go eat dinner together with your friends, remember?" Katrina reminded her.

"I remember."

"Sweetheart, what's wrong? What happened?"

"I" was all that Tiffany could get out. "I—"

Katrina went around the car and got in the passenger side. She then put the car in park and took the keys completely out of the ignition. "You what, sweetie?" Katrina prompted her.

"You're going to be mad at me," Tiffany responded.

Katrina pulled her head to her shoulder and embraced her. "I'm not going to be mad. Besides, I'm not your mother. You remind me of that quite often...remember?"

Tiffany lifted her face up to Katrina's with an expression of guilt for reminding Katrina of that particular fact. "I'm sorry."

"For what?"

"For saying that."

"It's okay."

"Can you be my mom?" Tiffany then asked.

"Tiffany, your mother has a special place in your life, and I don't ever want to take that away from her. But I'll be whatever you need me to be. So if that's what you need, then absolutely." Tiffany laid her head on Katrina's shoulder again. "So what happened, Tiffany?"

"I was driving past the coliseum, on my way home"—as soon as she said that, Katrina determined what she did, in part, but continued allowing Tiffany to tell her what happened on her own —"I just wanted to see him one more time."

"Joshua?"

"Yeah. And I kinda wanted to meet her too."

"Meet who?" Tiffany was unable to say her name, so Katrina assumed it. "His girlfriend?" Tiffany nodded, and then the tears began pouring out, and she again buried her face into Katrina's shoulder, sobbing uncontrollably. "Oh, Tiffany," Katrina consoled.

Tiffany then looked up at her and asked, sobbing, "Am I trash?"

"Tiffany, no. You're not trash. Did someone call you that?" Tiffany nodded. "Who?"

"She did." Katrina was almost ready to shed her own tears.

Tiffany continued crying on Katrina, sputtering random statements that were indicative of her emotional state. "I can't get her out of my head. And she's so pretty." The statement caught Katrina slightly off guard as Tiffany was a model.

"Tiffany, so are you."

"She's pretty without makeup though."

"It will still fade one day. But God doesn't look at our skin...*we're* the ones who do that." Katrina reassured her. "Tiffany, can I ask you something?"

"Yeah."

"I've been concerned about your infatuation with Joshua for a while. Please don't be offended, but you have been with a lot of guys and yet you seem *irrationally* stuck on Josh. Did something happen that caused you to become *this* emotionally obsessed with him? Besides his eyes and his physique?"

"I'm obsessed?" Tiffany asked.

"Yes, sweetie, this isn't love."

"But I do love him, I do," Tiffany adamantly responded.

"Well, okay, maybe you do, but why then do you love him?"

Tiffany got a bit anxious, but then explained to Katrina the reason. "Remember when we met at the restaurant, and I—"

"And you got us kicked out?" Tiffany nodded. "Yeah I remember that."

"I lied. I wasn't upset because of a dream I had. The night before, Joshua came over for dinner. But I didn't do a very good job of making it. He was going to leave, but I...well...convinced him to stay. So we—"

"Had sex," Katrina filled in the blank, to which Tiffany nodded.

"Well, while we were, Brett Karmel showed up with a gun. He wanted to kill us!"

"Oh my goodness, Tiffany! What happened?"

"Josh pushed me out of the way and stood in front of the gun. The gun, thank God, didn't go off, then Joshua beat him up and he left."

"Then what happened?" Katrina further inquired.

"Well, we—"

"Had sex again?"

"Yeah. But something was different. I felt safer than I've ever felt, ever since—"

"Since your parents passed?"

"Yeah. I felt like I finally belonged. Like someone wanted me. But then the next morning, he was gone again." Tiffany took her phone and showed Katrina the text message Joshua had left her: *Unless you have car problems, don't show up at my shop again.* "This is what he sent me."

"Oh, Tiffany. I'm so sorry."

"It doesn't make sense. He was going to take a *bullet* for me! How could you take a *bullet* for someone and not love that person? It's not logical...I can't comprehend it. He has to, somewhere inside, love me, right?"

Katrina then pulled her close again and held her while she continued crying. "Thanks for telling me. I understand now."

"I wish I was like her," Tiffany sobbingly told her.

"Tiffany! No! God made you the way you are for his glory. In fact, there's something I've wanted to do for a while. Let's go inside."

Katrina had Tiffany sit in front of a vanity where she proceeded to wash all her makeup off her face. Then she rummaged around Tiffany's seemingly endless supply of makeup and, finding an eye liner pencil, applied a small amount to her face. Katrina then pulled her lip gloss from her pocket and applied that to her lips as well—no other makeup was added to her face.

"Take out your contacts," Katrina directed Tiffany as she left the bathroom. Tiffany did and then Katrina returned with Tiffany's glasses—that she hadn't worn in a long time—and placed them on her. Tiffany then stared at her reflection as if finding a long-lost friend, for she hadn't seen that face in nearly three years. Katrina then took her own necklace off that had a shiny cross on it and put it around Tiffany's neck. "See, you don't need all that makeup."

Shortly thereafter, a knock came to the front door followed by, "Tiffany? It's us, Kara and Sandra!" Katrina and Tiffany left the bathroom to meet them in the living room. Upon seeing Tiffany, Kara and Sandra were stunned to see their former roommate looking remarkably average. It was, however, a pleasant surprise. "Wow! Tiffany! You look great." Tiffany smiled. Then Katrina reminded them of the dinner plans and soon after left.

While at the restaurant, a lot of laughter came from their table but mostly generated from Katrina, Sandra, and Kara. Tiffany simply smiled at many of the jokes, as the lack of public attention that she normally drew from her usual provocative appearance was almost insulting to her. Until, "Hi," an unassuming average-looking man approached the table and offered to buy Tiffany a drink. He was a little stocky and had some facial hair, but was well-dressed and groomed. Tiffany glanced at Katrina as normally she was quick to run off men who were obviously only interested in one thing. However, Katrina smiled and lightly nodded at her approving of the man's offer.

Tiffany then looked up at the man, smiled, and then responded, "No thanks."

"Okay, I like your glasses...they really bring out your eyes," for he was wearing glasses too. "Have a good evening, ladies," he commented, then went on his way.

Katrina was shocked at Tiffany's rejection of the man. Then Tiffany explained her response by simply saying, "He was fat." Then Tiffany got up from the table. "I'll be right back. I need some fresh air." She went outside then noticed that next door was a hair products store and went in to look around. She came to a box of brown hair dye and picked it up. She stared at the box for some time then finally took it to the register. After she bought it and turned to leave, Katrina was standing there.

"Brown, huh?" she said disapprovingly. Tiffany was silent. "Tiffany, sweetie, don't change your appearance for anyone."

"I just like the color," Tiffany responded, to which Katrina simply replied, "Okay."

PUZZLE PIECES

"Hello?" said a man, answering his cell phone.

"Hi, is this Nicholas Perry Jr.?"

"Yeah, but if you have a role, you need to get a hold of my agent—"

"No, no role. My name's Chris. I just had a quick question."

"Okay, quick," he replied.

"Do you know Tiffany Love by chance?"

The question stopped Nicholas in his tracks. "Listen, I was found innocent of that whole thing—"

"Yeah, I know, I'm just trying to get some more background information on her."

"You want background info on her? Here it is...*she's insane!* She *almost* cost me my acting career! If it wasn't for that entertainment company spending millions of dollars to get her off the hook, she'd be in an insane asylum—*where she belongs!*"

"All right, I hear ya."

Katrina then whispered, "Ask if he has silver eyes."

Chris thought the question was odd, but then asked him, "One more quick question, do you have silver eyes by chance?"

"What? Yeah, I do…they're an asset, to be honest. Now, do me a favor and lose my number." Click.

"What a jerk!" Chris responded after the phone conversation.

"Cut him some slack, the guy was accused of rape."

"True, I'd rather be charged with murder than with sexual assault," Chris admitted. "So what about the silver eyes thing? That was kind of weird to ask."

"It solidifies my theory about Tiffany."

"Which theory is that?"

"She's not sleeping around with guys just for sex, or to find a mate. She's trying to replace her father."

"That's interesting. Do elaborate."

"Well, her father was very *successful*, he was her *protector*, and in fact, he did literally everything for her. And he had silver eyes. Women generally are attracted to men who resemble their father. Even if they hated their father. For example, if they had an alcoholic for a father, it's not uncommon for them to wind up with a man who's an alcoholic in many cases. Not that they're cognitively searching for that…it's a familiarity. Conversely, women who've had great relationships with their father might, more intentionally, seek a man with similar qualities. With all that in mind, Tiffany brings home a lot of guys who are very *successful*."

"So why's she hung up on Josh?"

"Besides the fact that he's very successful—has his own business, he's popular, obviously in the UFC thing, *and* he has silver eyes—but I also just learned yesterday that apparently he nearly took a bullet for her."

"He protected her," Chris interjected.

"Exactly. And, speaking of Josh, how did the match go?"

"You didn't hear? All the sports networks have been talking about it." Katrina looked at him cockeyed, as she rarely follows sports. "Right, he did amazing. I was very impressed."

"That's good, but I wasn't talking about Josh and whoever he was competing against," she responded.

Then Chris looked at *her* cockeyed. "Babe, I know I'm a skin head, but that doesn't make my name Charles Xavier."

"Oh, trust me, I know," she further replied, sarcastically. "Tiffany was there too. Apparently."

"Really?"

"You didn't see her at all?"

"Babe, there were a few thousand people there. It would have been hard to effectively point her out...even in her normal apparel."

"She said that she and Jennifer had a conflict. I assumed Jennifer was with you two."

"Yeah, she was but"—then it dawned on him about some of Jennifer's behavior—"actually, now that I think about it, she was talking to someone behind the barricade. I had no idea who it was. She also made quite the scene in the cage with Josh," he explained.

"She called Tiffany trash apparently, and it had quite the effect on her. What do you think about that woman?"

"Jennifer? Well, she's only interested in Josh for attention. You would have thought the event was for her the way she threw herself in front of the cameras. But she has been a useful tool in getting him to commit to things. Unfortunately, she's going to break his heart real bad one of these days."

"Well, I can't say I'd be all that sympathetic toward him after what he's known for doing with girls. But I am curious to know what he sees in her."

"His mother."

"His mother?"

"Jennifer reminds him of his mother. He doesn't know it, but after meeting his mother and her telling me her story, there are a lot of personality similarities between the two, and a lot of physical similarities too—they both have brown hair and brown eyes for starters. The only difference, besides age, is that Trisha was essentially destitute raising Joshua and Jennifer lived in luxury her whole life."

"Why does Luke chapter 16 ring a bell?" Katrina retorted.

"Good point. Jennifer is highly agnostic, maybe borderline antitheistic...based on some of her comments."

"So is Tiffany. Well, I shouldn't say antitheistic, but she's pretty subtle about her rejection to receive Jesus. She always says *she will later.* Sometimes it seems like she wants to, but something is holding her back. Maybe fear that she'll have to let a lot of things go."

"Like her *daddy's* house?"

"Precisely. I've been praying that God gets her out of that house...and out of this company no matter what it takes. And this Glamour Entertainment business is pure evil. In fact, she has a show in Vegas tomorrow night. I offered to take her to the airport this afternoon when she told me about it a few weeks ago, but she said no."

"I wonder why. I thought she enjoyed being around you."

"I remind her a lot of her mother, but I talk a lot about Jesus. I can tell there's an internal conflict within her over those two things."

Then Katrina's phone rang. It was Tiffany. "Hey, Tiffany."

"Hi, I was thinking, I do want you to take me to the airport."

"Sure, I can do that," Katrina responded.

"Okay. I'll be ready."

"All right, I'll see you soon." The conversation concluded. "Like I said...internal conflict. Now she *wants* me to take her to the airport."

****

Katrina picked up Tiffany and pulled up to the airline entrance at the airport. Tiffany got out, got her suitcase, and headed toward the entrance. A sense of fear then came over Katrina. She then jumped out of the car. "Tiffany! Wait!" Tiffany stopped while Katrina ran up to her.

"What's the matter?" Tiffany asked as she could see Katrina was anxious about something.

"Tiffany, don't bring anyone back home with you," Katrina said adamantly. "I don't think it will turn out well for you."

"Okay," Tiffany responded, nodding.

"Can you promise me you won't?"

"Yeah, I promise."

"Okay." Katrina smiled as the answer relieved her. "Call me when you get to your hotel, okay?"

"I will." They then hugged and Katrina watched Tiffany enter the airport. "Jesus, please protect her. And get her out of this company...no matter what."

Then her phone rang. It was the attorney. "Katrina?"

"Yeah," she responded.

"Can you come down to my office? We've got some information regarding the contracts you gave me."

"Yeah, I'm on my way."

****

At the attorney's office

"Katrina, this is Priscilla Hovage. She used to be employed by Glamour Entertainment," the attorney, Joel, explained.

"Priscilla Hovage? That sounds familiar," Katrina responded.

"*Sexiest woman in America*...ten years ago," Priscilla replied with a rhetorical smile. Then Katrina remembered the name was among a few that came up when she was doing research on Glamour Entertainment.

"What did they do?" Katrina asked.

"Well, to give you some background, my parents were really wealthy. One night, a man broke into our house and killed my parents and my brother. I hid in the closet. But I lost everything in a moment. This company executive out of nowhere finds me and says they could take care of me. I just had to sign a contract. It sounded great...but I was desperate." Immediately Katrina remembered Tiffany's words the day she first met her. "All I had to do were take some pictures. It was kind of fun and exhilarating at first. Until the pictures got more exotic. Then another contract came around and I was hesitant to sign it, but by then everything I had was really theirs. So I did. I had to do some shows, usually big venues."

"Tiffany Love signed two contracts already."

"A third one's coming soon."

"What's that involve?"

"That's really when it starts picking up speed."

"What picks up speed?"

"The grooming process. They're going to make her do shows nude. And then the fourth contract they send you to parties...and not to dance or sign autographs."

"Oh my gosh! We need to get her out of this! I just dropped her off at the airport to do a show in Vegas tomorrow night. I wish I didn't take her. But she's so worried about losing everything if she leaves," Katrina hysterically explained.

"Well," Priscilla continued, "if she doesn't get out soon, she's going to lose everything anyway. You said she's been with the company for three years?"

"Yeah, about that," the attorney responded.

"My guess is she won't even be in the country by the end of the year."

"How did you get out?" Katrina further inquired.

"I and some other girls were shipped overseas. I don't know what happened to the others...I never saw them again. But I ended up in India. I was there for two years before a ministry that secretly finds trafficked girls and smuggles them out found me and got me back to the states."

"What can we do?" Katrina asked Joel.

"We're working on putting together a criminal lawsuit against the company to get this going."

"How long will it take?"

"These things can take time, Katrina. Sometimes a couple of years. These two contracts you gave me, they are very well-crafted. That's why we're going to need witnesses like Priscilla."

"Thank you, Priscilla, for sharing. I am so, so, so sorry you went through all of that."

"Thank you. I have been blessed with amazing friends that God has used to restore me. And I tell my story to get the word out about this company...and there are others like it. But they have a lot of allies—politicians, lawyers, you name it. The media won't even touch this. According to them I, and others like me, are basically a bunch of liars. I just pray that you can convince Tiffany to get out no matter what. There are people that will help her if she lets them."

"I know. She's such a stubborn girl."

"We all are," Priscilla added.

They conversed for some time before their conversation concluded. "Katrina, before you leave, I just want to say thanks...thanks for bringing this to my attention," Joel said. Katrina nodded then left the office.

SERPENTS IN SHINING ARMOR

Las Vegas

It was nearing show time. The auditorium was filled with a thousand hormonally driven men and some women. Tiffany was backstage in her white exotic outfit and drinking wine to knock off her edginess that she feels before these events. The president of Glamour Entertainment along with some of his associates and one of the company's attorneys were also backstage.

"Tiffany, baby! Looking amazing!" She smiled, but it wasn't her smile.

"Hey, Brad," she said, pre tending to accept the compliment.

"Oh, before you go on, we have an updated contract we need you to sign," Brad added, and his attorney brought a roughly two inch-thick stack of paper to the table she was near.

"You want me to sign this now? Just before I'm going out there?" She knew she couldn't read through the whole contract in ten minutes, and even if she could, much of the legal descriptions were tantamount to reading Latin.

"Why not?" Brad asked, somewhat rhetorically.

"I just signed an updated one six months ago."

"That was six months. Times change, sweetheart."

She stared at the front page, skimming over it as fast as she could. It appeared to match what she vaguely remembered from the last two contracts. "Does it say I have to—"

"No, no sex acts," he reassured her. Then the attorney handed her a pen. She then flipped to the last page and signed her name and dated it.

"Can you put the time on there too please?" Brad requested, and she did. The attorney then took the pen and the contract and left.

"See, that wasn't too hard. Oh, and by the way, tonight, you can go without the outfit...as stunning as that looks on you."

"What?" she exclaimed in horror.

"The outfit...it needs to go."

"You said to wear white!" she reminded him.

"I did, but I changed my mind."

"What am I supposed to wear?"

"I said without...or do you not know what that means!"

Immediately her anxiety shot through the roof.

"You said no sex acts," she added, nearly beginning to hyper-ventilate.

"Sweetheart, this isn't a sex act! Besides, from what I under-stand, half the men from where you're from have seen more of you than what these guys are gonna see...so I don't know what the big deal is, to be honest."

The words were like knives, and Jennifer's statement came to mind as she said under her breath, "I'm a paper cup."

Brad then turned to the producer and said, "She's going to be a couple of minutes late getting on stage, have the opening glam-our girls do one more act." He then took a bottle of pills out of his pocket and put two on the little table. "Here, these will take off the edge better than that wine. You got an extra fifteen minutes before you go on." She quickly took the pills and chased it with the wine. "Oh, and you're doing autographs tonight too," he added, then left to sit in the suite to watch the show. Autographs at times entailed signing not only provocative photos of her but also signing her name, sometimes with a comment, on a person's body part such as their arm or chest, so they can get it tattooed. And fifteen minutes later she went on stage in the manner which Brad told her to in a cognitive state of oblivion.

After the show and a couple of hours of autographs were over. She sat alone at a small round table in a corner next to the bar, staring at her drink.

"Hi. Tiffany, right?"

"Where do you want your autograph? On your abs?" she said rhetorically with a little aggression mixed in.

"Actually, I just wanted to see if you're okay," he politely responded.

"Why?" she asked with a hostile tone.

"I get it. I watched the show, and you assume I'm like the rest of these guys. Honestly, I don't really like these things. I got suckered into coming down here by some coworkers." Tiffany stayed silent, continuing to stare at her drink. Then he took that as a sign to leave her alone and began to walk off.

"Wait," she said. He stopped and turned back to her. "You didn't answer my question," she said firmly.

"Why I asked if you were okay?" She nodded. "Because you looked like you hated every second you were on that stage."

"Was it that obvious?"

"Well, apparently not, based on the reaction of the rest of the crowd. But I could just tell. I tend to analyze people's faces...just a weird talent I have I guess." His comment appeared to disarm her just slightly as her facial expression went from aggressive to somewhat sad.

"You know, you never answered my question either," he added. "Are you okay?" She still didn't answer, but it was obvious that she wasn't. "Do you want to talk?"

"About what?" she cautiously asked.

"Whatever you want. Heck, we can talk about physics even, if that helps," he said to lighten her up.

"I was going to be a physicist once," she said to him.

"Oh, really? I'm an engineer. In fact, that's why I'm here. My company sent a few of us out here to come up with some new schematics."

"They sent you to a strip show?"

"Huh, um...no. They sent us to the hotel. We're here for a month. My coworkers wanted to check this out. And to be completely honest with you, I didn't even know it was going to be a strip show."

Tiffany lightly nodded in agreement and said, "Yeah, either did I."

"Hey, can I sit with you?"

She hesitated to answer, but then said, "Yeah."

"And by the way, my name's Timothy." He held his hand out as a friendly greeting, but Tiffany didn't shake it, so he pulled it back. "If I may ask if you don't like what you're doing, why don't you just stop?"

"I can't."

"Why not?"

She squirmed in her seat a bit before answering. "The company I *work* for," she said, rolling her eyes, "own my house."

"Oh, wow! Don't you have a husband or boyfriend that could help you with all that?"

The first thing that popped into her mind at the word *husband / boyfriend* was Joshua Nickel. However, having come to some acceptance that he and she were never going to be, she simply said no.

"Oh, I was going to say if you had a guy that provided for your needs, then maybe you wouldn't have to do this...is all."

"Huh. Are you volunteering?" she said rhetorically, not expecting a response in the affirmative.

"Well, I'm not that much to look at compared to you obviously, but I'd definitely volunteer."

The statement fully captured her attention. She then noticed that he didn't once look below her face the whole time they talked. She also began noticing that he was pretty handsome and his eyes had a little green in them. Her guard had been knocked down, but then Katrina's words came to mind: *Tiffany, promise me not to bring anybody home with you.*

"Um, I just remembered that I told my friend back home that I would call her before my flight. It leaves in a couple of hours."

"Sure. I'll just hang out here if that's okay."

She smiled and nodded then took her phone with her to the restroom and called Katrina.

"Hello, Tiffany?" Katrina answered.

"Yeah, it's me. Hi," Tiffany responded.

"How did your show go?"

"Um, it was...okay."

"You're not sounding convincing, Tiffany. What's the matter? Did something happen?"

"I just met this guy—"

"No, Tiffany!" Katrina didn't even let her finish her sentence.

"He's really nice—"

"Tiffany, please, please, please listen to me. Something *bad* is going to happen. You're vulnerable. Please come back alone!"

Hesitantly, Tiffany responded, "Okay."

"Promise me that."

"I promise."

Shortly after, the phone call ended Tiffany went back to her table. Timothy was still there. "Everything okay?" he said.

"Yeah. I have a friend back home. She tries giving me advice. But I don't always follow it."

"Maybe you should start doing that."

"You should probably go. I got to get ready to go to the airport in a few minutes."

"Oh, okay. Well, it was nice to meet you. I really hope you find a nice guy to settle down with, and hopefully, you can get out of your situation."

"It was nice to meet you too," Tiffany slowly responded, glancing down at her cup of water. But Timothy got no more than a few feet from her table when she spun around and asked, "Are you lying to me?" in a firm, stern voice.

"Um, I haven't lied about anything. Is there something, in particular, you're talking about?"

"I don't want to be a paper cup," she said to him.

"Okay? I'm not sure what you mean by that," he responded, then noticing a single tear fall from her eye, he knelt down and looked up at her with a concerned expression.

"I don't want to be thrown away anymore," she explained to him.

"Oh, Tiffany, you're nothing to be thrown away."

She cracked a small smile at hearing that.

"You would actually move for me? And stay?"

"If that's what you wanted. I don't have anybody either. I would absolutely take care of you, protect you, and be anything you needed me to be for you."

Her smile couldn't get any bigger at that point. She was like putty in his hands. "Okay, I got to go get my things. You'll meet me at the airport in half an hour?"

"Absolutely. This is kinda exciting...like eloping, though I think usually people come to Vegas to elope, and we're doing the opposite."

The comment made Tiffany laugh and lifted her spirits as she got out of the chair to get her things from her hotel room. "See ya in a bit."

"Sounds good. I got to go tell my guys over there my updated plans."

Timothy then walked over to a large table across the room where several of his coworkers were. As he approached, his fellow engineers smiled at him, then said, "Took you long enough." Timothy shrugged his shoulders. "How did it go?"

"Piece-a-cake," he responded with a smirk. "You know these desperate, vulnerable types."

As promised Timothy met Tiffany at the airport where he bought a one-way ticket to fly with her home where she would later give herself to him.

THE DESCENT

Tiffany woke up with a smile on her face, but as in the past, it wouldn't last long. She stretched then reached behind her to feel for Timothy, but she couldn't find him there. She then sprung up to the horror of an empty bed, once again. Immediately, the feeling of life drained out of her.

"No, no, no!" she yelled. Anxiety and depression set in so fast she didn't have time to compensate for the bombardment of negative emotions. Briefly, Katrina's words came to mind again: *Promise me you won't bring anyone back with you, I don't think it will turn out well.* She grabbed her phone off her nightstand and called Timothy— somewhat anxiously as if calling a boy for the first time, fearful of a subsequent déjà vu. She collected herself, then calmly pressed *call.*

Timothy was walking through the Las Vegas airport toward the baggage claim when Tiffany called. He was hesitant to answer it at first, but then he did. "Hello."

"Hi, Tim, it's Tiffany. Is everything all right?"

"Yeah. But hey, Tiffany, listen…I'm really sorry, but the thing is, the boys and I had a bet, and I don't like to lose." The statement immediately caused her flesh to feel disgusting, adding to the other countless emotions she was already experiencing as well as causing her body to tremble, which was also evident in her following response.

"I was a bet?"

"Yeah, sorry about that. But hey, I had fun though. And I really hope you find someone, it's just not going to be me. Also, if you could do me a favor and lose my number, I'd appreciate that. I really don't want to go through the trouble of blocking you, all right, thanks. Bye now." He then hung up as he approached a woman and two younger children, who asked him with smiles, "How was your business trip, hunny?" to which he responded, "Great, I got a lot done."

Tiffany then stared at the phone, her lips quivering before she began screaming at the top of her lungs while shaking her head and slamming her arms viciously on the mattress—fluid poured from her eyes and nose.

"DADDY!" she shouted as her seventeen-year-old self, ran into the kitchen, and clung to her father.

"Tiffany! What's the matter?" her father replied.

"Jimmy broke up with me," she explained.

"Oh, sweetheart," he responded, embracing her. "He doesn't deserve you. You need an intelligent man. A hard-working man. A man who will protect you and never leave you."

"Like you, Daddy," she responded, looking up in his soft silver eyes.

After her trip back in time, she found herself staring at her reflection once again in the bathroom mirror. She got in the shower and scrubbed herself for an hour. Still feeling as though she had inches of grime on her flesh that bar soap couldn't get off, she left the shower then returned to the hot water with a heavy-duty scratchpad where she proceeded to scrub her body with it to the point blood was protruding through her skin. After another hour in the shower, she got out. The box containing the brown hair dye was still on the bathroom counter. Again the words of Katrina, who was with her when she bought it, rang in her mind: *Don't change yourself for anyone.* But finally, she tore into it and began the process of dying her hair brown.

After another couple hours, she had completed dying her hair, though it was obviously not professionally done as there was still plenty of red in it. She then began straightening her hair, putting makeup on, and dressing up in the most exotic apparel she had available. It was all black—a reflection of her internal agony complimenting the multitude of small cuts on her face, arms, and thighs from the use of the scratchpad on her flesh. She then walked out to her vehicle with a ratchet and opened the hood for a few minutes then shut it again. She then picked up her phone and called Joshua, who was at his shop.

"Josh's auto, this is Josh."

"Hey, Josh, it's Tiffany, Tiffany Love. You remember me, don't you? You only screwed me a couple of times, remember?" she said in a vindictive tone.

"Um, yeah. It's kinda hard to forget," he responded, but in a way that suggested he wanted to forget. The relentless inundation of Bible talk from Chris had since started having a real effect on his conscience. However, Tiffany smiled at the response, receiving it in a more favorable way.

"Oh, I'm glad to hear that. For a while, I thought I was just a piece of toilet paper to you," she responded rhetorically.

"Right. So, Tiffany, can I help you with something? Honestly, I'm in the middle of working on a transmission."

"Um, yeah. My car isn't working. I was wondering if you could come look at it."

Joshua's head sunk to his chest getting a feeling that it would be a bad idea to go over to her house, so he responded, "Well, I can send Lisa, one of my employees, over. She's an excellent mechanic. She can figure it out." But Tiffany didn't like that answer.

"I want *you* to fix it."

"Well, like I said it's going to be a couple of hours, I'm in the middle of working on another vehicle," he again responded, hoping she would reconsider his offer if she had to wait.

"That's okay, I'll wait."

"Tiffany—"

"Yeah?"

"Is something really wrong with your car, or are you making this up?"

"Why would you think that? Of course, something's wrong with my car. You're just the best at this stuff."

Joshua finally caved and said, "Okay, it's noon, I'll be there around two o'clock. Is that okay?"

"Yeah, I'll be here."

"All right, see ya then," he concluded before hanging up. He went to his office, sat down, and put his head in his hands. Brody walked in to check on him.

"You all right, man? You've been different lately."

"Yeah, I'm good. Did you install the electrical harness in the Subaru?"

"Heck yeah, piece of cake...only took forty-five minutes."

"Piece of cake for you, that thing was a mess when it showed up."

"Well, you know me, I live for the electrical work. I could build a bomb out of vehicle components," Brody said sarcastically, illustrating his skill in that particular area.

"Yeah, well, I wouldn't advertise it quite like that. Listen, I gotta go look at Tiffany's car...she just called. It's *apparently* not starting. I need you to finish up the transmission on the Plymouth, can you do that?"

"You know I can. But is this *Tiffany Love*?" Brody asked with a smirk.

"Yes, but it's not what you think. I'm actually trying to do right with Jennifer...I really like her."

"I'm sure you do," Brody again responded sarcastically. "Oh hey, I found another one for you, by the way." Brody pulled out a folded contract from his pocket and sat it on Joshua's desk. "It's a big one."

"Brody, I told you I wasn't doing that anymore."

"But listen, this guy is dropping twenty G's."

"Man, that's a lot of money," Joshua admitted.

"Right? And he's been cited for domestic violence like five times."

"Brody, listen, I'm not doing it anymore."

"What? I know you wanted a break, but—"

"Brody, are you not hearing me?" Joshua said firmly. "I'm done with all that! Besides, maybe you should be asking why these chicks are sticking around these guys who keep abusing them, to begin with."

"I can't believe I'm hearing this."

"Brody, why are you getting all upset over this? Unless it's because I give you a cut of the cash after I bludger these guys? If that's your concern, why don't you go fight him and take the whole twenty grand?" Joshua responded rhetorically.

"You know what I go through to find these guys?"

"Okay, fine." Joshua then went to his safe, opened it, and pulled out fifteen hundred dollars. He closed the safe and then handed Brody the cash. "This is for your trouble to find this guy, but no more."

"Uh-huh, and exactly what am I supposed to tell him?"

"I'm going to be out of town for a couple of days later this week...I'm going to a men's conference. Tell him I'm unavailable. Or better yet, tell him I chickened out."

"Men's conference? Whatever. You're making me look like a fool going back to this guy to say Joshua doesn't want to fight. Oh, and this isn't the first time either."

"All right, Brody, this conversation's over. I have to get some tools ready to go fix a car."

"I'm sure you do. Or more likely just another excuse to get your hard-on taken care of, right?" A few months earlier, that comment would have put Brody in the hospital—regardless if he was his best friend or not. Instead, he pointed his finger at him with a scowl across his face and said, "Watch your mouth. I have a good thing going with Jennifer, and I love her. Now, I need you to take care of the Plymouth."

"You know what? Take care of the Plymouth yourself," Brody responded, then left the office and the shop in anger.

Joshua stood in his office looking at the ceiling, then said to himself, "God, are you real?" He then called Jennifer, but he only got her voicemail. "Hey Jenny, if you get this within the next half hour, can you call me back, please? I was hoping you could go with me somewhere. Thanks." He then went out to the shop and explained to his techs the situation. Then he collected some equipment that he possibly might need for fixing Tiffany's car and put them in the back of his truck. After getting in, he just sat there, hesitant to see Tiffany again. His anxiety over going to Tiffany's house then compelled him to see if Jennifer was at her dorm and drove to the university.

He pulled into the university dorm's parking lot and parked next to Jennifer's car. He knocked on the dorm door, but no answer. He looked at the time; it was about one o'clock at this point. "They're all probably in class right now...darn it." He then got back in his truck. "What are you so worried about, Josh?" he said to himself. "You're just going to check out the car and, if need be, fix it. That's it." He then started back out on the road toward Tiffany's development on the other side of town.

Joshua got to Tiffany's house half an hour early and pulled into the driveway. The garage door was open and her convertible was inside. He exited his truck, grabbed the bag of tools, and headed toward the car. By the time he entered the garage, Tiffany, who had heard his truck pull up, also walked out into the garage to meet him.

"Hey, Josh," she simply said.

"Hi, ah...holy Mylanta! Grandma naked...grandma naked... grandma naked," was his reaction at her appearance, and his reaction was just as she had hoped.

"What's the matter, Josh? You act as you've never seen me before."

"Uh, yeah, well. New dress? If you call that a dress."

"Yeah. Do you like it?"

"Yeah, it looks nice. So where's the keys so I can see what it's doing?" he asked. She handed him the keys and he got in the car, turned the ignition, but nothing. "Hmmm, could be the battery." He then popped the hood, and upon opening it his eyes nearly popped out of his head. He looked straight up in the air in disbelief as both battery cables had simply been removed from their ports. "Definitely the battery," he said, faking a smile. "Did you deliberately unhook your battery?" She leaned over the engine provocatively then slowly shook her head. However, Joshua wasn't fooled, he just refrained from speaking about it any further as he was now excessively determined to get out of there as soon as possible.

"Can you fix it?"

"Yeah. I...sure...can." It took Joshua no more than ten seconds to hook the battery backup. He then got back in the car to make sure it started—it did—then he closed the hood. "Well, you're all set," he said, picking up his bag of tools and began to head back to his truck. She then came running out of the garage halfway toward him saying in an almost desperate voice, "Stop!" to which he did.

"Look at me," she said with a slightly firmer voice. But he remained facing his truck. "LOOK AT ME!" she then shouted. He then turned around but still wouldn't look directly at her.

"What?" he said. "Why won't you look at me?" He didn't answer. He just shook his head thinking of what to say that wouldn't be offensive. "WHY WON'T YOU LOOK AT ME?" she then shouted at the top of her lungs.

He finally looked directly at her and responded, "Well, for one thing, because you're standing in your driveway, practically naked!" Then, as she was in the sunlight, he noticed her hair. "Did you dye your hair brown?"

"Do you like it?" she asked. "I did it for you." He was about to respond but then noticed the many cuts all over her flesh.

"Did you cut yourself?"

"I was *really dirty*, so I scrubbed *really hard* to get the filth off my body," she responded.

"Tiffany, I really need to get back to the shop."

"Wait!" she again said in a somber voice. He stopped again.

"Can you do one more thing for me?" He exhaled deeply before answering,

"What is it?"

"There's a picture in my room. It's too heavy for me to hang up by myself."

He turned back around to face her in disbelief of the request— though perhaps he should have believed it. "You want *me* to *hang a picture* up in your room?" She nodded. "Your room? As in, your *bedroom*?" She again nodded. He sat his tool bag on the drive then walked up to her and asked again, "Is there *really* a picture you need hung up in your bedroom?"

"Yes," she said, this time timidly. "If you can do that for me, you can leave. I promise. Then you don't have to look at me ever again." He again refrained from commenting on her latter statement as to avoid an emotionally reactive argument.

"Okay, *real* fast," he said then walked back into the garage and into the house. Tiffany followed. He walked through the large living room, up the stairs, and into her bedroom where she followed then closed the door and stood in front of the doorknob. Joshua looked around the room—no picture.

"This must be gullible-Joshua day," he said to himself. "Tiffany, where's the picture?" he asked, figuring there was no picture.

"Look at me," she again said. Joshua was again hesitant. "LOOK AT ME!" she then shouted again. He turned around and looked at her. Same appearance but with the addition of tears welling up in her eyes. "Am I trash?"

"Tiffany, no, you're not."

"So *why* am I just something *everyone throws away*?"

"Tiffany. I didn't know. I found out just a couple of weeks ago. Chris told me—"

"Told you what?"

"That...you're...hurting," he responded, expressing guilt, knowing that he had contributed to aspects of her emotional distress.

Tiffany puffed out her chest and smiled but maintained her grip on the doorknob. "You know, I think I'm starting to like it," she said rhetorically. "Can you hurt me some more?" She then walked up to him and grabbed his hands softly then raised them and put them around her neck. But he then quickly pulled them away.

"Are you crazy? I'm not going to hurt you."

"Why? You have before. Just like everyone else."

"Okay. Tiffany"—at this Joshua's own eyes began to tear up—"I can't say this for anyone else, but I'm...sorry. I'm so, so sorry. I can tell you what type of woman I thought you were, but that's no excuse for me to treat you like that." After saying that, the realization that she wasn't the only woman he had hurt in the same fashion came to mind. "Oh my gosh, I've hurt so many people. I'm a horrible person. Tiffany." He then looked into her eyes as he asked, "I know I don't deserve it, but can you please...forgive me?"

Tiffany, with a feeling of vindication, then held his face, smiled and, with tears in her eyes, replied, "I can." She then pulled his face to hers and began pressing her lips to his, but then he pulled his head back and walked away from her.

"No, I can't. I'm seeing someone."

At that, Tiffany's smile fled and she scowled at him. Again the look of intense jealousy engulfed her body. "I *can* forgive you, but I'm *not* going to forgive you. And you don't *love* her! *You don't know how to love anyone*!" she shouted.

"You may be right. I grew up always being suspicious of every one...for my moms' sake. I learned to be tough. Not to show emotion. I had to be mean, to scare off guys who wanted to use my mom for—"

"Guys like you?" she interjected. The short phrase pierced Joshua. He had become a lot like the very people he hated and once hunted with his fists—though that's not all he had become.

"Please, Josh. I'll do anything for you to stay with me. I can't take it anymore, I feel like I'm losing my mind."

"Tiffany, since I've met Chris, and believe me, we've had some differences, but all his talk about God and faith and all that...well, it's really been getting me to think a lot."

"Think a lot about what?" she responded, having rolled her eyes at each mention of the word *God*.

"About...God. Maybe it's real. Some of the things he says, well, it's compelling. It makes a lot of sense."

"So what? You want to start going to church or something? If that will make you happy, we can go to church. I mean some people do that, right? I mean, my family never did, but I knew some that went and they were happy."

"Oh, Tiffany, that's not what I'm saying. What I'm saying is—"

"WHAT THEN?"

"I know I'm probably the last person you want to hear this from. In fact, I'm probably the last person on earth that should even be saying this, but maybe they're right, maybe we need God. Maybe, you...need God."

"I DON'T *WANT* GOD! I WANT *YOU*!"

"Okay, I'm not going to argue about this. You're obviously solidified in your thinking, and I have a lot of work to do at the shop."

At that Joshua attempted to make his way to the door, but Tiffany jumped up on him wrapping her legs around his waist causing both of them to fall on her bed. She then began shouting "I HATE YOU! I HAAATE YOU!" while profusely sobbing and slamming her fists onto his chest as hard as she could. He got a hold of her wrists as to get her to stop hitting his chest, but she resisted.

"That's it, hurt me!" she yelled, feeling the grip of Joshua's hands tight around her wrists. He was, indeed, hurting her, but obviously unintentionally. He finally, having no other alternative, tossed her off of him then dashed out of the room and out of the house.

Tiffany remained on her bed screaming at the top of her lungs with agonizing sensations of anguish, rejection, anger, heartbreak, and other emotionally debilitating feelings. She then began ripping what little clothes she was wearing before, on impulse, grabbing her cell phone and dialing a number.

"9-1-1, please state your emergency."

It took Joshua about thirty minutes to get back home. During that time Jennifer called. "Josh, what's going on? You sounded a little uneasy in your voicemail," she said.

"Can you come over? I really want to see you. I can tell you what happened when you get here."

"Yeah, I'll head over there now."

The incident with Tiffany was a new experience for him. He paced back and forth through his house repeating the word *God*, considering the possibility he himself might be going nuts, having now felt real conviction, but was currently unaware that that's what he was actually experiencing. He then went to his fridge and grabbed a beer, which his fridge was full of. He popped the top then set it on the counter. With the word *God* on his mind annoyingly pricking his conscience, he then looked up and said, "All right, *if you're real*, I won't be able to drink this beer." He then immediately picked it up, and right before it touched his lips, the doorbell rang. He sat the beer back down on the counter without having any and answered the door. It was Jennifer.

"Hey, babe, what's going on?" Jennifer asked. They both walked back into the kitchen.

"You won't believe it." He then picked up the beer bottle and just before putting it to his lips, again the doorbell rang. They both walked to the door. It was the police.

"Can I help you?"

"Joshua Nickel?"

"Yeah, that's me."

"You're under arrest for the rape of Tiffany Love."

"WHAT?" they shouted in unison.

CHAPTER

23

A CRUMBLING HOUSE OF LIES

Chris was standing on a chair in the living room replacing a light fixture.

"All done," he said, stepping off the chair then flipping on the light switch, making sure it was working.

"At this rate, you're going to have the whole parish updated by the end of the year," Katrina said to him. Then her phone rang.

"Hello? Tiffany, what's going—" Chris then witnessed his wife's jaw drop, expressing shock. "Are you okay? The police are there? Yeah, I can come over. I'll be there soon, okay. Okay, bye."

"What happened?" Chris asked.

"She said Joshua sexually assaulted her."

Chris's face then morphed into that of a serial killer, which he was not of course. "I'm gonna kill him—"

"Wait!" Katrina rebuked, having a bit of skepticism over Tiffany's accusation. "Remember, she's said this before," Katrina reminded him.

He nodded in agreement. "I'm going to give him a call." When he attempted to call Joshua, there was no answer. "I'm going to his house," he then said.

"Okay. Drop me off at Tiffany's."

****

Meanwhile, at the police station

"I swear...I never touched her! Except to get her off of me to get away from her," Joshua said adamantly to both—the detective, a public defender—and even more so, to Jennifer.

"They found DNA on her bedding, bruises on her wrists, and her clothes were ripped indicating someone was forcing them off of her," the detectives said.

"Did you see the clothes she was wearing? She hardly had anything on to rip off," Joshua retorted.

"DNA from another individual," the public defender rebutted.

"We contacted him. His wife wasn't too happy," the detective admitted.

"This Tiffany won't even let the medics do an examination on her to confirm her accusation...oh, and don't forget that this is the third time she's falsely accused someone of sexual assault," the public defender added. "Tell them again, Josh, what happened," he said to Joshua.

"Okay, for the second time, she called me at work. Said her car wasn't working. I offered to send one of my other techs out, but she wanted me *specifically* to go. That's when I called Jennifer, hoping she could go with me, 'cause I really didn't want to go there myself, but Jennifer was in class." Jennifer smiled at hearing that and grabbed his hand. "So I went and then found that she removed the battery cables from the terminals, so I just put them back on. I didn't say anything about it 'cause I wanted to get out of there ASAP. When I was leaving, she chased me down the driveway yelling at me to look at her. When I finally did, I noticed she dyed her hair brown"—he looked at Jennifer when mentioning her colored hair—"and she looked like she just finished filming a *Slasher* movie, to be honest. But then, she pleaded for me to hang a picture up in her bedroom. And *stupido* me fell for it. I went to her bedroom. Sure enough, no picture. She blocked the door then started talking crazy about wanting me to hurt her. I tried talking sense into her. I told her I was taking mine and Jennifer's relationship seriously, and that's when she lost it—jumping on me and banging my chest." He primarily maintained eye contact with Jennifer as he described the sequence of events. Then he lifted up his shirt to show them his chest. It was still swollen with fresh bruises. "You know for a hundred-and-twenty-something-pound girl, that chick hits pretty hard. But yes, I did grab her wrists, only to stop her from hitting me. Then I tossed her off me and hightailed it out of there. I could even hear her screaming from my truck."

The public defender sat back in his chair, assured of himself. "This seals the case."

"That's what he says," the investigators responded.

"This is what I think," the public defender continued. "My client has a rap sheet, of which, and I'll remind you, he successfully completed the court-mandated restitution for. But you still don't like him, therefore someone accuses him of something, so let's run with it. You must be taking your cues from CNN."

While the public defender and investigators continued arguing, Jennifer said to Joshua with a smile, "You've changed a lot."

"All this stuff about God that Chris has been talking to me about...I can feel it having an effect on me," he responded.

"Or you know what I think? I think I'm changing you," she said, prideful, dispelling any notion of God being a force for positive change.

Joshua's lack of theological knowledge prompted him to respond, "Yeah, maybe." But then there was a knock on the door and one of the investigators opened it.

"Excuse me," a police officer said, "there are two ladies here with something to show you." Then Sandra and Kara walked in, to the shock of both Jennifer and Joshua.

"What do you have?" the public defender asked.

"What Tiffany did was messed up," they said to Joshua. They then handed a DVD to one of the investigators who promptly put it in a DVD player. "We didn't know Jennifer was going to be here though."

"Why shouldn't I be here?" Jennifer asked.

"Tiffany and Joshua are on the DVD. It's all together we didn't have time to edit it. Sorry, Jennifer."

"What are you talking about?" Jennifer asked.

One of the investigators then began the video, and to Jennifer's horror, it started right in the middle of an exotic activity featuring Tiffany and Joshua from several months ago. Kara picked up the remote in an attempt to fast-forward it, but even fast-forward it was pretty clear. Jennifer turned her eyes to Joshua, who, embarrassed, stared at the desk. Jennifer's smile melted and an expression of discussed enveloped her face.

"You talk about *change*, and *God*, and doing *something right!*" She exhaled through her teeth. "You don't *change*. I'm an idiot for having ever allowed you to touch me." "That was months ago. Before you and I—" he attempted to explain.

"I don't *care*." She then began punching his arm, which neither the investigators nor public defender said anything against as if they felt she was vindicated in her action. Jennifer then got up, grabbed her purse, and walked to the door. She turned to her two roommates and glared at them then viciously said to them, "You can *have* your *whoremonger* back...*enjoy*."

"Jennifer!" Joshua said, to which she turned and simply said, "Strike two! I'm done with you! Don't ever talk to me again." The investigator then opened the door and she stomped out.

"Here it is," Kara said ironically right after Jennifer left. She hit play, and a recording of what took place between Tiffany and Joshua that afternoon resumed. It was exactly how Joshua described it.

The investigators then asked Kara and Sandra, "How did you get this video?"

Hesitantly, they explained. "Okay, so we were asked to keep an eye on her a long time ago. Because, you know, she has some problems. She's a really big asset to that company she's with, apparently. That's why we visit her a lot. But then we thought it would be easier if we could monitor her without being there so often."

"So you two just put a video camera in her room? Without her knowing."

"Well, we gave her a present a couple of years ago. And it had the camera in it. We didn't know where she was going to put it honestly. Admittedly, we didn't fully think it all the way through."

"That's for sure," one of the investigators said. "So this present with a camera in it makes it to her bedroom, where she obviously has a lot of sex. What do you do with the video feed?"

"Okay, so we didn't have this in mind at the time. But we found that we could make some money off of them, so like once every couple months we edit it some and sell them on a website we cre- ated. It actually helps pay some of our tuition," they continued, somewhat ashamed. The investigators looked sternly at the two girls. "But honestly, we have been feeling *really guilty* about it re- cently. So much so that we were actually going to stop. In fact, we were in the process of deleting it all when we saw this. Then we saw on social media that Joshua got arrested for this and knew we had to get it down here."

"What's the name of the site?" the investigator asked. They told him. "We're going to check it in twenty-four hours. It better be gone!" the investigators demanded of the girls.

"Yeah, okay. It will be." The girls then left, without the DVD. "Josh, we're sorry about Jennifer," they said on their way out. "I kinda don't want to go home now," they said to each other walking down the hall.

One of the investigators then walked over to Joshua and sat on the desk looking down at him. "Can I give you a real simple piece of advice?" Joshua nodded. "I'm telling you this as a friend. Until you have a ring on a lady's finger, keep your pants on. And if it helps...get a belt."

"Right," Joshua responded, taking the investigator seriously.

"All right, you're free to go."

"Wait!" the public defender interjected.

"What?" Joshua asked.

"We need to discuss the charges against Ms. Love."

"Charges? I'm not pressing any charges against her," Joshua made clear.

"No? She just falsely accused you of rape. That's serious. And this is the third time she's done this," the public defender continued.

"Listen, I feel partly responsible for the underlying cause. And aside from all that, I just chose to forgive her. I mean, what is a jail cell going to do for her anyway? What she needs is a good counselor."

"Josh!"

"I said no. Thanks for sticking up for me though. If it's all well and good now, I'd like to go home and stare at the ceiling for the next six hours." Joshua then left.

The public defender then turned to the investigators. "Well, what are you going to do?"

"About what?" they responded.

"This is the third time she's done this. Joshua can *choose not* to press charges, but the *state can choose* to press charges. This has to stop, and you know it—whether or not she is some high-priced supermodel."

The investigators glanced at each other, then responded, "We'll get a hold of the DA."

The public defender, with a smile, closed his briefcase, got up, and headed to the door. "Good."

****

While Joshua was being interrogated

"Tiffany, someone's here to see you," said an officer outside of her bedroom. Tiffany nodded, still pretending to be shaken up. She had changed her clothes since Joshua was there. Katrina then walked into the bedroom. She had a look of a concerned mother as she embraced Tiffany on the bed in which the sheets and blankets had been removed by the medics.

"Sweetheart, what happened to your face? And your arms?" Katrina noticed the small scratches with dots of dried blood all over her.

"I guess I kind of scrubbed a little too hard in the shower this morning," she simply explained.

"I see. And it looks like you colored some of your hair brown," Katrina also noticed. Tiffany nodded. Then Katrina asked her about the accusation. "Now, tell me what Josh did."

"I must have left the garage door open because he just showed up inside my house. I tried running from him, but he carried me to my room and held me down." Tiffany then showed Katrina her wrists. Katrina acknowledged they looked a little bruised.

"Tiffany, Josh admitted to the police that he grabbed your wrists, but he said it was to stop you from beating on his chest and to get away," Katrina said as gentle as possible.

"Well, I was trying to get away from him."

"So you were beating his chest, while he was holding you by your wrists," Katrina interpreted Tiffany's statement back to her. Tiffany's eyes moved back and forth as if attempting to find another avenue to make her accusation believable. However, a female police officer entered her room with a notepad and a disgusted look on her face. She began reading the information from the notepad.

"Ms. Love," the officer said in a stern voice. "According to Joshua Nickel's cell phone call log, you called him around noon today. And his employees said you asked *him specifically* to come and look at your vehicle."

"Oh yeah, I forgot. He did come to look at my car, but it ended up being okay—nothing major—but then he took me inside."

"Sweetheart, that's an awful lot of information to forget, don't you think?" Katrina asked. Then the officer continued.

"Also, Ms. Love, your neighbor across the street heard yelling from outside. He said he saw, from his living room window, a guy out in your driveway, as well as you. And he said you were dressed pretty sleazily. His words, not mine. Then watched Josh walk into the garage and *you followed him in.*"

Katrina then gently turned Tiffany's face toward hers and asked bluntly but as gentle as possible still, "Tiffany, tell me the truth, did Joshua do those things?" Tiffany hesitated, exhaling heavily, but Katrina's non-condemning glow led Tiffany to tell the truth by lightly shaking her head. "Tiffany, this is serious. I'm afraid this is not going to turn out good for you. Why did you say these things?"

"I don't know. I just reacted."

"Reacted over what? What happened?"

"He was so nice. So nice," she began telling Katrina about Timothy.

"Who was?"

"Remember, I called you about Timothy?"

"That was the guy you met in Vegas?"

"Yeah. But he said he would move everything here...for me. He said he would never leave. He bought a one-way plane ticket and came back with me." Katrina could almost feel Tiffany's pain as she listened. "And when I woke up this morning, he was gone. I called him to see if everything was okay. He was already back in Vegas."

"What did he say?" Katrina asked.

"That I was a bet. *I'm a bet. I'm a paper cup. I'm trash*, Katrina. I thought of Joshua. I wanted him so bad. I thought if I did my hair like Jennifer, he would love me."

Katrina put her arms around her, then responded, "No, you're not those things. You have value and purpose. You're letting your emotions dictate you. Why didn't you call me instead of Joshua?"

"Because—" Tiffany was hesitant to explain her reasoning.

But Katrina pressed for that reason. "Because...why?"

"Because all you ever want to do is talk about God. And I told you, I don't want God."

"And you never tell me why you don't."

"Because! I can't feel him, Katrina! I can't touch him! There's nothing physical about him!" Tiffany grabbed Katrina's arm as a demonstration of the physical touch that God doesn't provide her.

"That's not what he's about," Katrina responded with a more firm tone.

"Then what *is it* about?" Tiffany asked, getting contentious.

"He's about restoration. That's why he *physically* came to this place. That's why he *physically* died and shed *real* blood on a *physical* cross. And the fact that *he* was *physically* restored means that we can be restored too," Katrina explained.

"I don't need restoration, I need—"

"*No*! What you *think* you need, is nothing more than a *delusion*. You, *my dear*, are taking your father's characteristics and projecting them on *every man* that winks at you, which then fuels an *infatuation* over the *idea* of being loved. That is what you are doing."

"I just want to be loved."

"Tiffany, do you even know what love is?"

"Yes. Ask Joshua how much I *loved* him," Tiffany responded antagonistically.

"*No*. That is *not* love. *God* is love. Why do you think I'm here? Do you really believe that I'd just show up randomly at some house where *ironically* the resident is an emotional wreck? No. I'm here because God loves you, and I love you. In fact, I loved you before I even knew you. If I didn't, I would have just ignored God's direction to come here!" Katrina explained sharply. "You want physical? Touch me again...I'm physical. But you keep *rejecting* that *love*, and why? Because I *don't have a penis*?" Tiffany looked away as Katrina's words were convicting. "That's the world's love," Katrina continued. "And you want to know what that leaves you with?" Katrina then grabbed Tiffany's arm, pointing to all the blood-dotted scratches on her body. "*This* is the world's love— skin deep. *And* if you *really loved* Joshua, you would never have accused him of sexually assaulting you. In fact, you would *respect* that he has a girlfriend and is *actually trying* to turn his life around, to be a better man—and you would *encourage that*, even if it was painful. Because love is *selfless*, and love *sacrifices*— sometimes physically, sometimes emotionally. I know that firsthand. I've experienced heartache, crushing depression. Remember my horror story? How I woke up on a bathroom floor in my own vomit and pregnant not remembering the night before, then having my baby murdered? And I was seventeen? And my father was the associate pastor of our church. How's that for screwed-up?"

Katrina's words again triggered the flow of tears, and then Tiffany leaned into Katrina who held her again. Katrina saw that the police officers were not happy at all with Tiffany. Then one of them spoke up receiving more information about the accusation.

"Joshua was just let go. Apparently, two ladies showed up with video evidence of what actually took place in this bedroom this afternoon." At hearing that, Tiffany's face instantly changed from sorrow to aggression over the new knowledge that she's being watched. She then began looking around the room for a camera. "They want to talk to you at the station," they added.

Katrina asked, "Can I go with her please?"

"Yeah, you can ride with me to the station," agreed one of the officers.

JOSHUA VERSUS JESUS

When Joshua walked out of the police station, Chris was waiting for him, leaning up against his car with his arms crossed.

"Need a ride?" he said.

Joshua wasn't surprised to see Chris at the police station, though he wasn't expecting it either. The sense that Chris was possibly dis appointed in him welled up inside. They got in the car and left the station. The drive was silent for a while, only with Irwin Lutzer playing through the radio on low. After several minutes of driving, Chris spoke.

"What happened?" Chris asked, having a general idea.

"I already explained this twice," Joshua responded.

"Not to me, you didn't."

"She called me. She said her car wouldn't start and asked me to come fix it," Joshua explained.

"Did it have to be you?"

"Apparently so."

"Why didn't you call me?"

"I called Jennifer. But she was in class."

"And if she wasn't, you would've probably made a bigger problem."

"A bigger problem than Tiffany accusing me of raping her?"

"Josh, Tiffany is hurting."

"And that makes it okay?"

"No, it doesn't, but come on, man, how did she sound on the phone?"

Joshua thought back for a moment when Tiffany called him at the shop. "She sounded angry."

"That should have been your first clue. But then you call another woman instead of me."

"Jennifer's my girlfriend, I thought you approved of us."

"Approved of you sleeping with a woman who's not your wife? Nah, man, I never approved of that. Besides, Josh, you're just a trophy to her."

Joshua's head fell to his chest. "I know," he admitted. "But it doesn't matter now. She broke up with me at the police station. She saw...well, that doesn't matter either."

Chris deduced a depressed tone from Joshua and responded, "Josh, I'm sorry."

"You ain't got nothing to be sorry about, Chris. I'm sorry though. I'm sorry for breaking your rules."

"Josh, those rules weren't for me. They were for you. To show you what you couldn't accomplish without the Lord. You know, Josh, he's trying to get your attention. Sometimes in order to do that he removes people from your life. And the more joined you are, the more painful it can be."

"I know he is," Joshua responded, looking down at his feet. Chris stopped the car and parked.

"So go to him."

"I want to. I want what you got. I've never seen anything like it. But I can't."

"Why, Josh?" Joshua didn't say anything but continued staring at the floor with the appearance of contemplating. "It's your father, isn't it?" Chris determined.

Joshua turned his face to Chris. His eyes appeared to be filled with pain, then he replied, "He called me a mistake. He said I was an accident. That I ruined his life."

Chris put his hand on his shoulder, then said, "Let's go inside." Chris got out of the car, then Joshua looked up and saw that they were in front of the community center. He then got out as well.

"What are we doing here?" Joshua asked.

"I think it's time you have a conversation with someone," Chris replied, heading to the entrance.

"Okay?" Joshua followed.

Inside, Chris got into the boxing ring. "Come on," he said to Joshua.

"I thought I was going to have a conversation with someone."

"You are," Chris reassured him, then Joshua got into the ring as well. Chris put a stool in the middle of the ring and sat on it. "So, Josh, what do you want to say to your dad?"

Joshua thought the question was odd. He didn't know what to say and walked around the ring thinking about it. "Come on, son, what do you have to say to me?" Chris said, imitating Joshua's father. The phrase propelled Joshua's memory back years ago to when he was last in his father's shop. He saw his dad sitting on a stool next to an old car that was in the middle of being repaired. "Do you got something to say to me, Josh, or what?" his father said.

Joshua looked around the garage. It was just as he remembered it. Tools scattered around. The benches weren't organized. Oil on the concrete and the smell of hard alcohol in the air. "Yeah, I got something to say to you. What did I do? What did I do to make you hate me?" His father didn't respond; he just sat there with a disgusted look on his face. "Well? ANSWER ME!" Joshua yelled.

Still no answer. "Everything I ever did was to get your approval! I tried so hard to get you to notice me. Every time I came to see you, you were either banging some girl on the hood of a car or you were drunk beyond imagination trying to get information out of me about my mother. You didn't care about me. You didn't even care about my mother. *I* was the one who stayed up at night watching over her. *I* was the one who took care of her when she was sick. *I* was the one who listened to her crying when she didn't have enough money to buy food for us, and held her, telling her it was going to be okay. You weren't there for us. We needed you! *I* needed you, but *you were never there for me*!"

Still, his father remained silent, sitting there on his stool. His continual lack of communication incited Joshua's anger even more, to the point he was even beginning to shed tears of rage. "ANSWER ME! ANSWER ME!" Finally, Joshua walked up to his father and, in a rage, picked him off the stool by his shirt. "ANSWER ME!" But still no response. Then Joshua hit him in the stomach. He buckled over. Joshua then threw him up against the car and again shouted, "ANSWER ME!" Just silence still. Then he punched him in the face then the stomach again. Joshua then did a roundhouse to his head, and his father fell to the ground. He got on top of his father and attempted to strike his face again, but his father put his arms up to block his fists, so, instead, Joshua continued to pummel his stomach while yelling at him.

"Joshua?" a small voice then penetrated Joshua's eardrum. He turned his head to see some kids standing outside the boxing ring with a look of shock. His name being called drew him out of his fantasy, then saw that he was on top of Chris. His lip was bleeding and his cheek was bruised. He then saw that Chris's shirt had come up, and for the first time Joshua saw the countless scars that covered his abdomen and sides.

"Chris?" Joshua simply said with his own look of shock.

"It's okay, Josh, it's okay. Now...forgive him." At that, Joshua fell onto Chris's chest, sobbing. Chris patted his back. "It's all right, man. It will be all right. Jesus can heal you."

Through his tears, Joshua stuttered, "I w-w-want h-h-h-im too."

"Tell him that then," Chris instructed Joshua.

And through the tears, Joshua said, "Jesus, I need you. I'm sorry for what I've done. Please forgive me." And he sobbed. Chris gestured for the kids to get in the ring, and soon the ring was filled with many of the neighborhood kids. They came and embraced Joshua, many with tears of their own over the scene.

"Okay, Josh, I need some oxygen," Chris finally said. Joshua managed to crack a bit of smile at the statement, then pulled himself off of Chris.

"Sorry," Joshua responded.

"Don't be sorry. I told you, I'd be whatever you needed me to be," Chris reminded him. They backed up to the side of the ring leaning against the ropes. "But I'm definitely regretting teaching you that roundhouse at the moment."

"Ha ha," Joshua lightly laughed.

Then one of the younger kids asked Joshua, "So you didn't have a relationship with your dad either?" The statement pierced Joshua's heart, and he shook his head, then held his arm out to the young boy.

Another kid said, "My parents dropped me and my sister off at a fire station when I was seven."

Yet another said, "My mommy took me to my aunt's house so she could go get drugs, and she never came back." It seemed like every kid in the center had a story like Joshua's—some worse, others not quite as bad but still emotionally damaging.

"See, Joshua? This is what you can be. You can be for these kids what I've been for you. I'm not going to be here forever, Josh, so I have to hand you off to the Lord."

The statement gripped Joshua's heart. "What? You're going to leave me?"

"Believe me, Josh. If it was up to me, I'd live forever. Ha ha. You have to get to know the Lord now. But as long as I *am* here, I'm not going to leave you. Have I broke a promise to you yet?"

"No," Joshua admitted. He looked at the back of his hands. His knuckles were banged up and swollen with many scars. "I don't want to fight anymore," he added.

"Oh, man, Frank's going to love hearing that," Chris responded. "Frank?" Joshua glanced at Chris who nodded at him then looked back down at the mat. "He sponsored me, didn't he?"

Chris again nodded, then said, "See, Josh. There are people who love you." Joshua and Chris sat in the ring, continuing to listen to the kids' stories and talking to one another for some time.

"Now I get to explain these bruises to Katrina when I get home. Ha ha ha."

THE GOOD NEWS

Frank and Trisha had just been seated at a nice restaurant as they were on a date. Before long Trisha's phone rang.

"It's Josh," she said to Frank then answered the call. "Hey, hunny, how's it going?" she said. "Yeah, he's here." She then had a fairly shocking expression on her face as she handed her phone to Frank. "He wants to talk to *you*."

Frank was shocked as well as he took the phone. "Hey, Josh, how's it going?" There was a pause as Joshua spoke to him. A look of astonishment accompanied by a smile enveloped his face. "Joshua, that's great news." There was another pause as Joshua continued speaking. Trisha was anxious to know what was being said. "Joshua, you're welcome. Your mother and I just sat down to eat, would you like to join us?" There was another short pause. "Oh, okay, Josh. Well, let us know if we can do anything for you." Then one last pause. "We love you too, Josh. Talk to you soon." He then hung up and handed the phone back to Trisha.

"Well!" Trisha said, anxious to hear what Joshua had to say to Frank.

"He got saved!"

Trisha's eyes immediately welled up with tears of joy as her hands flew to her mouth. "Oh my gosh. I can't believe it."

"He said thanks for sponsoring him and that he's not going to fight anymore, and he asked us to pray for him."

Trisha could hardly hold in her excitement at the news. Frank then said, "You know, I'm not that hungry. You want to go for a walk in Canyon Park?" Katrina emphatically said yes. Some of the other guests turned to their table as their excitement over the news was difficult to contain. As they got up to leave, the server approached their table, to which Frank quickly pulled out a bill and handed it to the waiter. "The water was excellent," he said as they left. The server unfolded the bill. It was a fifty-dollar bill. He looked at it in shock.

****

Frank and Trisha arrived at the park entrance. A path led down into a small valley that connected to other dirt paths that swerved around huge rocks and other cave-like holes within some of the boulders. They frequently visited the park, especially in the evenings when the sun was setting over the horizon. It was always a breathtaking scene and a reminder of the creative mind behind it all. They began their descent into the valley. They were upbeat and talked about Joshua and his newly professed faith.

As they rounded an enormous rocky structure, Frank saw an opening into the rock. The adventurer in him said to Trisha, "Let's go explore the cave." However, Trisha wasn't that adventurous and was uneasy about it but finally agreed. They had just walked into the cave when Frank tripped over something. He found that he tripped over a small wire.

"That's weird," he thought out loud. At that, Trisha became increasingly uneasy about being in the cave. "Come on, Frank, let's get out of here," she insisted.

"Oh, it's all right. Some kids were probably playing in here and left this as a prank." Then Frank went further in, using the flashlight on his phone to look around. Trisha continued to follow but nervously. They came to another opening in the wall of the cave that led into another cavern. Frank went in then immediately stopped.

"Maybe you're right, Trisha," he said as she walked in behind him. Old clothes, a makeshift bed, a small crank radio, and a little propane stove were in there. Obviously, someone lived in the cave.

They turned around to exit the cave, but a mammoth of a man with multiple layers of ace bandages wrapped around his head stood in the way.

"AHH!" Trisha yelled in terror.

"WHAT ARE YOU DOING IN HERE?" the giant said.

"We didn't know anyone lived here. We were just checking out the cave," Frank explained.

"GET OUT!" he demanded, then they ran out of the cave.

Upon exiting the rock, Trisha balled her fist and slammed it into Frank's arm, saying, "I told you we shouldn't go in there. We could've been killed."

"All right, you were right. I just felt like I had to go in there."

"Yeah, well, next time you're going alone. After you increase your life insurance policy."

They then left the park a bit rattled.

CHAPTER
26

TIFFANY REJECTS KATRINA

Tiffany and Katrina sat in the interrogation room in which Tiffany got the opportunity to watch the video that was earlier shown to prove Joshua's innocence over her false accusations. She watched it intensely, focusing more on the angle of the recording than that of the content as she attempted to determine where the camera may have been located in her room.

After the video, the investigators attempted to get her to explain why she did what she did. However, her only response was, "I'm not saying anything until my attorney gets here." The investigators accepted her request then left the room leaving the two women alone. Katrina, sitting next to Tiffany, grabbed her hand, indicating she wouldn't leave her. Tiffany looked away from Katrina, for being in her presence appeared to increasingly invoke a greater sense of conviction in which she was trying to escape from.

"Why are you pulling away from me all of a sudden?" Katrina asked, noticing Tiffany's avoidance of her. Tiffany didn't answer then pulled her hand away from Katrina. "Tiffany, please look at me. I'm trying to help you," Katrina said, but again, Tiffany didn't respond. "Tiffany, look at me."

"I don't want to," Tiffany finally said aggressively, still looking away.

"Why?"

Tiffany finally faced her with slight aggressiveness and responded, "Because it hurts to look at you."

"God's trying to get a hold of you."

"Okay, since you *love* to talk about *God* so much, if you answer me this with assurance, then I'll *receive* your *God*. Is my family in heaven?" Tiffany demanded.

"Is that what you're concerned about?" Katrina responded.

"Just answer the question," she further demanded of Katrina.

"I don't know where they are," Katrina answered truthfully.

"Isn't that *convenient*," Tiffany replied, crossing her arms, a further sign of deflecting Katrina's kindness.

"Tiffany, listen to me," Katrina said in a firmer tone. "I don't know where your family is. But I can tell you this, they may be in a far better place than where you're heading right now." Tiffany turned and looked at Katrina as she continued, "Because, while some people hit rock bottom, for others, there is no bottom— and that's where you're headed." Tiffany then looked away from Katrina again as if not caring, and then an attorney entered the room.

"Ms. Love?"

"Hi, Justin," Tiffany responded with a somewhat apologetic expression over the reason for him being there. She then avoided eye contact with him as well.

"Are you the public defender?" Katrina asked.

"No, he's my attorney from the entertainment company," Tiffany answered. Immediately Katrina's eyes narrowed having developed a deep antithesis toward the company which has essentially enslaved Tiffany.

"So the devil does wear a suit," Katrina said to the attorney.

"Excuse me?" he responded, caught off guard by the comment. Tiffany informed him,

"Don't mind her...she's religious."

"Ah, I see. Well, Ms.—?"

"Mrs. Belvu," she corrected the attorney with her arms crossed.

"Well, Mrs. Belvu, if it makes you feel any better, my firm is subcontracted, we don't work directly for the company," he explained.

"Yes, you do," Katrina responded firmly.

"Well, I can see your set in your opinion and I obviously can't change that, nor am I here to do so. But if you excuse us, I need to discuss a few things with Tiffany."

"Can't I stay in here with her?"

"To her, you are—"

"Her friend," Katrina affirmed.

"Well, Tiffany, do you want Mrs. Belvu to stay?" he asked.

Tiffany looked straight ahead at the wall then said to Katrina, "Remember the day I found you in my house? And I asked you what you wanted?"

"I do remember that. I said I wanted to know if you were okay."

"And do you remember my response?"

"Yes, you said you were okay."

"You want to know something?"

"What?"

Tiffany then faced Katrina and, with tears in her eyes, said, "I meant it."

That cut Katrina to her core, and she placed her hand on her chest as if she was just stabbed through the heart. "I'm not your friend, and you're not my mom," Tiffany again verbally stabbed Katrina.

"You're right, I'm not your mother. And I never pretended to be. And I'm sorry you lost your family. But as much as you complain about your pain and how people hurt you...you're not innocent. You hurt people too."

Katrina then walked to the door and knocked on it to be let out. The police officer opened it, but before exiting, she turned to make one last comment. "Oh, and being that I'm *so religious*," she said sarcastically while faking a smile through her tears, "you may have heard of the devil being called the destroyer. But sometimes he doesn't destroy anything...sometimes he just kicks back in his recliner comfortably, laughing, as he watches *you* destroy *yourself*."

Tiffany continued slouching in her chair, with her arms crossed, staring at the wall. She paid little attention to the statement contemplating the video instead.

"Katrina!" Tiffany then said, to which Katrina stopped in the doorway. "If you ever see Joshua, tell him...I hope someone rips his head off."

"Tiffany!" the attorney shouted. "Not now!"

Katrina's eyes fixed on Tiffany until the door was shut, which was like watching a casket close on an unsaved loved one. She began weeping over the thought of losing Tiffany to the devil. Then she went home.

In the interrogation room, Tiffany's attorney was looking over notes from his briefcase. "I might not agree with your *friends'* ideology, but she's not wrong...you're not innocent, Tiffany. Why did you do this?"

"I don't know," she responded. "When do I get to leave?" she added.

Justin looked up at her sternly and said, "What makes you think you're leaving any time soon?"

"But last time—"

"Last time? You act like this is not a big deal. Ms. Love, you're not leaving any time soon. The district attorney is pressing criminal charges against you."

"What?" Tiffany responded in shock.

"I can probably get the charges dropped, but it's going to cost you."

"Cost me what?"

"My services are two-hundred and fifty dollars an hour after a three-thousand-dollar retainer fee."

"What? But the company pays you!" Tiffany responded anxiously.

"Yes, they do. And they paid me to come here. Because you signed a contract that, among many other things—of which I don't agree with admittedly—essentially says, if you do something like this again your employer has the right to let you go without notice." He then showed her the paragraph and section in the contract to which he was referring. She read it, fearful that everything she had was going to be taken away from her—her daddy's house being at the top of her list.

"Are they going to take my daddy's house?"

"It looks like it."

Tiffany then appeared as though she was about to hyperventilate. Then in desperation she said, "Can you talk to them, please? Tell them I promise I'll be good for now on. I'll do whatever they want. Just not to take my daddy's house."

Justin's heart sunk a little at Tiffany's response, then further explained, "Unfortunately I can't do that for you. But even if I could, it's doubtful it would do any good. The company made a statement that, at this point, you have cost the company more than what you're worth to them. Between your multimillion-dollar house, along with all of your expenditures to suffice your shopping habits, your last two accusations alone cost the company five million dollars, between legal fees and to keep the media quiet. However, Tiffany, I think you will be better off, because secondly, and I shouldn't tell you this, because its attorney-client privilege, but I think this company is under a criminal investigation. I'm telling you this as a friend. Now I can't represent you beyond this point without a retainer. My advice to you is to ride this thing out...it's not like you murdered anyone, but you're going to have to face some consequences. The courts will get you a public defender." Tiffany's mouth hung open as she appeared to be unable to breathe. "Tiffany! Take a breath! This isn't the end of the world!" Then she began yelling and crying and banging on the table like a toddler on steroids having the mother of all temper tantrums. Her reaction to the news caused the investigators and police to rush into the room, and the attorney got up and left. Tiffany began to get violent with the officers forcing them to arrest her and put her in a holding cell.

****

The police gave Katrina a ride back to the parish, and Chris soon joined her there. He could tell she was very upset.

"Babe! What's wrong?" he said. She looked up at him then got up and clung to her husband. He put his arms around her tight. "What happened?" he, again inquired. She was so distraught that she couldn't speak. In an effort to cheer her up some, he told her about Joshua. "Katrina. Josh accepted Jesus."

She then looked up at him and attempted to make a smile and look joyful at the comment. "That's wonderful, hunny." She then told him about what happened at the police station with Tiffany. "She rejected him again. And me." The tears multiplied with her words.

"I'm so sorry," Chris consoled her. "I know you did everything you could for her."

"Did I?" She began questioning that very idea. "I feel like I failed. Maybe I should have pressed her more? Maybe I pressed her too much. She said she didn't want to see me anymore. Do I accept that?"

"Remember that young girl back home. She was on drugs and kept getting into bad situations?"

"Yeah, I remember her."

"And she wouldn't listen to you. Remember we prayed for God to get her off the drugs and out of the situation, no matter what?"

"She went through hell, but she came out of it," Katrina remembered.

"Remember what we prayed for Tiffany?"

Katrina nodded her head. "That God would get her out of that house and out of that company...*no matter what*."

"Maybe this is how he's going to do it," Chris optimistically responded. The idea did lift Katrina up a bit, however, Tiffany's words—*I don't want to see you anymore*—still had a grip on her heart.

"What am I going to do without you?" Katrina then said.

"Hey, I'm right here. I thought we weren't supposed to live in the future," he reminded her. She smiled and nodded, then Chris took her hand and put it over his heart. "See, it's still beating." She then rested her head on his shoulder, and he held her, as they swayed in the living room.

THE BROAD AND NARROW

It was morning and the day before the men's conference. Joshua was up early to meet the contractors at the community center to have the new windows installed in the facility. As he conversed with the contractors the neighborhood kids spotted him and came to meet him. Since he received Jesus, many of the area residence were even more attracted to him than previously. As he was laughing and talking to the kids, a familiar shout came from down the street.

"JOSHUA NICKEL!"

"Uh-oh," one of the kids said. "It's Trevor."

Trevor came up to Joshua shouting, "I still got a bone to pick with you!"

"Listen, man," Joshua responded. "I don't want to fight."

"I wouldn't want to fight me neither!" Trevor said. Joshua gave him a cockeyed look, as he knew full well that he could win a fight with Trevor.

"So how's your arm?" Joshua asked, in reference to when he had dislocated his arm in their last conflict several months back.

"Oh, you're about to find out."

"Look, man, listen...what I did...was a horrible thing. I'm sorry I messed around with your lady. I was stupid."

The kids were impressed, and Trevor was even somewhat taken by his apology. But without warning, Trevor threw a fist into his gut and Joshua buckled over onto the ground. About that time, Chris had rounded a corner and saw Joshua on the ground with Trevor standing over him. He then ran to the conflict. A moment of rage welled up in Joshua, but then before he lifted himself off the ground he whispered through his clenched teeth, "Jesus, give me strength." He felt the anger flee, then he got up. He just stood there. Then Trevor hit him across the face with his fist. His head went to one side, but he didn't fall. Chris arrived at the conflict just as Trevor said to Joshua, "Apology...accepted."

He then turned around, and Chris asked Trevor, "Feel better now?"

"Oh yeah," Trevor responded, then went on his way.

"You all right, Josh?" Chris asked.

"Yeah, it's not the first time I got hit."

"But probably the first time you didn't hit back," Chris added, to which Joshua nodded. "Well done, son," Chris complimented.

"For some reason, I thought that whole thing was behind me."

"Joshua, just because you're a Christian now doesn't mean you won't face consequences from previous actions. The past sometimes has a nasty way of showing up again. The key now, though, is to know that Jesus will go with you through it, if it does," Chris explained. "So what's going on here that you were eager for me to see?"

"This was the surprise I had for you," Joshua explained what the contractors were doing there. Then Joshua showed him and the kids around. They were all excited to see the new windows going into the building.

"Josh," Chris said, "I think this should be yours." The statement gripped Joshua's heart as he knew it was in reference to the fact that Chris believed he wasn't going to be around long. "I want you to lead the youth group for now on."

"Are you kidding? I don't know what to do?"

"Yeah, you do. Besides, these kids look up to you." Chris then asked the kids, "You guys want Joshua to lead youth group for now on?"

And the crowd of kids roared, "YEAH!"

"It's your playground again," Chris added.

"Nah, its Jesus's playground," Joshua corrected him.

"Speaking of Jesus, you ready to give your testimony to a thousand people?"

Joshua looked at Chris, cockeyed, and then said, "No. It's one thing standing in front of a camera, another in front of ton of people."

"You'll do great. Katrina's waiting at home with food for the drive. Let's hit the road." Then they climbed into Joshua's truck, stopped to pick up Katrina, as she was to be a greeter at the conference and left on the eight-hour drive. They were planning on getting hotel rooms that night, for the men's conference was being held at a coliseum the evening of the following day.

****

Brett showed up at the police station per Tiffany's request, though he wasn't thrilled to see her. She was brought out of the holding cell, and the two of them sat on opposite sides of the glass.

"What do you want?" he said.

"I don't like it in here?" she said. "They're taking my daddy's house."

"You called me a loser," he reminded her.

"I'm sorry. I didn't mean it. I miss you," she continued, manipulatively. "Joshua took everything from me. He took everything from us."

"You'll lose everything," he explained.

"I already have."

"No, you haven't," he assured her. Then he stood up and said, "It's going to hurt," then turned and left. Tiffany didn't fully understand the comment, though implied it to mean he was going to get her out. An officer then took her back to the holding cell where she sat until evening. She spent most of the day crying in the corner. From time to time, another individual was placed in the cell, and others would be released. Later that evening a woman was added to the cell. She was a tall, stocky woman and looked mean. There were only a couple of other ladies in the cell with them. The big girl kept staring at Tiffany until she finally said, "That's a pretty face you have there."

"Thank you," Tiffany responded timidly.

"You wouldn't be that *Tiffany Love*, would you?" Tiffany nervously nodded as she was curled up on the bench in the corner of the cell. "Did you hear that, ladies?" the big girl said to the other girls. "This is the *sexiest woman in America*!" The others laughed at the antagonistic comment. The big girl then got up and sat back down next to Tiffany, who then began breathing rapidly. "You know, I think I see a flaw in that face of yours. We should remove it," she continued intimidating her to the laughter of the other ladies. Tiffany then slid herself away from the big girl who then got up, walked over to her, then grabbed and dragged Tiffany to the center of the cell.

"Please! Not my face! It's all I have left!" Tiffany pleaded. The others continued laughing. Then the big girl pulled a knife out. Tiffany yelled for help as the big girl ran the blade across one of her cheeks, leaving a bloody cut wide open.

"Now you've lost everything," the big girl said. Hearing that statement, Tiffany then knew this was Brett's attempt to get her out of the police station. Some officers rushed into the holding cell. The big girl dropped the knife next to Tiffany who quickly grabbed it and hid it in her long sleeve. The officers lifted Tiffany off the ground and, seeing the gaping wound on her face, took her to the nurses' station. Once Tiffany was at the station, the big girl then began attacking the other couple of women in the cell, which drew the officers back to the cell, leaving Tiffany alone with the nurse.

"Have a seat on the exam table," the nurse said. Then she took a quick look at the gaping cut in her face. The nurse then turned her back to Tiffany to go to the cabinet for some supplies. Immediately Tiffany hopped off the table, grabbed the aluminum tray next to her, and as the nurse turned around, Tiffany slammed the tray into the side of the nurse's head, causing her to stumble to the wall. Tiffany rushed to the nurse pushing her hand over her mouth so she wouldn't scream and held the knife to her torso. The nurse unable to breathe and in shock over the unexpected action, flung her hands to Tiffany's face, her nails dug into her skin.

"I'm so sorry," Tiffany said to the nurse. She slowly pushed the knife harder. "I've never hurt anyone before," she added. "But I can't stay here." Finally, the knife began penetrating the nurse's flesh, which was evident by the nurse's expression and tears. The feeling of intense grief welled up inside Tiffany as well over what she was doing. The entire blade had been buried in the nurse's body, and soon her eyes stared at Tiffany lifelessly and her hands fell from Tiffany's face. Tiffany let go of the nurse, and the body slid down the wall and fell over on its side. Tiffany looked in disbelief at the blood on her hands and sobbed. The idea of confessing what she did briefly came to mind as she was aghast at what she had just done. But then the lights went out throughout the police station, and she immediately knew that was her only chance to get out of the building without getting caught. And she stealthily made her way down the halls in the dark, while police were still dealing with the towering woman in the holding cell. She found the exit and fled. A car was waiting for her. Brett was in the driver seat, then another person showed up from disabling the electrical system to the police station and got in the back then they sped off.

"I need to go to my daddy's house," she said.

"That will be the first place they look for you," Brett responded.

"I need to find something, and you need to pick someone up for me. Then we have to find a place to hide."

"I have a place," Brett explained.

Tiffany glanced in the back seat, then asked, "Who's this?"

"A fan," Brett answered. "He knows electronics."

The third person then introduced himself, "I'm Brody."

Tiffany was dropped off at her daddy's house and immediately rushed to her bedroom. Having memorized the angle of the video that captured the incident between her and Joshua, she began moving in the direction that appeared in the recording. When she finally determined from what direction the video had come from, she bent down until her view of the room was exactly how she remembered it in the video. Then she turned her head.

"Oh, Snuggles," she said, disappointed in the stuffed bear. "Have you been watching me?"

****

Meanwhile, there was a knock on the dorm door. Kara and Sandra weren't home, so Jennifer answered it. It was Brett. He immediately walked into the dorm.

"Who are you?" she asked angrily.

"I'm here for Joshua's girlfriend," he replied.

"HA!" she responded. "I'm not his *girlfriend* anymore. I could care less about that jerk! If you want him, he's on his way to some *stupid* Christian men's conference!"

Brett observed the flowers in the vase and the card. "But he cares about you."

"What are you doing?" Jennifer asked as he approached her, causing fear to suddenly grip her.

****

Kara and Sandra showed up at Tiffany's house. The door was unlocked like it usually was when they came over, so they stepped inside and called for her. "Tiffany? It's us, Kara and Sandra." Tiffany came running to meet them. She looked horrible, as she was covered in blood and the gashing bloody slash across her face was prominently displayed. Yet she was enthusiastically smiling as she embraced the two of them. "Hey, Tiffany," they said with concerned expressions. "We were surprised to get your phone call," Kara said.

"Yeah, we thought you were in the slammer," Sandra added.

"Obviously I'm not," Tiffany responded. "I just realized I never thanked my *best friends* for my present," Tiffany said. Then grabbing the stuffed bear, she ripped the head off of it revealing the camera. Tiffany's smile then vanished, and a look of hostility replaced it. Kara and Sandra then felt both guilt and fear over the situation.

"We were only trying to help," they responded. Brett and Brody then walked in the house with Jennifer, who was gagged.

"You're going to help," Tiffany explained to her *friends*. Then she walked over to Jennifer with the knife in her hand. The fear in Jennifer's eyes as Tiffany approached her instilled a sense of power over her. "Hi, Jennifer." Tiffany smiled. "You know, at our last meeting, I could see in your eyes that you didn't have any feelings for Josh. So when you did what you did, in front of everyone, part of me wished I could save him from you. I have a friend...had a friend...who said to me that the devil shows up dressed in light...to deceive people. That's you. Your pretty hair, your pretty face, you look so innocent. Unfortunately, you have two roommates that like to gossip."

"Please don't hurt her," Kara pleaded with Tiffany.

"Oh, I'm not going to hurt any of you. There's only *one person* I want to *hurt*. But I do have a question for Jennifer." Turning back to Jennifer, she asked, "Tell me, am I *trash*?" Jennifer rapidly shook her head no. "I like her." Then to Brett and Brody she concluded, "Now you two have a conference to get to."

THE MEN'S CONFERENCE

The number of visitors to the coliseum grew as the time for the men's conference got closer. Upon walking into the atrium, Pastor Wesley met the three of them.

"Joshua, this is our pastor from back home—Pastor Wesley," Chris introduced.

"It's great to meet you. I've heard a lot about you," Pastor Wesley said to Joshua.

"Is that a good thing or a bad thing?" Joshua sarcastically responded.

"Ha ha ha...well, we all have baggage in some shape or fashion. There's a lot of men here today anxious to hear the story of a new and former MMA fighter."

"New and former, huh? I guess two fights don't make it a career, does it? Ha ha ha." They laughed.

Wesley then asked Chris and Katrina, "So how are you two doing?"

"I'm doing great," Chris emphatically replied. Katrina wasn't as enthused as she was still upset over the thought of losing Tiffany to the devil.

"I've been better," she said. Chris put her arms around her then asked her, "is she dead?" to which she answered, "no."

"Then there's still hope. I still think you give up too easily some times," Chris said to her.

"Oh, you and your optimism. Okay, you boys get going. I got to do some greeting," she responded, cracking a smile. Chris kissed her and he, Joshua, and Wesley headed to the auditorium, while Katrina stayed with the ladies talking and greeting others coming to the conference.

The auditorium seated thousands. Down in the center of the auditorium was a circular stage above which hung a video cube. Additional video monitors hung from the ceiling as well as lined the perimeter of the auditorium. Christian music was playing through the many PA speakers. The three of them found their seats. Joshua sat closest to the aisle so he could easily get up when prompted to give his testimony.

Shortly after sitting, an older gentleman walked up to Joshua and said, "Joshua?"

"Yeah, that's me."

"There's a young lady over there who wants to talk to you," he said.

"Okay?" Joshua then left his seat to talk to the young lady. As he walked up the aisle, he spotted Sandra sitting alone in the last row of one of the sections.

"Sandra? What are you doing here?" He immediately noticed her clammy skin and anxious look. She turned her head and looked down between the seats as a prompt for Joshua to do the same. He spotted a couple of wires and a blinking light. He was about to put his hand between the seats, but Sandra stopped him, saying, "Don't touch it!"

"Is that what I think it is?" She simply nodded. "Can you get up?" She then shook her head. Joshua was going to look under the seat when she further said, "Don't make a scene. They're watching." Joshua saw the many cameras that were intended to live stream the conference all over the auditorium.

"Watching through the cameras?" he further inquired. She nodded. "Who's watching?"

"She *really* hates you now."

"Are you *kidding* me?" Joshua responded. "I'll be right back." Joshua went back to Chris and Pastor Wesley. "We have an *enormous* problem," he said. Chris and Wesley followed Joshua to Sandra's seat and began explaining the issue. Then Joshua realized something. "Sandra, I never thought you and Kara left each other's side."

Sandra looked at him intently and then responded, "Seat G-33." Joshua walked as quickly as he could to the opposite side of the auditorium. As he approached Kara, she spotted him.

She was far antsier than Sandra, saying, "Josh, Josh! What are we going to do?" Joshua looked between her seat and the seat next to hers and, sure enough, the same thing.

"We're working on it. I need to go back to the other side. I have a couple of guys trying to figure out what to do."

"Don't leave me here!" she said.

"I'll come back or I'll have someone else come over. I promise," Joshua responded.

"Okay, come back, please come back."

Joshua then headed back to Sandra's chair. When he returned, a couple of security guards were informed of the situation. They and Pastor Wesley stood behind Sandra's seat, appearing as though they were talking casually while Chris was looking under the seat. Chris then got up and said to Joshua and the security guard, "She's sitting on a pressure mechanism made out of car parts, and there's a hole in the concrete that a wire harness is running through." The guard radioed the maintenance workers to investigate below the auditorium.

"Car parts!" Joshua said, then he got down and looked at the mechanism. "Clutch plate, master cylinder." He then got back up and said to Chris, "Brody did this."

"Brody? Your best friend?"

"We sorta had a falling out recently." He then asked Sandra, "Why does Jennifer hate me so much?"

An expression of shock came across Sandra's face. "Wait, you think Jennifer did this? Ha ha ha. You know, once you get passed your *pretty face* and your *six-pack abs*...you're an *idiot*. Jennifer doesn't *hate* you, Josh. Because she never loved you. She loved the attention she got from your popularity. You cannot *hate* some body this *passionately*, without the capacity to *love* with the same *intensity*."

Joshua glanced at Chris, who nodded in agreement with Sandra. A sense of guilt welled up inside as he figured who she was talking about. "I thought she was in jail."

"She got out," Sandra responded.

The maintenance workers found the cables running beneath the auditorium hooked to explosives. Sensors prevented the tampering of the explosives. They reported their discovery to the security guards, who in turn shared the information to Chris and Joshua.

"We need to start an evacuation," one of the guards said.

"No!" Sandra responded emphatically. "If they panic, they'll remotely set it off."

"What about shutting the cameras down?" Chris considered, to which Sandra shook her head again. Then Joshua got an idea.

"We at least need to contain this." He then suggested to the guards, "Close off the building, make sure no one else comes in. The conference doesn't start for another forty-five minutes—people are still coming and going. Start at the back and have people leave, but not fast." The guards agreed. Then Joshua asked Pastor Wesley, "Can you go to seat G-33? Kara's over there in the same situation...freaking out. I told her I'd send someone to calm her down." Wesley agreed and headed that way.

Shortly thereafter, the noise level from the current crowd of attendants began increasing closer to the stage as a single random individual with the top of his head bandaged up, got on the platform, intimidating the workers who were setting up mics and other equipment off of the stage. He was carrying a suitcase of some sort and set it down.

"Who in the world is that?" Chris asked. Joshua then took his attention from Sandra and put it on the stage. "You got to be kidding?"

"Is that who I think it is?" Chris inquired.

"That's Brett Karmel." Joshua then asked Sandra, "What do they want to do?"

"I'm not sure. We've been in here for fifteen hours though. I'm scared."

Then Brett grabbed a microphone on the stage and shouted through it, "JOSHUA NICKEL! COME ON DOWN!"

"You might want to do what he says," Sandra suggested. Joshua then began slowly making his way down the aisle toward the stage. Chris came with him.

Meanwhile, in the video and sound booth, the techs had been locked out of their software as a foreign signal had accessed their computers remotely. Brett glanced up and down each aisle looking for Joshua. Once he spotted him, he then shouted through the PA system, "THERE YOU ARE! THIS IS THE LAST PLACE I'D EVER EXPECT TO FIND YOU HIDING!" Then he said to the visitors, "YOU ALL WANT TO KNOW WHO JOSHUA NICKEL REALLY IS?" Then the video monitors throughout the coliseum began running a montage of Joshua's former lifestyle: lude pictures of him with girls, bodies beat to a pulp by his fists, police photos and records of Joshua, and his contracts between him and those he beat up. Joshua and Chris continued down the aisle, and as he walked up onto the stage Brett then asked him, "now that they see who you *really* are, who's going to stand next to you?" Chris then came up and stood next to him on the stage. Brett laughed.

Joshua felt overcome with shame as he was sure no one else would. Brett's smile then left, and Chris nudged Joshua to look behind him and, to his amazement, men all over the auditorium were standing and migrating to the stage to stand with Joshua.

"Whoa. I thought they were supposed to be evacuating," Joshua said to Chris, to which he responded, "Only wimpy Christians run, Josh. This is what *muscular* Christianity looks like."

It appeared as the entire crowd was going to charge on Brett, but then through the PA system, a woman's voice said, "No, no, no, no. Only Josh gets the stage!"

The attention of the auditorium was at that moment directed to a live stream of Tiffany Love on the monitors throughout the building. Her appearance could have placed her in a psycho movie —as her being the psycho. "Hi, Josh!" she said with a remarkably large grin—though the statement was obviously antagonistic. "Guess what?" Her smile then fled as she continued, "I don't love you anymore. I *haaaate* you!"

"Oh no, Tiffany!" Katrina responded, watching the scene in the atrium.

Meanwhile, Joshua's stepsister was in the middle of watching a television program when a piece of breaking news interrupted her show. She then ran upstairs to her father and Trisha. "Hey, where was that men's conference that Josh was supposed to be at today?"

"Why?" they responded.

"Oh nothing, just that Tiffany Love is back in the news—"

"They took everything from me, Josh! *Everything!* They took my *daddy's house!* And look at my *face.* I don't even have *that anymore*!" Every outburst was accompanied by tears. "I'm desperate, Josh... desperate for you to feel what I feel. But you can't feel. You have no feelings for anyone. Or so I thought." Then the picture zoomed out just a bit to reveal another individual.

"Jennifer!" Joshua shouted as the picture of Jennifer incapacitated to a chair and gagged gripped his heart. "Tiffany! Please don't do this!"

"You know what the irony is, Josh? You actually love this person, but she doesn't care about you. *Sound familiar*!" "Tiffany! I'm sorry! I'm begging you to let her go! I'll do whatever you want!"

"Oh, really? Okay, let me think. Oh, I know what I want. Since you *crushed* my heart...I want yours to be *crushed* too." Then she pulled out a knife and put it to Jennifer's throat. "After you stop *breathing*, I'll let her go. So, *Joshua Nickel*, fight for Jennifer. Fight for the girl you love...but who doesn't love you."

"No! Tiffany, I'm not going to do it," Joshua responded in defiance.

"Oh, really?" She then held up to the camera the detonator associated with the bomb under the auditorium. "Well, if you don't, then...*boom*! And Jennifer's insides will be outside. So fight for Jennifer, Joshua." Tiffany then pulled Jennifer's gag out of her mouth and told her, "Tell him to fight for you, Jennifer." "No! That man can go to *hell*!" she responded.

But in a rage, Tiffany screamed at the top of her lungs directly into Jennifer's ear, "*say it*!" Then liquid oozed out of Jennifer's ear from her eardrum bursting.

Then with trepidation in her voice, Jennifer obeyed and timidly said, "Fight for me, Josh."

"This is a no-win situation," Joshua said to himself. Brett opened the case he had brought onto the stage, and inside were what looked like boxing gloves.

"Boxing gloves?" Joshua and Chris said in unison.

Then Chris said to Joshua, "Don't let him hit you with those."

"Right. You wouldn't by chance have an encouraging Bible verse for this, would you?"

"Not off the top of my head, no."

"Let's get this started!" Brett shouted at Joshua. He slammed his fists, encased in *gloves*, onto the floor of the stage. Two holes were left when he pulled his arms up, indicating that there was nothing soft about them.

"Brett," Joshua began attempting to reason with him, "you're really going to do this for her? Risk jail time, or worse?"

"The enemy of my enemy is my friend. I'm not *doing* this for *her*," Brett replied. "You took everything from me!"

"I beat you fair and square."

"ENOUGH TALK!" Then Brett jumped at Joshua bringing his arms down like hammers at him. Joshua quickly maneuvered out of the way. Joshua had the advantage of being faster than Brett since it could be easily determined that the gloves were heavy and slowing Brett down. However, Brett's rage was like a super drug that bolstered his strength and relentlessness.

While the fight progressed, one of the security guards came up to Chris and explained the progress they were making on resolving the bomb situation.

"One of the techs found the location of an IP address. The police are headed to Tiffany Love's house."

Frank was watching the simulcast of the event on a computer, focusing primarily on the video showing Tiffany. "Why does her background seem familiar to me?" Frank said to himself. Trisha was hysterically frantic. Janice was trying to calm her down. An entourage of police vehicles, bomb squad, and EMTs showed up outside the entrance of the coliseum. Katrina ran outside to meet them. "You can't go in the auditorium yet!" she informed them. "She'll blow it up if the police go in there."

Meanwhile, the police had arrived at Tiffany's mansion. They broke in and swarmed the house. They found the computer associated with the IP address and other hardware in the dining room, but no one was in the house. A software expert discovered that the IP address was a decoy. The police also noticed that the wall was spray painted in red: "I'M SORRY, DADDY."

Back at the coliseum, Joshua continued dodging Brett's encased fists, occasionally getting in a punch between Brett's irrational swings. However, he was primarily avoiding getting crushed. Tiffany encouraged Brett by shouting "GET HIM! GET HIM!" As the fight progressed, the security guard with Chris informed him that the IP address location was not correct.

Meanwhile, Frank continued watching the simulcast, paying close attention to her background. It was fairly dark, and the texture of the walls seemed deformed. Then as the camera moved slightly, he spotted a makeshift bed and a crank radio. "I KNOW WHERE SHE IT!" he exclaimed. "Come on, we have to get to the police station!"

Back on the auditorium stage, the fight was getting more intense as Joshua threw some kicks to Brett's gut, then as Brett swung at Joshua, Joshua punched Brett's forearm then threw a right hook at Brett's wrapped wound.

"Aah!" Joshua exhaled as pain surged in his hand from contacting something hard under the bandages and dropping to the ground.

"HA HA HA!" Brett laughed. "You never did knock me out!" He then unwrapped his head, and there was a metal plate over the wound that Joshua left on him months ago.

"Josh!" Chris shouted, wanting to rush onto the stage to help, but knowing he couldn't without risking Tiffany blowing up the auditorium, he remained at the edge of the stage. Joshua's hand was broken and Tiffany laughed. Witnessing Joshua in pain filled her with some sense of vindication.

Frank, Trisha, and Janice arrived at the police station and went directly to the captain. "I know where Tiffany Love is!" Frank told him.

The captain quickly got some officers together, and Frank led them to Canyon Park and to the cave that he knew they were in. As the police entered, Trisha reminded Frank, "The tripwire."

Frank then ran in and stopped them. "Wait," he said. Then he got down and showed them the tripwire that they didn't see. This time it was attached to some explosives. The officers quickly disabled the explosives and the tripwire, then frank led them to the hollowed-out cavern farther down. As they approached, they could hear Tiffany yelling one thing or another. Jennifer's cries were also audible. Peaking in, they confirmed that they had found Tiffany and Jennifer. Brody was also there as he set up the bomb, the phony IP address, and was the one holding the video camera.

"They found them," the security guard informed Chris. Joshua was rolling around on the ground as Brett kept jumping at him and attempting to slam his fists into him.

"STAND STILL YOU PARASITE!" Brett shouted. Joshua held his broken right hand to his chest. Chris's concern for him grew by the minute as he could see that the combination of pain and exhaustion was taking a toll on him.

In the cave, the police gathered just outside the opening of the hideaway. Then, unsuspectingly, a Taser struck Tiffany, temporarily paralyzing her. As she collapsed to the ground, the police rushed in. They secured the detonator and quickly subdued her and Brody.

"They got her and the detonator! Go! Go! Go!" the security guard exclaimed, then Chris dashed toward Brett with a shout and plowing into him just before he was able to strike Joshua. Chris then began pulverizing Brett, engaging with speed and power that even drew the astonishment of Joshua.

"Where'd that come from?" Joshua exclaimed.

Brett was completely unprepared for the offensive—a knee to his abdomen, then an elbow to his head, a foot to his chest a fist to his jaw, then to his lats. Lastly, Chris grabbed the top of Brett's head and slammed, his face into his knee, sending teeth and blood flying out of his mouth as he fell onto his back and Chris landing on his chest. Brett's gloves slid off when his arms hit the stage floor with a bounce.

"YEAH!" Katrina shouted in the atrium, having watched the action on the TV screens. The unexpected outburst startled the other ladies. "Ladies, that is *my* husband. *Mmmhmmm*, that's right," she added proudly.

Chris then stepped off of Brett, and as he was walking over to Joshua a gunshot went off. Chris immediately froze. Joshua stared at him as his demeanor instantly changed. Then blood came out of his mouth. Brett had shot him in the back. Brett then got up and aimed at Joshua, but Chris turned and leaped in front of Brett as he pulled the trigger a second time, taking another bullet then falling to the stage.

"CHRIS!" Joshua shouted. Dozens of men rushed the stage and attempted to subdue Brett, holding his arm up so the gun was pointing to the ceiling. Joshua then shot up and rushed at Brett while others were holding his arm in the air, drawing his left arm back as he approached then threw a left hook at Brett's head that knocked him out, collapsing him to the floor motionless. Several first responders then rushed to the stage.

Joshua then ran to Chris's side. "Chris!" he said. "Why'd you do that?"

"There's no greater love than one who lays down his life for his friends," Chris responded. Shortly thereafter, Katrina rushing onto the stage.

"Chris!" she said. "Is he going to be okay?" she asked the EMTs. They responded in the negative. "No, I'm not prepared for this," she said to Chris.

"I know," he responded, then reached up and pulled her face to his, and he kissed her, then said, "Don't give up on her." Katrina nodded, beginning to cry. Chris then looked up at Joshua and said, "Take care of those kids." Joshua nodded as tears fell from his eyes as well. "I love you two. I'll see you there." Chris's head then fell to one side as he exhaled his last breath.

AS THE SUN SETS

After Joshua returned from the botched men's conference, he rushed to Kara, Sandra, and Jennifer's dorm, but his intention was specifically to see Jennifer. He parked and got out of his truck. His hand was in a cast. She was carrying her belongings out of the dorm and placing them in her car. She was obviously not very happy. When Jennifer came back out with another box, she saw Joshua waiting for her. The sight of him intensified her anger.

"Jennifer," he said sorrowfully. She initially ignored the fact that he was even there. "I'm sorry," he said.

Then with pent up aggression, she yelled, "WHAT DID YOU SAY? I CAN'T HEAR YOU! OH THAT'S RIGHT BECAUSE SOME CRAZY WOMAN YOU WERE SCREWING AROUND WITH BLEW MY EARDRUM!"

"Is it going to heal?" Joshua asked.

Jennifer folded her arms and took a breath and nodded. "The doctors said it was torn, but it will heal."

"Oh, good. I'm just so glad that you're okay."

"You're *glad?*" Jennifer then began screaming again. "You *caused* all of this! Look at my hands, Josh!" She showed him her hands; they were shaking. "I can't stop shaking. It's been two days, and *I can't stop shaking*!"

"So I guess then there's no chance we could—"

"If you finish that statement, I'm going to run you over with my car. In fact, It's a really good thing that my hands were tied in that cave because if they weren't I would've grabbed that detonator just to blow *you* to hell! So no—infinity times, no. Remember, I said you only get one strike. This whole thing is like strike ten...*billion*! TO THE SIXTY-FOURTH AND A HALF POWER!"

"But I—" Joshua couldn't even get another word in, Jennifer was so irate.

"Shut up. This is what I want from you, okay? You...stay away from me. I'm moving back to Florida, and I never, *ever* want to see you *again*, hear from you *again*, or speak to you *again*. You got that?"

"Yes," he said softly, to which she responded, "WHAT? I CAN'T HEAR YOU!"

"I said yes! I got it. I'm still going to pray for you though."

"No! I don't want your *stupid* prayers." At that comment, it finally dawned on him why he got attached to Jennifer in the first place. "I just realized that you remind me a lot of my mother."

"Your mother? Who goes to church and is all goody-goody?"

"She wasn't always that way."

"I don't *care*, Josh. You know what? In fact, I don't *care* about your *mother*, I don't *care* about your *sister*, and I don't *care* about your *dead mentor's widow*! And I *especially* don't *care* about *God*!"

Every word broke his heart even more. "Now, Josh, in case you haven't gotten the hint...due to the thickness of your skull, I. Want. You. To. Leave. Now. That's what I want you to do. You can come back to visit your *old flings* or whatever *after* I'm gone.

They were right. You are a nightmare...*my nightmare*. I don't want to see you anymore. So can you please do that for me? Please?"

Joshua, having determined that he would not be able to convince her otherwise, simply nodded his head and then entered his truck and slowly left, never to see, hear, or speak to Jennifer ever again.

****

The following day was sunny and cool. However, the beautiful weather didn't stop the tears from flowing at the funeral. Pastor Wesley shared Chris's testimony and a sermon about death and that those who put their hope in Jesus Christ will have eternal life. Most of the funeral attendants were those whose lives were impacted by Chris over the years, including Joshua, who, after Pastor Wesley spoke, also shared how Chris impacted his life in such a short amount of time.

In a way, Joshua felt somewhat responsible for Chris's death, but Katrina continuously reminded him that it wasn't his fault. After the funeral, the attendants slowly vacated the cemetery giving their condolences to Katrina. Kara and Sandra were there and also came up to Katrina with tears. "Can you still visit with us on the weekends?" they asked.

"Of course." Then they embraced each other.

Lastly, Joshua and his family approached Katrina to further express their condolences as well. "I don't know what to say," Trisha said to her. "What your husband did with my son...it was miraculous."

"You know, you sound a lot like me. My husband would say...*you give up too easily*," Katrina responded through her tears. "And that sounds like my husband. If there's anything we can ever do for you, just ask. And don't be a stranger, you're welcome over any time," Trisha continued.

"I appreciate that. I just wished I would have prepared for this. Chris would try telling me that I should prepare myself for his departure. I would get so angry with him because I didn't want to live in the future. But it's here now," Katrina explained.

"Did Chris know this was going to happen?" Joshua asked.

"Ha ha, no," Katrina replied. "He's not a prophet. He was diagnosed with leukemia about a year and a half ago. It was in an advanced stage by the time we found out. They gave him two years, and treatment was unlikely to be effective."

"Why didn't he tell me that?"

"How would you have dealt with that knowledge?"

"I would have at least been easier on him. Instead of such a jerk."

"Exactly," she responded. Joshua then understood.

"Are you going to move back to the Midwest?" Frank inquired.

"No. The church is giving me the parish. Besides, I don't think Chris would be too happy if I didn't finish."

"Are you referring to Tiffany?" asked Trisha.

"Yeah. Someone's got to help her find the way. What are you going to do, Josh?"

"Chris wanted me to lead the youth group at the community center for now on. So that's what I'm going to do."

"You're going to do awesome, Josh."

"Are you going to go see her this afternoon?"

"Yeah," Katrina replied.

"Well, after your visit with her, you should join us to watch the sunset," Frank invited.

"That sounds wonderful."

Later that afternoon, Katrina was led into a small room with padded walls. She took a seat at a small table and opened her Bible. Shortly thereafter, Tiffany was brought in by two guards in a strait jacket and placed in a seat facing Katrina.

Katrina smiled at her, then said, "Hey, sweetie, how are you?"

Tiffany leaned over the table, opened her mouth allowing saliva to run out, then she spit in Katrina's face and laughed. "Ha ha ha!"

The guards would have disciplined Tiffany for the action, but Katrina stood up with her hand out and shouted, "No! Let her do that, please." She then sat back down. "I'll just have to remember to bring a raincoat next time," she said, attempting to make humor out of it. Then Katrina proceeded to read her Bible to Tiffany while she rambled, "Blah-blah-blah-blah-blah."

After the hour with Tiffany was over, Katrina said a prayer over her then told her, "I love you, Tiffany," to which Tiffany responded with profanity and dark humor. Katrina smiled as she left the room, then the door was shut, leaving Tiffany rambling on nonsensically alone. The warden took Katrina aside and said to her, "Looks like a lost cause for you to come back after that, am I right?"

Katrina smiled and replied, "She's a little lost right now...true. But she's not a *lost cause*. I know you're burned up because the state's secretary of corrections overruled your attempt to keep me away from her. And I was given power of attorney over her too. So I will be here tomorrow, and the next day, and the day after that. However long it takes, I will be here. So I guess you and I are going to get to know each other really well."

"You know," responded the warden, "if you succeed, she could get the death penalty."

Katrina thought for a moment before saying to him, "So basically you're saying that as long as she remains in her current mental condition, she's *saved*? Listen, I know the risks, but I have something for her that you don't—hope. Oh, and by the way, I thought you *humanists* were opposed to the death penalty," she added rhetorically.

"We're in favor of it for some," he responded.

"I couldn't imagine who those would be. See you tomorrow." Katrina then left the asylum and drove to meet Joshua and his family to watch the sunset over Canyon Park.

"How was she?" they asked her.

"Crazy," she honestly responded.

"Just pray for her. And me too."

"We will," they reassured her.

"Wow, you're right that is a beautiful sunset."

"Hey," Frank interjected, "how about we go explore the caves?" Joshua, Katrina, and Janice replied, "Sure, okay, sounds fun."

"No!" Trisha emphatically answered.

EPILOGUE

For two years Katrina faithfully visited Tiffany at the asylum where she read the bible, prayed, and reminded her that she and Jesus loved her. Tiffany's irrational, profane, and sometimes wet, utterances continued for a time, but eventually died down until Katrina's visits found her silently curled up in a corner. Sometimes the routine would become so mundane that Tiffany's minor changes came unnoticed to Katrina who also had to remind herself of why she was even doing this in the first place.

Another day came when Katrina entered the room in the asylum. Tiffanys' iconic red hair was to her waist with more of an orange tint to it than red and with a million different types of curls—evidence of lack of maintenance. Katrina got on the floor, opened her Bible, and began reading as per usual. Tiffany again simply stared at her as she read. The hour had passed and was prompted by the warden that it was time to leave. Katrina said her prayer over Tiffany, then closed her Bible concluding with, "I love you, Tiffany." Then as she began lifting herself off the floor she heard a soft stuttering voice respond, "I love you too."

Katrina froze, staring at the floor analyzing what she had just heard. She then lifted her eyes to Tiffany to see a single tear fall from an eye. "Tiffany?" Katrina said in shock.

"I miss you," Tiffany added, accompanied by another tear.

Immediately Katrina's eyes welled up with tears and rushed to her. The security almost stopped her, but Katrina pressed them to release her arms so she could embrace her, saying, "Please let her go so I can hold her! She's okay now!" The guards did as she asked to the initial objection of the warden.

It had been two years since the two embraced each other. As the tears fell, Tiffany asked her, "Can you ask me again?"

Katrina nodded with a smile that could wrap around the earth a dozen times. "Will you receive him?"

"Yes," Tiffany quickly replied without hesitation and with a dozen nods. Katrina then told her what to say, and Tiffany repeated the prayer of salvation. After that Tiffany also asked, "Can you be my mom again?"

Katrina emphatically responded, "Yes, yes."

****

Over the five years since Chris Belvu passed, Joshua Nickel grew in his faith exponentially, having converted the community center into the Belvu Faith Center. The center had been expanded to house kids who've come from broken homes with a boy's wing and a girl's wing. A wall in the office had articles following Katrina and the rise of her ministry to reach incarcerated women with the love and hope of Jesus Christ that began with Tiffany Love's Salvation.

Article:

> Accused murderer, Tiffany Love, has a new psych eval. After deemed competent to stand trial, she's convicted of first-degree murder and attempted domestic terrorism. Widow, Katrina Belvu, stood in the courtroom next to Tiffany as a death sentence was handed down.

****

Joshua Nickel opens two more auto service centers within the city limits. Joshua is the first to financially support Katrina Belvu's incarcerated women's ministry and other supporters soon follow.

****

A three-year-long criminal investigation against Glamour Entertainment president, Brad Stone, his company executives, and organization affiliates, led by several Christian legal organizations, ends with a multitude of criminal charges involving sex trafficking. Discovery revealed that the company routinely lured hundreds of vulnerable women, many in crisis situations, into their enterprise over several years where they were groomed for sexual exploitation, and in many instances sold as sex slaves in other countries.

****

Tiffany Love was among the hundreds of witnesses listed in the action against Glamour Entertainment. Evidence of emotional and psychological trauma was submitted in an appeal, which, in a controversial decision, a judge reversed Tiffany's sentence from capital punishment to life in a maximum-security prison.

****

Several state secretaries of corrections allow "Love Incarcerated Women Ministries"–a Christian outreach organization founded by Katrina Belvu–to minister to the inmates of woman correctional facilities.

****

"I really shouldn't be doing this," Tiffany said to Katrina. The two of them sat in front of a yard field with women in orange jump suits surrounded by both guards and several women with black shirts that read *Love Incarcerated Women, Ministries*. "I've done so many horrible things," she continued.

"It's okay, just start from the beginning," Katrina encouraged her.

"I thought I had a perfect life. My family was really wealthy. But in a second it was gone. When my family died, it was like the ground vanished. I had nothing to stand on. And grabbing the first thing I thought could hold me up. But everything I clung to...it was like, hanging onto dead and rotting branches...that simply snapped, and I would fall further." She detailed her time with the entertainment company and her desperate search for love—or what she thought was love.

"One day I walked into my daddy's house, and Katrina was standing just inside the door, in front of the fire place, looking at the pictures of my family. I didn't know it at the time, but she was what I was waiting for. She told me about Jesus. And I kept rejecting him, and every time I rejected him I'd fall further." She shared how her false accusations led to the murder of a nurse followed by the conspiracy that resulted in Katrina's husband's death.

"When I was in the asylum, it was like being in a forest where the trees spanned for miles. I couldn't find my way out." She analogized her time in the psychiatric hospital. "I'm so sorry I said those things to you and spit on you," she said to Katrina with tears. "But I heard your voice, and you showed me the way." Then she glanced at her fellow inmates and concluded with a smile that was her own, "She showed me the way. And Jesus...Jesus is the way."

Article:

> Thousands of incarcerated women come to faith in Jesus Christ after Tiffany Love shares her testimony from the yard of a maximum security prison.

Florida; 2:00am

It was dark and humid. A sports car pulled up to the curb of a small, old house, that was in desperate need of maintenance. The passenger door opened and Jennifer stepped out. The woman driving said to her before leaving, "Sorry you had another rough night and that your car broke down again. Maybe you'll have better luck tomorrow." She then drove off.

Jennifer opened the rusted mailbox next to the curb. It looked like it could fall over at any moment. She rummaged through the mail: overdue student loan bills, credit card bills, and utility shut-off notices were the bulk of the letters. As she approached the house, she looked up to see her old tattered furniture, much of which appeared to have been bought from garage or yard sales, were sitting on the front lawn. "What?" she said to herself. She sat her purse down on the arm of the love seat that was inundated with tears and permanent stains then went up to the front door. The lock was changed and there was a paper stuck to the door. She grabbed it and read it. It was an eviction notice for not paying her rent for the last few months.

Two guys in hoodies were walking down the street and spotted the purse sitting on the arm of the love seat. They sprinted for it. Hearing someone running she looked up just as they grabbed her purse and took off with it.

"HEY! THAT'S MY PURSE!" She ran out after them but fell face first, for she was in high heels. Then looking toward the heavens, she raised her fist, shouting, "*I HAAATE YOOUUU!*"

Lucas Gorton McIntire grew up between Denver, Colorado, and Wichita, Kansas. *The Way* is his second book after his debut novel, *The Sentient*, which is a speculative-science-fiction narrative in to the superhero genre.

Though Lucas has found an interest in writing fiction, specifically speculative-sci-fi, his personal reading selection is non-fiction, which he weaves throughout his stories. Studying Christian apologetics was instrumental in him transitioning from atheism to faith in Jesus Christ.

As a musician, he enjoys recording instrumentals and occasionally distributes them online for fun. He's played the bass guitar since he was seventeen and the electric guitar since he was twenty-nine. Additionally, he finds enjoyment in fishing, camping, and other outdoor-related activities, or with family.